THE SEA MONSTER

It loomed before them, shrouded in the mist, its teardrop-shaped hull like a steel island rising out of the waves. They could see the huge conning tower with its winglike sailplanes and tall periscopes, the flattened top portion of the deck with ominous round hatches, beneath which lurked ballistic missiles in their silos.

"Mon Dieu!" Verne whispered, awestruck. "What is that?"

"A submarine," said Lucas. "We came here looking for it. Well, now we've found it . . . "

The Time Wars Series by Simon Hawke

THE IVANHOE GAMBIT
THE TIMEKEEPER CONSPIRACY
THE PIMPERNEL PLOT
THE ZENDA VENDETTA
THE NAUTILUS SANCTION

5 TIMEWARS
THE NAUTILUS SANCTION

BY
**SIMON
HAWKE**

ACE SCIENCE FICTION BOOKS
NEW YORK

For Natasha and Andrei

This book is an Ace Science
Fiction original edition, and has never
been previously published.

THE NAUTILUS SANCTION

An Ace Science Fiction Book / published by arrangement with
the author

PRINTING HISTORY
Ace Science Fiction edition / December 1985

ISBN: 0-441-56566-2

Ace Science Fiction Books are published by
The Berkley Publishing Group,
200 Madison Avenue, New York, New York 10016.
PRINTED IN THE UNITED STATES OF AMERICA

With special thanks to Bill Bondie, Edward Bryant, Bill and Lola Molner of The Gun Room in Denver, CO, John Dunning and The Old Algonquin Bookstore in Denver, Leanne Christine Harper, Michelle Hughes and, last but by no means least, the mysterious Dr. Darkness.

A CHRONOLOGICAL HISTORY OF THE TIME WARS

April 1, 2425:   Dr. Wolfgang Mensinger invents the chronoplate at the age of 115, discovering time travel. Later he would construct a small scale working prototype for use in laboratory experiments specially designed to avoid any possible creation of a temporal paradox. He is hailed as the "Father of Temporal Physics."

July 14, 2430:   Mensinger publishes "There Is No Future," in which he redefines relativity, proving that there is no such thing as *the* future, but an infinite number of potential future scenarios which are absolute relative only to their present. He also announces the discovery of "non-specific time" or temporal limbo, later known as "the dead zone."

October 21, 2440:   Wolfgang Mensinger dies. His son, Albrecht, perfects the chronoplate and carries on the work, but loses control of the discovery to political interests.

June 15, 2460:	Formation of the international Committee for Temporal Intelligence, with Albrecht Mensinger as director. Specially trained and conditioned "agents" of the committee begin to travel back through time in order to conduct research and field test the chronoplate apparatus. Many become lost in transition, trapped in the limbo of nonspecific time known as "the dead zone." Those who return from successful temporal voyages often bring back startling information necessitating the revision of historical records.
March 22, 2461:	*The Consorti Affair*—Cardinal Lodovico Consorti is excommunicated from the Roman Catholic Church for proposing that agents travel back through time to obtain empirical evidence that Christ arose following His crucifixion. The Consorti Affair sparks extensive international negotiations amidst a volatile climate of public opinion concerning the proper uses for the new technology. Temporal excursions are severely curtailed. Concurrently, espionage operatives of several nations infiltrate the Committee for Temporal Intelligence.
May 1, 2461:	Dr. Albrecht Mensinger appears before a special international conference in Geneva, composed of political leaders and members of the scientific community. He attempts to alleviate fears about the possible misuses of time travel. He further refuses to cooperate with any attempts at militarizing his father's discovery.

February 3, 2485:	The research facilities of the Committee for Temporal Intelligence are seized by troops of the TransAtlantic Treaty Organization.
January 25, 2492:	The Council of Nations meets in Buenos Aires, capital of the United Socialist States of South America, to discuss increasing international tensions and economic instability. A proposal for "an end to war in our time" is put forth by the chairman of the Nippon Conglomerate Empire. Dr. Albrecht Mensinger, appearing before the body as nominal director of the Committee for Temporal Intelligence, argues passionately against using temporal technology to resolve international conflicts, but cannot present proof that the past can be affected by temporal voyagers. Prevailing scientific testimony reinforces the conventional wisdom that the past is an immutable absolute..
December 24, 2492:	Formation of the Referee Corps, brought into being by the Council of Nations as an extranational arbitrating body with sole control over temporal technology and authority to stage temporal conflicts as "limited warfare" to resolve international disputes.
April 21, 2493:	On the recommendation of the Referee Corps, a subordinate body named the Observer Corps is formed, taking over most of the functions of the Committee for Temporal Intelligence, which is redesignated as the Temporal Intelligence Agency. Under the aegis of the Council of Nations and the Referee

Corps, the TIA absorbs the intelligence agencies of the world's governments and is made solely answerable to the Referee Corps. Dr. Mensinger resigns his post to found the Temporal Preservation League, a group dedicated to the abolition of temporal conflict.

June, 2497–
March, 2502:

Referee Corps presides over initial temporal confrontation campaigns, accepting "grievances" from disputing nations, selecting historical conflicts of the past as "staging grounds" and supervising the infiltration of modern troops into the so-called "cannon fodder" ranks of ancient warring armies. Initial numbers of temporal combatants are kept small, with infiltration facilitated by cosmetic surgery and implant conditioning of soldiers. The results are calculated based upon successful return rate and a complicated "point spread." Soldiers are monitored via cerebral implants, enabling Search & Retrieve teams to follow their movements and monitor mortality rate. The media dubs temporal conflicts the "Time Wars."

2500–2510:

Extremely rapid growth of massive support industry catering to the exacting art and science of temporal conflict. Rapid improvement in international economic climate follows, with significant growth in productivity and rapid decline in unemployment and inflation rate. There is a gradual escalation of the Time Wars with the majority of the world's armed services converting to temporal duty status.

Growth of the Temporal Preservation League as a peace movement with an intensive lobby effort and mass demonstrations against the Time Wars. Mensinger cautions against an imbalance in temporal continuity due to the increasing activity of the Time Wars.

September 2, 2514: Mensinger publishes his "Theories of Temporal Relativity," incorporating his solution to the Grandfather Paradox and calling once again for a ceasefire in the Time Wars. The result is an upheaval in the scientific community and a hastily reconvened Council of Nations to discuss his findings, leading to the Temporal Strategic Arms Limitations Talks of 2515.

March 15, 2515–
June 1, 2515: T-SALT held in New York City. Mensinger appears before the representatives at the sessions and petitions for an end to the Time Wars. A ceasefire resolution is framed, but tabled due to lack of agreement among the members of the Council of Nations. Mensinger leaves the T-SALT a broken man.

November 18, 2516: Dr. Albrecht Mensinger experiences total nervous collapse shortly after being awarded the Benford Prize.

December 25, 2516: Dr. Albrecht Mensinger commits suicide. Violent demonstrations by members of the Temporal Preservation League.

January 1, 2517: Militant members of the Temporal Preservation League band together to form the Timekeepers, a terrorist offshoot of the League, dedicated to the complete destruction of the war machine. They announce their presence to the world by assassinating three members of the Referee Corps and bombing the Council of Nations meeting in Buenos Aires, killing several heads of state and injuring many others.

September 17, 2613: Formation of the First Division of the U.S. Army Temporal Corps as a crack commando unit following the successful completion of a "temporal adjustment" involving the first serious threat of a timestream split. The First Division, assigned exclusively to deal with threats to temporal continuity, is designated as "the Time Commandos."

PROLOGUE ═══════════

The lookout in the crow's nest of the *H.M.S. Avenger* had been the first to spot him, clinging to a floating piece of wreckage off the port bow. They sent a boat out and discovered he had lashed himself to a large section of what had once been the mainmast of a ship. He was half dead from thirst and badly burned, both by fire and by the sun. His lips were cracked and parched and his skin, where it had not been blackened by flames, was red and blistered, oozing with infection. They feared they would lose him. Admiral Lord Hood, anxious to learn the fate of whichever ship it was the poor devil had come from, gave strict orders to the *Avenger's* surgeon to call him at once should the man regain the power of speech. No such summons proved necessary. The entire ship's company heard it when, on the second day following his rescue, the man began to scream.

They had managed to calm him down somewhat by the time Hood arrived in the sick bay. The man was thrashing on the surgeon's table, and for all that he was little more than skin and bones, it took two men to hold him down. He was struggling against them, his eyes rolling wildly, while Dr. Graves attempted to administer some laudanum.

"Belay that!" Hood said firmly, though without raising his voice. "The man is of no use to me drugged."

Something in Hood's voice penetrated through the ship-

1

wreck victim's terror and he ceased to struggle against the two sailors. His eyes became fixed upon Hood, who met his gaze steadily and nodded reassuringly.

"You're safe, man," he told the shipwreck victim. "You're aboard the *Avenger*, bound for Bristol."

"Thank God," the man whispered, his voice now barely audible. "Thank the Almighty God!"

"What happened to your ship?" Hood said gently.

"Destroyed," the man said, shutting his eyes. His chest rose and fell unevenly as he breathed laboriously. "It was the beast," he said, with a shiver.

Hood frowned. "The *Beast*? I know of no such ship."

"A sea beast!" said the man, opening his eyes wide and staring at Hood with the gaze of a lunatic. "The *Covenant* was destroyed by a monster from the depths!"

"Monster?" Hood said, glancing at the doctor. "What monster?"

"Perhaps he means a whale, Your Lordship," said Dr. Graves.

"*No!*" The man struggled to rise, finally managing to prop himself up slightly on his elbow. "No, not a whale!" he said, fervently. "A beast, I tell you! A veritable leviathan! A great, horrid, monstrous thing from the very jaws of hell!"

"Come, man, what nonsense is this?" said Hood. "We are not children to believe in sea dragons. Even schoolboys know such creatures do not exist."

"I *saw* it, I tell you!" said the man, his voice rising. "It churned the sea all round as it thrashed its mighty tail. It sounded and we heard it scream! I will hear that dreadful sound for all the days and nights left in my miserable life!"

"The man's a lubber," Dr. Graves said. "It must have been a whale he saw."

"Not this one," said the first mate, who had helped hold him down. "There's tar in his hair and those were good seaman's knots he lashed himself to the mast with." He glanced up nervously at Hood. "No seaman gets himself frightened senseless by a whale, Your Lordship."

"Lubber, am I?" said the sailor, his voice rising in pitch as he neared hysteria. "Whale, was it? Aye, you show me the whale that can hole a man-o'-war and then spit fire into its hull! Aye, the very flames of hell! One instant, there was a mighty ship, the next, there was nought but flaming splinters! The creature spat at us and we were consumed! Not a man jack left alive to tell the tale save me!''

"The poor man's daft," said Dr. Graves. "He's lost his mind."

"Aye, call me mad! Any sane man would. But I know what I saw, and I only pray to God I never lay eyes on it again!''

"Steady, now," said Hood, bending down close to the man. "You have been through an ordeal enough to make any man half-mad. Try to remember. Think, could it be that a whale struck your ship or was struck by it? Perhaps the shock caused a lantern to fall and ignite the powder magazine?''

"I tell you, it was no whale!" the man shouted. "Think you I do not know a whale when I see one? We thought at first it *was* a whale when we glimpsed it on the surface, but no whale could swim with such unholy speed or give vent to such a cry! No whale spits fire at a ship!'' He reached out and grasped the lapels of Hood's seacoat with shaking hands. *"Pray!"* he said, his eyes glazing over, staring not at Hood, but at something else that none of them could see. "Pray you do not cross this creature's path! Tell your lookouts to keep watch! Tell your men to keep their eyes upon the sea! If they should sight a dark shape in the water with a fin very like a shark's, but larger than any shark that ever swam the ocean, tell them to make their peace with God! For you can turn your ship; you can put up every foot of sail in the strongest wind and flee, but it will avail you nought! The hell-spawn swims with a speed beyond belief! You shall hear its awful cry and it will sound and the sea will roil with its passage!''

The man began to laugh hysterically.

"Aye, a whale, you say. A whale!''

Hood firmly grasped the man's wrists and pried himself loose from his hold. He stood, watching sorrowfully as the shipwreck victim alternately laughed and sobbed.

"Do what you can for him, Graves," he said. "Poor wretch. I fear he is beyond your help.''

"Aye," said the doctor, shaking his head. "Sea monsters.''

The mate looked up at Graves and Hood, then glanced back down at the shipwreck victim and quickly crossed himself.

Later in the day, they lost him. That evening, Hood himself
said the words as they put the poor man's weighted body over
the side. By then, there was not a man aboard who had not
heard the story. When the *Avenger* made port, the tale began
to spread throughout the pubs of Bristol, a tale of a leviathan
that had risen from the deep. Sailors prayed and watched the
sea with fear.

The entire division had been called in for the briefing. Every
single temporal adjustment team was in attendance save the
ones clocked out to Minus Time on missions. The briefing
room on the sixty-third floor of the Temporal Army Headquarters Building at Pendleton Base was packed and buzzing
with an undertone of conversation rife with rumors. Moses
Forrester was not the sort of division commander who rou-
tinely called the troops out for mass briefings, so there was a
great deal of speculation about the reason for the muster.
Rumors circulated about everything from a new security
evaluations program to a battery of proficiency examinations
for the Time Commandos ordered by the Referee Corps. In
the Temporal Army, such things were known as "mickey-
mouse," a term whose origins were lost in military antiquity.

Lucas Priest, Forrester's exec with the rank of major,
spotted Finn Delaney near the front of the briefing room and
made his way to him. Slender, very fit and elegantly handsome, Priest walked with a slight limp, favoring his left leg.
The plasma burns he had received on his last mission to Minus
Time had completely healed, but there was still considerable
soreness there. He wore a black patch over his right eye. His
real eye had been melted right out of its socket by the heat
wave from an auto-pulser blast. He was fortunate. He had
only lost an eye and sustained serious burns upon his face. A
direct hit from an auto-pulser would have cooked his head off.
Cosmetic surgery had restored his features to their original appearance and the doctors had replaced the hair he lost, but
Lucas had chosen a bionic optic unit instead of an organic eye
replacement. It was superior to a natural eye in a number of
ways, but he had not yet had it long enough to grow accustomed to it. Using it together with his natural left eye for more
than half an hour gave him a slight headache.

"Finn," he said, touching Delaney on the arm, "you know what this is all about?"

Sergeant Major Finn Delaney turned to face him with a frown. Massively built, the red-haired Irishman somehow always managed to look less like a non-com than like a technician in his uniform. No matter how sharply creased, and they rarely were, his black base fatigues always looked like workmen's coveralls when he wore them. He never buttoned up his blouse all the way, and more than one officer had learned the hard way that Sergeant Delaney had a tendency to back up his recalcitrance with his fists. In any other outfit, Finn would long since have become a casualty of military regulations, but Forrester valued a soldier's performance in the field above all else. His frequent, grudging intercessions on Finn's behalf kept him from being drummed out of the corps, although they did not prevent his being busted down to private time and time again. It was a never-ending cycle. Finn would return from a hitch in Minus Time and his exemplary performance would result in a promotion, but sooner or later, he would run across some officer who had not been advised to steer clear of him. The result was usually an injured officer and Finn's being busted down to private once again. He was still a sergeant major only because the members of the Temporal Army officers' corps, in the interests of self-preservation, were learning to give him a wide berth. In that respect, Finn Delaney epitomized the nature of the Time Commandos. The regular troops respected them tremendously, but rarely socialized with them. Forrester's people had a reputation for being mavericks, more than a little crazed.

"Do *I* know what this is all about?" said Finn, looking at Lucas with surprise. "Hell, I was going to ask *you*. You're the exec, I figured you would know."

Lucas shook his head. "Not me. You seen Andre?"

"Right here," she said, from behind him. "What's going on?"

Biologically, Andre Cross was the youngest member of the First Division, with the rank of corporal. Chronologically, however, she was by far the oldest, having been born in the 12th century, where she once held the rank of mercenary knight. She was not pretty. Her features were plain and somewhat on the sharp side, yet there was something about them that was very striking. Her hair was straw-blond and she paid an absolute minimum of attention to it, less than most men. She wore it a bit longer than most soldiers did, partly because she had worn it short for many years to aid in her passing as a male in the time from which she came. She filled out her uniform quite well, but with muscle rather than soft, feminine curves. Her shoulders were quite broad and her biceps, when flexed, had a surprising peak to them. Her legs were long and shapely, but with mass and definition that a triathlete would have envied. Her breasts, though small, appeared somewhat larger than they were due to her pectoral development. Her waist and hips were narrow, without an ounce of surplus fat. She had the poise of complete self-assurance and the animal sexuality that came with being in peak physical condition, though her deltoids had still not quite recovered from the wound she received when a nysteel rappelling dart had been fired into her shoulder, severing muscle and shattering bone. Their last mission had been a bad one. Lucas had been seriously injured. Finn had also been hurt, nearly killed, when a thrown dagger struck him in the chest, coming perilously close to his heart and pulmonary artery. Only the density of his muscle mass had saved him. All three of them were walking wounded, but the army doctors had pronounced them fit enough to return to active duty. Civilian doctors would have been a great deal more conservative in their decisions.

"I heard something about a new battery of psych tests," Andre said.

"Who the hell knows?" Finn grumbled. "I guess we'll find out soon. Here comes the old man. Better get the rabble in some sort of order, Major."

Lucas turned to face the room. "Ten-*hut!*"

Several hundred boot heels cracked in unison as the soldiers of the First Division snapped to. Lucas about-faced and climbed up the steps to the rostrum, saluting the old man smartly.

"First Division all present or accounted for, sir!"

The craggy Colonel Forrester returned his salute. "Thank you, Major. You may step down. At ease, people. Please be seated."

He waited a moment for them to take their seats.

"I am in receipt of a Priority One, Code Red directive from the Referee Corps," he said without preamble.

They all tensed. This wasn't mickey-mouse. A Priority One, Code Red meant very serious trouble. It was an order for total mobilization.

"About three weeks ago," said Forrester, "a portion of a shipment destined for the Temporal Army P.O. was stolen from the warehouses of Amalgamated Techtronics, in spite of the most rigid security precautions. In all, some five thousand temporal transponders, ranging in classification from P-1 to V-20, were stolen by persons unknown."

The reaction was instantaneous and tumultuous. "As you were!" shouted Lucas, surprised to hear his own voice crack. *Five thousand temporal transponders!* It was a crime of unprecedented and staggering proportions with consequences that could be cataclysmic.

The transponders, or warp discs in soldiers' parlance, were the most recent development in military applications of Einstein-Rosen Bridge technology. Not all temporal units had them yet, but every temporal army in the world—and on other worlds—was in the process of converting to them to supplant the already obsolete chronoplates.

Originally, Einstein-Rosen Bridge technology had been developed in the latter half of the 26th century, based on the theory developed by Albert Einstein and Nathan Rosen in 1935, in which they postulated the existence of a "corridor" in space-time. It took the discovery of white holes, cosmic gushers of pure energy exploding into the universe, and the technological advances of some seven hundred years before their corridor in space-time, or "worm hole," became accepted as a reality. In 2645, Bell Laboratories developed the first working model of the Einstein-Rosen Generator at their Bradbury facility on Mars. Using particle-level chips, the device was still of mammoth size, much like the earliest computers. It was designed to tap into the energy field of an Einstein-Rosen Bridge between two universes. The Einstein-Rosen Generator, or ERG, was in fact misnamed. It did not actually *generate* power. Rather, it acted as a power dilator, in a manner similar to how a black hole "dilated" the universe in the vicinity which it was located, with a gravitational field so great that not only could light waves not escape from it, but the fabric of space-time itself was torn, disrupted in that region to open up into another universe as a white hole. The purpose of the ERGs was to tap into that maelstrom of power and then "feed" the energy to appropriate the transponders, in this way providing free energy for everything from powering orbital colonies to turning on a light switch in a New York conapt.

Eventually, the ERGs made possible the creation of a bridge to neutron stars within the galaxy and a number of on-line ERGs were bridging to Orion. It was not until a research scientist in the Ordnance Section of Temporary Army Headquarters came up with the idea of reversing the process, in 2615, that the principles of Einstein-Rosen were applied to military weaponry. The result was the warp grenade—a combination nuclear device and time machine.

Lucas had used one for the first time on his last mission. Since then, they had already been refined to achieve pinpoint intensity control. The device was called a grenade only because it approximated ancient hand grenades in size and general appearance. A warp grenade could be set manually with a timer or thrown set for air burst. The result was instant holocaust—only, capable of being totally controlled. It could be set to wipe out a city, a city block, a building on that block, a room within that building, or a spot within that room no larger than a fist. The variable factor in the classification of warp grenades was one-to-nine megatons. Lucas had used one of the least powerful ones and the thought of using a nine-megaton grenade made his knees weak. He could not imagine a situation in which such a necessity could arise. At the instant of detonation, the particle-level chronocircuitry within the device clocked the "surplus" energy of the explosion—that which was not needed to do the job—through an Einstein-Rosen Bridge via transponder link to an on-line ERG. In the case of a nine-megaton grenade, 90 percent of the explosion's energy could be clocked to the Orion Nebula, safely out of harm's way. Or, more to the point, to where it could safely do no harm. Nevertheless, the remaining energy would be equal to the blast that had destroyed Hiroshima, and the thought of carrying such power in his pocket was enough to make Lucas break out in a sweat. The blast he had set off on his last mission was nowhere near as powerful, but its results had been frightening just the same. Lucas had caught some residual radiation, though not enough to cause any more damage than prolonged exposure to the sun during a beach vacation in St. Croix. Yet, somewhere in the Orion Nebula at that instant, there had been one whale of a big bang. All Lucas had done was use an infinitesimal part of it.

As the upshot of that flash of insight on that research scientist's part, the brains in the Army think tanks suddenly realized the obvious possibilities for further temporal-military applications of those same principles. Even while the warp grenades were being perfected, the Temporal Army research scientists at Heinlein University on Dyson were already constructing the prototype temporal transponders to replace the chronoplates. Utilizing the same Einstein-Rosen Generators that provided power for utilities, they made some inspired modifications (the plans for which were immediately classified Top Secret) to enable the power drawn through time and space to provide the energy for travel through time and space via temporal transponders designed on the micro-molecular or particle level. Each soldier of the First Division, chosen as the first to be issued what the commandos quickly nicknamed "warp discs," now wore a temporal transponder on his wrist. If necessary, the warp disc could be taken off its bracelet and worn on a neck chain, camouflaged as some other piece of jewelry or hidden somewhere on one's person. Now, instead of a bulky chronoplate and flexible, bimetallic border circuits, all it took to transport a man of approximately six feet and two hundred pounds through time was a wafer-thin transponder disc no larger than an ancient twenty-five-cent piece. The transponders were made correspondingly larger according to their purpose, hence their classification designations. Lucas wore a P-1 disc. An entire battalion of soldiers could be teleported via a field provided by a T-25, a disc no more than eight inches in diameter. The actual power dilator, or ERG, could be anywhere—at Pendleton Base or even in ancient Mesopotamia. Theoretically, since the power supply was limitless to all intents and purposes, the entire planet could be teleported elsewhere with a large enough temporal transponder, though that was a possibility no one seriously entertained. Soldiers joked about it, but the laughter always had a slightly strained note to it. On that scope, it was just a bit too weird to even think about.

Every soldier of the First Division had been issued an "Eyes Only" Top Secret manual to scan, or rather, they had been given access to the data under top security conditions. Lucas had studied his while actually under armed guard. It did not escape his notice, or anyone else's for that matter, that the research scientist in Ordnance who had started the whole thing was never named. All attempts at discovering his or her identity were summarily discouraged in no uncertain terms. Finn had made a comment that the poor bastard was probably hiding under a rock somewhere, terrified out of his wits. The comment had been flippant, but it brought to mind immediately the fate of Albrecht Mensinger, who committed suicide when he realized the full implications of his work in refining the chronoplate.

Now, those same implications were forcibly driven home to each and every soldier in that room. The theft of five thousand temporal transponders was unsettling in the extreme. Lucas realized his mouth had gone completely dry and no one had paid any attention whatsoever to his shout of "As you were!" They were all talking at once, shouting and creating a din that drowned him out. How in hell had the theft been accomplished? Amalgamated Techtronics was a Top Security plant —*the* Top Security plant. Whoever accomplished the daring theft would still need an ERG, properly modified, for the transponders to be keyed to. But if they were able to hijack a shipment from Amalgamated Techtronics, right from under the very noses of crack troops, how difficult would it be for them to obtain the necessary plans to adapt an industrial ERG for temporal translocation? The very fact the warp discs had been stolen suggested that whoever had them also had the means or the means to get the means of using them. The transponders that were stolen varied in classification from P-1 to V-20. *V-20!* Lucas shuddered. Just one of those was big enough, at a diameter of about twelve inches, to transport something the size of, no, *bigger* than the Washington Monument!

"They must have stolen them for ransom," Finn said,

standing beside Lucas. "They couldn't possibly *use* them."
He licked his lips and glanced at Lucas. "Could they?"

Forrester waited patiently for them all to become quiet.
It was hardly the sort of news he could expect them to take
calmly. When the noise died down at last, he continued.

"I don't need to tell you people the potential for danger this
situation represents," he said gravely. "If any word of it
should happen to leak out, the media is going to play it up for
all it's worth and we'll have a disaster on our hands. And
that's not even counting the disaster we're already faced with
in terms of the potential for temporal contamination. The
entire Observer Corps has been placed on the alert for temporal anomalies and the TIA has been working around the
clock, correlating all the data from field stations reporting in."

He paused significantly.

"I realize it's going to be difficult, people, but I'll expect
you to restrain yourselves when I report their conclusions. No
computer data this time. Word of mouth only. We've got
some very frightened people on this and the levels of paranoia
have reached new heights. So listen carefully and I'll open up
the floor to questions when I'm through. I want no further
outbursts. I trust I've made myself quite clear."

Forrester waited a moment while they watched him with
tense anticipation. He took a deep breath.

"On November 12, 1993, the Soviet Union reported the disappearance of their new Typhoon-class ballistic missile nuclear submarine, *Vostochnaya Slava*, off Jan Mayan Island in
the Arctic Ocean—"

Lucas felt Finn Delaney's hand grasping his forearm in a
viselike grip. He glanced at Finn, seated beside him, and saw
that all the color had suddenly drained from his face. They exchanged quick glances and Lucas saw the fear in Finn Delaney's eyes. He tried to swallow and found himself unable to.
His throat felt constricted. The realization struck them both at
the same time.

Whoever had stolen the warp discs had used them to hijack
a Soviet nuclear submarine, a mobile, submerged and therefore practically undetectable strategic missile base. And with a
V-20 warp disc, the Russian sub could be equipped for time
travel and teleportation.

1 _____

"Apparently," said Forrester, "no one knows exactly when the Soviet sub disappeared. Its disappearance was officially reported on November 12, but the Kremlin was aware of it as early as two weeks prior to that date. The head of the Observer Corps outpost in that time period and location is Lieutenant Colonel Powers, whose cover is that of an agent for United States Central Intelligence functioning as a mole within the KGB headquarters in Moscow. From him, we have the following:

"Jan Mayan Island is a small spit of rock of about 145 square miles located in the Arctic Ocean between the northern part of Norway and Greenland. The island is owned by Norway and its remote location, as well as the savage climate, in which temperatures fall between 40 and 50 degrees below zero with a windchill factor of over 100 below, make it an ideal place for submarines keeping an eye on the passage from beneath the Arctic icecap. There is no sloping continental shelf, just vertical cliffs rising up out of the sea and dropping off rapidly to great depths, making it ideal for a large submarine to lie close in, completely undetected. A perfect location for a hidden missile base. There was nothing on Jan Mayan at the time except for a small meteorological station. The last coded radio transmission from the *Vostochnaya Slava* was a routine message on October 28, and then the submarine disappeared without a trace. The United States denied any involvement in the disappearance of the sub. This information was backed up by CIA reports to which Powers, of course, had access.

"Subsequently, the TIA compiled data from other stations in *other* time periods, among which were the following reports. In July of 1783, the British man-of-war *Avenger* picked up the sole survivor of another British man-of-war, the *Covenant*. The shipwreck victim died soon after being rescued,, but not before claiming the *Covenant* had been sunk by a 'sea monster' capable of great speed which spat fire at the ship. He described it as being larger than a whale, with a fin very like a shark's. Clearly, it could have been the sail of a nuclear submarine.

"In August of 1652, during Britain's war with the Dutch over the First Navigation Act, the Dutch ship *Amsterdam* was blown out of the water and completely obliterated while in a naval engagement with the British ship, *Albatross*. The *Albatross* was destroyed in a flash burn, going up like a tinderbox. The survivors who managed to get away in boats all died of what was reported to be scurvy, although the symptoms were far more indicative of radiation sickness. Nearby ships reported the explosion of the *Amsterdam* as being 'cataclysmic,' surmising she was loaded to her gunwales with powder. However, the powder magazine's explosion would not have accounted for the flash burn of the *Albatross*. An atomic torpedo would.

"Numerous sightings of a maritime phenomenon variously described as 'an enormous thing,' a 'long, spindle-shaped object,' and an 'aquatic mammal of unknown origin' were reported in the 19th century, beginning in the year 1866, when the steamer *Governor Higginson* of the Calcutta and Burnach Steam Navigation Company encountered a 'moving mass' five miles off the coast of Australia. On the 23rd of July of that same year, a similar sighting was reported in the Pacific Ocean by the *Columbus*, of the West India and Pacific Steam Navigation Company. At the time, it was noted that these two sightings were separated by a period of three days and a distance of over seven hundred nautical leagues. About two weeks later, the *Helvetia*, of the Compagnie-Nationale and the

Shannon, of the Royal Mail Steamship Company, both sighted a 'monster' in the Atlantic between the United States and Europe, estimating its length at over five hundred feet, which would either have made it a whale of unprecedented size, a sea monster of some sort, or a submarine. Several of these sightings also reported the 'creature' was capable of astonishing speed, others reported that it submerged immediately.

"Finally, the most telling piece of evidence was uncovered on Jan Mayan Island, when a TIA surveillance team, clocked back to the site of the Soviet sub's disappearance, found an abandoned Spatial Anomaly Displacement Detector. Needless to say, they did not have SADD's in the 20th century. Temporal Intelligence fed all available data into their computers and, given the available evidence, they have recreated a scenario of the most likely possibility for what occurred in the Arctic on or about October 28, 1993 . . ."

The Arctic Wind howled through the rocks of the barren, ice-encrusted island, making it next to impossible for the men to remain standing upright. They crouched behind an outcropping, huddled close together in their temperature-controlled suits, looking like slick sea lions as the spray glistened on polymer fabric, making droplets on the visors of their form-fitting helmets. One man bent low over the Spatial Anomaly Displacement Detector, adjusting the directional and depth scan and watching the screen intently, his eyes locked onto the soft, green-glowing grid coordinate lines that crisscrossed the monitor. A low, deep, resonant voice spoke over the headset inside his helmet.

"Anything yet?"

"Not yet. She's down there. It's just a matter of time. You can't hide something that displaces 28,000 tons from this instrument. All we need to do is—"

A softly glowing red outline in the shape of a submarine suddenly appeared upon the grid screen.

"Got her! Look at that! Isn't she a beauty?"

"You can admire her at your leisure later," the voice came back over his headset. "Right now, I'd appreciate having the transition coordinates. I would prefer a more hospitable environment.''

"Coming right up . . . Captain," the man said, glancing over his shoulder and grinning behind his faceplate. "Stand by. We're going down and under!"

There were fourteen men seated in the wardroom of the submarine. They were all young, ranging in age from twenty-two to thirty-five, and dressed in dark-blue, short-sleeved jumpsuits. The temperature inside the submarine was a comfortable, constant 70 degrees and the fluorescent lights were white, for day cycle. At the end of the watch, they would go to red interior light to simulate nighttime. Several of the men were eating snacks; others were drinking coffee and smoking cigarettes. Valentin Mikhailov watched Aleksander Muraviov's face intently as the latter frowned down at the pieces of the chessboard, pursing his lips thoughtfully. At twenty-nine, Mikhailov was senior to the younger Muraviov by seven years. He smiled, slightly. Muraviov was going to lose again. Still, he got better every time. He had the makings of an expert player and Mikhailov knew it would not be very long before he would be giving him good matches. He picked up his package of American cigarettes, unfiltered Camels, and lit one up, drawing the smoke in deeply and exhaling it through his nostrils.

"*Davaye, davaye, Sasha,*" he said, addressing Muraviov by the affectionate diminutive of his first name, "*ni kopaisiya.*" (Come on, come on, Sasha, don't dawdle.)

"*Zatknise, Mikhailov. Uspakoisya. Ya dumaiyu.*" (Shut up, Mikhailov. Calm down. I'm thinking.)

"*Sleduistchi budiet mat.*" (Next move will be mate.)

"*Yob tebyeh, Valentin.*" (Fuck you, Valentin.) Muraviov compressed his lips into a tight grimace and shook his head. "*Aah, nyet smisla.*" (Aah, what's the use?) He knocked over his king.

"*Istcho raz?*" said Mikhailov. (One more time?)

Muraviov grinned and began to set up the pieces for a new game. Suddenly, he looked over Mikhailov's shoulder and his eyes grew wide. "*Chiyort vazmi!*"

Two men dressed head-to-toe in weird-looking, shiny suits materialized in the wardroom out of thin air. In the split-second instant of shocked hesitation by the members of the submarine's crew, both of them twisted something in their hands and gently lobbed two slender tubes onto the floor. There was a hissing noise. Mikhailov shot out of his chair, but didn't even take two steps before his eyes rolled up and he collapsed. It took only a matter of seconds. All fourteen men were unconscious. At that same moment, the exact scene was replayed when one man materialized in the submarine's control room, another in the engine room and one in the crew's quarters. The invisible gas spread rapidly throughout the sub. There was never any chance of giving an alarm. The five men moved rapidly through the boat, already familiar with its layout. They released more gas, just to be safe, making certain that each member of the submarine's crew was incapacitated. In less than five minutes, they controlled the boat.

"All right," said their leader, over the comcircuit in their helmets. "Nicely done. Now let's get that equipment on board."

When Forrester had finished, one of the soldiers raised her hand.

"Sergeant Chan," said Forrester.

She stood as she was called on. "Sir, assuming a small strike force of some sort actually did manage to overpower the crew of a Soviet submarine, how would they plan to operate it? Wouldn't it require highly specialized training of the sort no longer offered in present time?"

Forrester nodded. "An excellent point, Sergeant Chan. We have two possible answers to that one. One, it is not beyond the realm of possibility for this to have been a long-range plan on the part of the hijackers. With access to warp discs, they could easily have clocked back to Minus Time, to the 20th century, and enlisted in the United States Navy, for example. The Navy had a nuclear-powered submarine training school in Idaho Falls and they might have obtained the necessary knowledge in that manner. However, that would have been doing it the hard way. If we are to presuppose an extremely organized, highly skilled group, then it makes more sense to assume at least one of their number was a therapist trained in re-education procedures. Getting their hands on the necessary equipment would have been child's play after what they've already accomplished. Once they had overpowered the submarine's crew, they could then condition them at their leisure to follow orders unquestioningly. Given the mentality of the Soviet military, that would not have been terribly difficult to do. The predisposition for unquestioning obedience would already have been there."

Another soldier raised his hand. "Lieutenant Bryant?" said Forrester.

"Is there any indication of the purpose behind this act?" said Bryant.

"As of right now, no," said Forrester. "There has been no contact, no demand for ransom, nothing. Temporal Intelligence believes the group is putting the sub through its paces, giving it a shakedown cruise while they familiarize themselves with its capabilities."

Lucas raised his hand. "Major Priest," said Forrester.

"Just what *are* it's capabilities, sir?" he said.

"The Soviet Typhoon-class subs were capable of sustained underwater cruising speeds in excess of sixty knots. Their titanium double hulls rendered magnetic detection virtually impossible and they were extremely quiet-running. They carried a full complement of ordnance, ranging from standoff missiles with a reported range of about 125 kilometers to cruise missiles, so-called "smart" missiles capable of being fired from the submarine's torpedo tubes and flying as low as ten feet above the water, thereby defeating radar. They also carried a full range of torpedoes, from homing and wake-following to antisubmarine and conventional type. Last but not least, they were equipped with twenty ballistic missiles, capable of being launched from silos via hatches in the deck. These were of the MIRV type, or Multiple Independently Targeted Reentry Vehicle, with as many as fourteen or fifteen warheads on one missile, aimed at different targets hundreds of miles apart. These were launched when the missile reached the top of its trajectory, from the nose cone. This method was facilitated by use of an inertial guidance system. Measuring devices known as accelerometers recorded movement in every direction aboard the submarine and sent signals to the missile computers, which translated those signals into the sub's exact position at any given time. Consequently, there was never any need to aim the missiles. If an order for launch was received, it would take only moments, if not seconds, to go through the procedure necessary to fire the missiles. One such MIRV missile could be fired every minute. No input into the ballistic computers was needed. The missiles would already know where they had to go."

Finn expelled the breath he had been holding in a soft *whoosh*. He raised his hand. "Delaney?" said Forrester.

"How deep could these things go, sir?"

"The Typhoon sub could dive to a depth of over four thousand feet," said Forrester. "However, that is a conservative figure. We don't know what the crush depth of the Soviet subs was and there's every reason to believe they were capable of going deeper. Also, due to the fact the Soviets were always classification-happy, and due to the fact no one had ever succeeded in actually capturing a Soviet nuclear sub—"

"Until now," Andre said, softly.

"—there is very little known about their actual capabilities. Without a pipeline into the KGB, we would have known even less."

There was a profoundly uneasy silence in the room. Forrester glanced about grimly at all the tense faces.

"If there are no further questions for the moment, I'll continue. I've received an order for complete mobilization of the First Division. Both Temporal Intelligence and the Referee Corps are proceeding on the assumption the object of the hijacking is blackmail, on a nuclear scale. It's the only scenario that makes any sort of sense. We—"

Andre raised her hand. "Yes, Corporal Cross?" said Forrester.

"Excuse me, sir, but it occurs to me that we should have the means of dealing with a threat of this nature. Satellite detection, combined with BPW technology would—"

"If I may anticipate you," Forrester interrupted, "there's a basic flaw in your reasoning. It's essentially good reasoning and it would certainly solve the problem if it were not for the submarine now being capable of temporal translocation. We can't exactly put satellites in orbit in every conceivable period of time where the submarine might show up. It simply isn't practical. Moreover, even if we had the logistics to accomplish such a task, there exist certain insurmountable problems. While Beam Particle Weaponry might well neutralize a ballistic missile threat, there are certain scenarios in which we would not be able to employ BPWs. For example, suppose the submarine was clocked into the 20th century. Its advanced design would still enable it to avoid detection by the world powers of that time. However, keep in mind the technological capabilities of the governments of the 20th century. It's extremely doubtful we'd be able to deploy surveillance satellites and BPWs without their being alerted. The United States had their space shuttle already operational by the early 1980's. The Soviets also had orbital vehicles of their own. If we put up so much as one orbital satellite, chances are it would be discovered fairly quickly and orbital missions would be launched to investigate. Do you really want either the 20th-century Americans or Russians to find a Beam Particle Weapon in orbit?''

Andre grimaced and nodded. ''Yes, sir. I see your point. I'm sorry.''

''Don't be. What we need now are ideas. If anyone has a brainstorm, fire away. The worst that will happen is your idea will be shot down. Meanwhile, we will proceed with the only other option currently available to us. Several teams are going to be held in reserve, in case any temporal adjustment missions come up that require immediate action while all this is going on. The rest of you are going to be clocked to various locales in Minus Time to investigate reports of sightings that could be the submarine. It'll be like looking for a needle in a haystack, people, but there isn't much else we can do at the moment. We have to locate the sub first. Then it has to be destroyed. I have here a list of assignments which I will give to Major Priest. Immediately upon receiving your assignment, you will report for mission programming, then draw your equipment and clock out to your designated time periods. You will have full Observer Corps and TIA support. In the meantime, there is already an extensive effort under way to locate the ERG these people are drawing on for power. *If* it can be located, then it can be destroyed or taken off-line, and at least then the submarine will no longer be capable of time travel or teleportation within any specific time period. However, I don't need to remind you of the odds for locating their ERG. The trouble with an Einstein-Rosen Bridge is that it's trans-temporal. It could be in our time period or in Minus Time. For that matter, it could be on another planet or on an asteroid or even aboard a ship somewhere in space. Don't hold your breath waiting for it to be found. It ain't very damn likely."

Finn raised his hand. "Yes, Delaney?" Forrester said.

"What happens if these people start issuing demands before we're able to do anything about them?"

"In that case," said Forrester, grimly, "we're going to do exactly what they tell us to. The situation's just too damn scary to attempt calling their bluff."

Another soldier raised his hand. "Captain Sullivan?" said Forrester.

Sullivan stood up. "What about clocking a warp grenade out to Jan Mayan Island and blowing it off the face of the map before the hijacking could occur? Then the hijackers would wind up materializing in the middle of the Arctic Ocean. They wouldn't survive more than a few minutes, at the very most."

"The trouble with that suggestion is it would also kill the personnel at the meteorological station there," said Forrester. "The question of whether or not that could be justified under the circumstances is highly debatable. It would entail some risk, in any case. However, what makes the point moot is the presence of the Soviet sub just off Jan Mayan. The last thing we want to do is set off any large explosions in the vicinity of a strategic missile carrier. It could have unfortunate consequences. Besides, any interference with the hijackers before the fact would raise the possibility of creating a timestream split. We already have proof they've managed to bring off the hijacking successfully. If we go back and prevent it, we'd be creating a temporal disruption and risking the creation of a parallel timeline in which there was a nuclear sub on the loose."

Sullivan made a wry face. "I'm sorry, sir, I should have thought of that."

"Nothing to be sorry about, Captain. You have a few things to learn yet about this unit. When you transferred in from

Ordnance, you left the regular corps behind. In the First, no one's going to jump on you for making mistakes. Here in Plus Time, it'll only help you learn. In Minus Time, it'll cost you. Don't be afraid to make mistakes, Captain. Just be sure you make them here."

"Yes, sir. Thank you."

"All right then, if there are no other questions, let's get the show on the road. We've got us a submarine to sanction. Dismissed."

2

"Professor—"

"Please," said the thin, elegantly dressed neatly bearded man, smiling in a self-effacing manner and holding up his hand. He spoke in English, but with a French accent. "While I am flattered at having a professorship thus conferred upon me, I do not merit the title. I am trained as an attorney. Besides, I am only thirty-eight years old. Being addressed as Professor makes me feel rather like a hoary academician."

The reporter from *The New York Times* smiled. "All right, then. But you did write *Mysteries of the Great Submarine Grounds*, so let's not be too modest about your reputation in academic circles."

"Only in a somewhat obscure branch of natural history," said the man, with a slight smile. He was all too well aware of how American reporters had a tendency to blow things out of proportion. One small, theoretical work, published in France in two slim volumes in an exceedingly small print run, and they were ready to seize upon it as an excuse to quote him as an expert. He had far too many friends in the scientific community and far too much respect for their accomplishments to want to be cast as a colleague on an equal footing.

"Well, we won't split hairs," said the reporter from *The New York Times*. "The point is you *have* been invited to represent your country on this expedition and obviously—"

22

"No, no, *please*," said the man, looking pained. "Really, sir, you quite embarrass me. I beg you to communicate the details correctly to your readers, if only to spare me future discomfort when I arrive back home. In point of fact, the kind invitation from Secretary Hobson *did* mention your government would be pleased to see France represented in this enterprise, however, he was speaking purely as a matter of form, you understand. In truth, it was I who requested permission to sail with Commander Farragut aboard the *Abraham Lincoln*. I practically *begged* myself a berth. Your government was merely humoring a somewhat presumptuous novelist who only dabbles in scientific matters."

"Nevertheless, Mr. Verne," the reporter persisted, "the very fact your request was granted obviously indicates that your opinion as a 'dabbler in scientific matters,' as you say, is valued. In that context, surely you have some theories as to the nature of this phenomenon?"

"Well," said Jules Verne, "I prefer to keep an open mind. However, I do have some ideas, and I stress that they are merely ideas, theories, you understand. We have, as yet, no empirical evidence to support them, so making any sort of conclusions would be extremely premature."

"Yes, well, what do you *think* it might be?" the reporter pressed him, anxious for a good quote.

Somewhat hesitantly, Verne replied. "After examining one by one the different theories, rejecting all nonsensical suggestions, it seems necessary to admit the possibility of the existence of a marine animal of enormous power."

The reporters on the dock scribbled hastily.

"The great depths of the ocean are entirely unknown to us," continued Verne. "Soundings cannot reach them. What passes in those remote depths—what beings live, or can live, twelve or fifteen miles beneath the surface of the waters—is something we can scarcely conjecture. Either we do know all the varieties of beings which exist upon our planet or we do not. If we do *not* know them all, if Nature still has secrets in the deep for us, nothing is more conformable to reason than to admit the possibility of the existence of fishes or cetaceans or even of new species heretofore unknown inhabiting the regions inaccessible to soundings. It is certainly within the realm of possibility that an accident or an event of some sort has brought such a creature at long intervals to the upper levels of the ocean.''

"So you're saying a sea monster, then?" said another man, from the *Tribune*, excitedly.

"No, sir, I said no such thing," said Verne, carefully. "I merely said the possibility exists that there are creatures on the ocean floor belonging to species which have not as yet been discovered. If, on the other hand, such is not the case, which is *also* a possibility, we must necessarily seek for the animal in question amongst those marine beings already classed. In such a case, I should be disposed to suspect the existence of a gigantic narwhal.''

"What exactly is that, Professor?" one of the other reporters called out.

Verne winced slightly. "The common narwhal, or unicorn of the sea, is a large mammalian creature which often attains a length of sixty feet. Increase its size fivefold or tenfold, give it strength proportionate to its size and you will have the animal required. It will have the proportions determined by the officers of the *Shannon*.''

"So you're saying it's just a big whale and that's all?" said the man from *The New York Times*, with some disappointment. "How would you account, then, for the sinking of the *Scotia* just last week?"

"I do not account for it," said Verne. "I do not have access to all of the details. True, the last transmission from the *Scotia* did report the sighting of a 'monster,' however, we have no evidence suggesting it was this so-called monster which caused the sinking of the ship.''

"But suppose it *was* the monster," the man from the *Telegraph* called out. "I mean, how could a whale sink a steamship? How do you account for the explosion witnessed by the *Moravian* from several miles away?"

"Well, so long as we all understand that what we are dealing with here is merely supposition," Verne said, "we can suppose the narwhal—if it is a narwhal—might have caused the sinking. Such a creature would be more than just a big whale, as you say. The narwhal is armed with a sort of ivory sword, a halberd, according to the expression of certain naturalists.

The principal tusk has the hardness of steel. Some of these tusks have been found buried in the bodies of whales. Others have been drawn out, not without trouble, from the bottoms of ships, which they had pierced through and through. The Museum of the Faculty of Medicine in Paris possesses one of these defensive weapons, two yards and a quarter in length and fifteen inches in diameter at the base. Very well.''—He paused for breath—''Suppose this weapon to be six times stronger and the animal ten times more powerful. Launch it at the rate of twenty miles an hour and you obtain a shock capable of producing the catastrophe required. As to the explosion, there is a better explanation for that than to imagine some sort of sea monster capable of breathing fire. Remember the *Scotia* was a munitions ship. Given an accident, something undoubtedly caused a fire on board, thereby resulting in the powerful explosion which the men of the *Moravian* saw from their great distance. Until further information, therefore, I shall be predisposed to suspect our phenomenon might be a sea-unicorn of colossal dimensions, armed not with a halberd, but with a real spur, as the armored frigates or the 'rams' of war, whose massiveness and motive power it would possess at the same time.''

''What about some of the other theories, Mr. Verne?'' another reporter called out. ''What about this business that it's a floating island of some sort or maybe even a submarine boat?''

Verne chuckled. ''Well, there have been quite a number of theories proposed, true, but I prefer to deal with rational scientific inquiry rather than wild speculation. Islands do not float. Rock and earth cannot float in water. Islands are simply the projecting tips of submerged land masses or mountains, if you will. Someone, as I recall, suggested that we could be confronted with the floating hull of some enormous wreck. While this may sound somewhat plausible upon the surface, this theory collapses under careful scrutiny. What would provide the motive power for this floating hull that would enable it to act in the manner described in the various sightings? Moreover, what would keep this hull afloat, if it were, indeed, a wreck?

''As to the question of a submarine boat, I must admit to

being personally quite intrigued by such a possibility. However, keep in mind that a submarine vessel of such enormous power could hardly remain secret against inquiries made both here and abroad. That a private gentleman should have such a machine at his command, while smacking of romance, is certainly quite unlikely. Where, when, and how could it have been constructed? And how could its construction, ambitious an undertaking as it would have to be, be kept a secret? It is possible a government might possess such a destructive machine; however, it is quite unlikely in view of what we know of submarine boats coupled with the technological capabilities we have.

"Not to dismiss your question out of hand, sir," Verne continued, "consider the history of the so-called submersible boat. Alexander the Great is said to have had himself lowered into the sea while encased in a barrel of glass. Leonardo da Vinci also experimented with the idea of an undersea craft. In the 16th century, an English carpenter named William Bourne designed a submersible boat, but was unable to provide it with any means of propulsion. Drebbel likewise constructed several watertight boats capable of being submerged and propelled by means of oars, with air supplied by tubes reaching to the surface. Not a very practical device. The first real step in the development of submarine boats occurred during your American Revolution, when Colonel David Bushnell built his *Turtle*, which rather resembled two large turtle shells joined together. Propulsion was achieved by means of a crude hand crank, which turned a propellor. It was quite an ambitious device.

"In order to submerge, the vessel's lone crewman operated a valve which would let water into a ballast tank. To reverse the procedure, the water was pumped out. A pair of brass tubes admitted fresh air into the vessel and, upon submergence, these tubes were closed with cork valves. That would leave enough air inside to allow for a submerged period of some thirty minutes. The purpose of the vessel was to approach British ships unseen and attach an explosive device to their hulls by means of a screw device. However, the *Turtle* never succeeded in its task, was slow and crude in the extreme and subject to navigational problems due to the effect of currents. Now this was the first practical submarine boat for which any record exists. The second was also built by an American, your Mr. Robert Fulton, of steamboat fame.

"In 1800, he designed and built the *Nautilus*, expanding upon the same basic principles developed by Bushnell. He was unable to gain support in the United States, so he came to my country and tried to interest Napoleon in his vessel. He was given some funds, with which he managed to stage a demonstration in which he successfully sank a wreck placed at his disposal. However, Napoleon branded it a dishonorable device and, fearing that Napoleon intended to steal the *Nautilus*, Fulton destroyed it. He then tried to interest England. He failed there, as well. At that point, he apparently gave up in disgust and returned here to build his famous *Clermont*.

"The most recent use of submarine vehicles was also in your country, during the recent war among your states. Doubtless, you gentlemen will recall the story of the *Hunley*, a Confederate craft some forty feet long and four feet in the beam. Its propulsion was provided by eight men, sitting side-by-side and operating a sort of crankshaft which turned a screw propellor. I believe it was on the seventeenth of February, in 1864, that the *Hunley* managed to sink the *Housatonic* in Charleston Harbor by means of a gunpowder torpedo on the end of a long pole. Given the nature of the craft, the attack had to be made with the hatch open so visibility would be possible. As a result, the *Hunley* was swamped when the torpedo exploded and it sank with all hands. To that extent, it is somewhat debatable as to whether or not this was a successful attack and even whether or not it can properly be called a submarine attack.

"Now, gentlemen, the *Hunley* went down a mere two years ago. Are we to believe it is within the realm of possibility for science to have progressed so far as to enable, in two years, a submarine boat to be constructed which is capable of remaining submerged indefinitely and of attaining the sort of speeds reported in the sightings? Even if we were to accept such an astonishing development, well then, how would this submarine be able to resupply itself? What fantastic method of propulsion could it employ to attain such enormous motive power? How could it hope to attack other ships without risking damage to itself? How could its crew survive such long periods of submersion, even given the ability of storing oxygen in some manner which would enable such submersion, without being poisoned by the gases of their own exhalations? No, gentlemen, glamorous though the idea might be, it is quite ludicrous when examined from a practical standpoint. The technology simply does not exist which would allow for the construction of such a craft. That smacks of the sort of fantasy disreputable novelists such as myself indulge in." He smiled. "What we are concerned with here is a scientific expedition, not one of my *voyages extraordinaire*. Although, I must confess, I find the idea of a submarine boat constructed by means of some sort of super science to be quite appealing. I may even write about it someday. However, it's all nonsense, I assure you."

They addressed him as Professor once again when they thanked him for his statements and Verne slowly shook his head as he watched them rush off to file their stories.

"Newspapermen," he mumbled to himself. "Doubtless, they'll get everything all wrong, as usual, and confer a doctorate upon me to validate their stories."

He went on board the frigate and one of the sailors conducted him to the presence of the ship's captain, a tall and handsome officer with ramrod straight posture and a no-nonsense manner.

"Commander Farragut?" said Verne.

"You must be Mr. Verne," said Farragut.

The author looked surprised. "You know me, sir?"

"I have seen your photograph and I have had the pleasure of reading your *Five Weeks in a Balloon*. It's a pleasure to have you aboard, sir. Can it be you are considering turning your talents towards nautical adventure?"

"I have been giving the matter some thought," said Verne, smiling. "Perhaps this voyage will provide me with some necessary background. I'm afraid I'm liable to make quite a nuisance of myself, pestering everyone with questions. Please do not hesitate to tell me if I begin getting in your way."

Farragut grinned. "Think nothing of it. You go on ahead and make as much of a nuisance of yourself as you care to. My men know what they're about. I doubt answering a few questions will get in the way of their performing their duties. They're all quite looking forward to this venture. It will be something of a pleasure cruise for them.''

"A pleasure cruise? Do I take it, then, you do not believe in this so-called sea monster we are hunting?''

"Quite the contrary. I have been at sea long enough to know that one can never truly know the sea. I think there is something out there, although I doubt it is anything like some creature out of Greek mythology. Whatever it may be, I intend to hunt it down and rid the seas of it.''

"You mean to kill the creature?'' Verne said, aghast. "But why? Think of the importance such a find would have to science!''

"With all due respect, Mr. Verne, I strongly suspect your scientific-minded friends would be far happier to have this creature spread out on their dissecting tables rather than have it swimming about on the bottom of the ocean, inaccessible to them,'' said Farragut. "As for myself, my first responsibility is to the shipping companies. All this publicity and speculation about a sea monster is causing companies like Lloyd's to raise their premiums. No one is very happy about the prospect of having to pay more in order to have their ships insured against destruction by some sea monster.''

"Yes, but—but I was under the impression this was to be an expedition of scientific inquiry!'' protested Verne.

"And so it is,'' said Farragut. "You will find quite a diverse group on board for this voyage. We have sailing with us representatives of the New York Museum of Natural History, the Smithsonian Institution, the Royal Zoological Society and members of the faculties of several universities. I should think you'll be at no loss for stimulating company. As a matter of fact, if you have not yet had time for dinner, I would suggest you hasten to the wardroom, where our passengers are being served at this very moment. Now if you will excuse me, we shall have to continue this discussion at a future time. I must make preparations for getting under way.''

Verne paused only long enough to check his cabin, which he found he was sharing with someone else judging by the belongings placed there along with his, then proceeded to the wardroom. The other passengers were already sitting down to dinner when he entered. Upon seeing him standing in the doorway, one of the diners stood and beckoned him forward.

"Ah, I see we have a late arrival," said the man, speaking with a British accent. He was dressed in tweeds and wore thick wire-rimmed glasses. "Please, there is a place beside me here. You are only just in time."

The other diners started to rise, but Verne quickly waved them back down. "No, no, my friends, please, do not get up on my account."

He walked over to the seat indicated by the Englishman.

"Permit me to perform the introductions," said the Britisher. "This is Dr. Samuelson, of the Smithsonian." He indicated the man to his immediate left, a dapper, distinguished-looking gentleman with thinning gray hair, horn-rimmed glasses and a moustache. "Dr. Vandenburg, of the Museum of Natural History here in New York." The man he indicated nodded briefly, gazing out at Verne from beneath large, bushy black eyebrows. There were bread crumbs in his walruslike moustache. "Professor Priest of the University of Maine." Lucas nodded at him with a smile. "Dr. Delaney of the University of Boston and his associate, Professor Cross; Mr. Ned Land—"

"Of the university of hard knocks," said the brawny Land, with a wide grin, his blue eyes glinting with amusement at being included among such distinguished company.

"And, of course, myself. My name is Devries. Dr. Reginald Fitzhugh Devries, of the Royal Zoological Society."

"I am pleased to meet you all," said Verne, taking his seat. "My name is Verne. Jules Verne. And that would be Mister, not Doctor or Professor, please."

Priest and Delaney exchanged quick glances.

"Ah, yes, the eminent author," said Samuelson. "I had heard you would be sailing with us. It's a pleasure to make your acquaintance, Mr. Verne. Tell me, did those newspapermen outside descend upon you, as well?"

"I am afraid so," said Verne. "I attempted to reply to their queries to the best of my limited ability, but I was left with the feeling I had not told them quite what they wished to hear."

"What did you tell them?" Devries said.

Verne sugared his coffee and briefly recapped the interview for their benefit. Samuelson chuckled.

"What do you want to bet tomorrow's papers carry drawings of behemoth, horned whales with tusks like woolly mammoths beneath the headline, 'Eminent Author and Scientist Describes Sea Monster'?''

Verne looked wounded.

"Oh, now don't look that way, Verne. It wasn't your fault. Newspapermen hear only what they want to hear and they write it up the way they feel their readers will wish to read it."

"Never talk to 'em, myself," growled Vandenburg.

"This is most distressing," Verne said. "I was most careful to say I was only speaking in terms of theory and supposition—"

"Don't you worry about it, mate," said Land. "It'll all be old news in another week or so and nobody'll remember it."

"Well, what did *you* tell them, Mr. Land?" said Verne.

Land threw back his head and laughed. "What, *me?* Hell, they didn't want to talk to me! I'm no scientist fellow like you folks and I'm no famous writer, either. I ain't important enough for them to bother with."

"May one inquire, then, what it is you do, Mr. Land?" said Verne, politely.

"Me, I'm a harpooner by trade."

"A harpooner!"

"That's right. Best there is, too." In French, he added, "I'm the one that's going to catch that fish so these stuffed shirts here can fillet it."

Lucas, Finn, and Andre smiled, while Devries cleared his throat softly.

"I'm afraid one of the hazards of associating with learned people is they might be multilingual," Verne said, smiling and giving a sidelong look to Devries. Vandenburg alone seemed to have missed the comment. "You are Canadian?"

"Quebec, born and bred," said Land, not at all apologetic for his comment. "I come from a long line of whalers. Makes no difference to me whether this whale has tusks or horns or what-have-you. A fish is a fish, far as I'm concerned."

"Mr. Land, here, does not believe in our aquatic mammal," said Devries. "It seems only we stuffed shirts are quite so gullible as to give credence to such a theory."

"Is that so, Mr. Land?" said Verne.

"Just call me Ned," said Land. "All this Mister this, Professor that, and Doctor whoever makes my head swim.''

"Well, all right, then, Ned. And you must call me Jules.''

"And a fine French name, it is,'' said Land. "My grand-father was named Jules. But to answer your question, no, I do not.''

"But, Ned, you, a whaler by profession, familiar with all the great marine mammalia, surely *you* ought to be the last to doubt under such circumstances!''

"That's just the point, Jules,'' Land said. "As a harpooner, I've followed many a whale, killed a great number, too. No matter how strong or how large or, like your narwhal, how well armed they may have been, not a one of 'em would ever have been able to scratch the iron plates of a steamer.''

"But, Ned, they tell of ships which the horns of the narwhal have pierced through and through,'' said Verne.

"Wooden ships, may be,'' said Land. "Me, I've never seen it done. Till I see some proof, I deny that whales, cetaceans, sea-unicorns or whatever you want to call 'em could ever do what you say.''

"Well, Ned, I repeat it with a conviction resting on the logic of facts,'' said Verne, while the others followed the animated exchange. "I believe in the existence of a mammal powerfully organized, belonging to the branch of Vertebrata, like the whales, the chachalots or the dolphins, and furnished with a horn of defense of great penetrating power.''

"Humpf!'' said Land.

"Keep in mind one thing, my Canadian friend,'' said Verne. "If such an animal exists, it inhabits the very depths of the ocean, frequenting the strata lying miles below the surface. It must, therefore, necessarily possess an organization the strength of which would defy all comparison.''

"And why would that be?'' Land said.

"Because it would require great strength in order to survive in those depths. Allow me to explain. I am certain our friends here will bring me up short if I am in error. Let us imagine the pressure of the atmosphere is represented by the weight of a column of water 32 feet high. Now, Ned, when you dive, as many times 32 feet of water as there are above you, so many times does your body bear a pressure equal to that of the atmosphere, which is 15 pounds for each square inch of surface.

At 320 feet then, this pressure would equal 10 atmospheres, at 3,200 feet, 100 atmospheres and at 32,000 feet, the pressure would be equal to 1,000 atmospheres. By simple arithmetic, we can determine that if you were able to attain this depth, for every foot you were to go down, your body would be subject to a pressure of approximately half a ton. Now, to a certain degree, this pressure is negligible because the air penetrates the interior of your body with equal pressure. This is why you are able to walk about without perceiving the effects of atmospheric pressure. This is also why you are able to dive down into the water, to a certain depth, and not be crushed. However, the deeper you dive, the more the pressure increases. At 32 feet beneath the surface of the sea, you would undergo a pressure of some 97,500 pounds. And, despite this pressure, pearl divers, for example, are able to survive at such depths. But the pressure increases correspondingly the deeper you go, so that at 32,000 feet, it would be some 97,500,000 pounds —with the result that you would be flattened as if you had been caught between the plates of a hydraulic machine.''

"The devil!'' said Land.

"Now,'' said Verne, "if some vertebrate, several hundred yards long and large in rough proportion, can survive in such depths, consider then what must be the resistance of its bony structure in order to withstand such amazing pressure.''

"Why,'' said Land, "it would have to be as strong as an armored frigate, plated with iron eight inches thick!''

"Exactly,'' Verne said. "And think what destruction such a creature would cause if it propelled itself with the speed of a locomotive against the hull of a vessel!''

"Yes, well,'' said Land. "Could be. You argue your case most convincingly, *mon ami*.''

"So have I convinced you?'' Verne said.

Recalcitrant to the end, Land shook his head. "I follow your reasoning,'' he said, "and you have convinced me that *if* such creatures exist at the bottom of the sea, then they must needs be as strong as you say. But I will still hold my judgment till I have seen some proof that there are, indeed, such creatures. I've spent forty some odd years upon the sea and I have yet to see one.''

Samuelson laughed. "It is quite obvious, Mr. Land, that

you will never make a good newspaperman. You are far too pragmatic."

"And what about you, my friends?" said Verne, turning to the incognito Time Commandos. "You have said nothing. Have you any ideas to contribute to this discussion?"

Lucas cleared his throat. "Well, I am a simple university biology professor. I hesitate to speak in such learned company. However I am of the same opinion as Mr. Land, here. I prefer to reserve judgment until some tangible evidence is at hand. There have certainly been enough curious reports to warrant an investigation, which is why we are all here, but none of us have any idea, really, just what it is we are investigating. I am enthusiastic over the possibility of there being some unique aquatic form of life heretofore unknown, but then the ocean is quite large and for all we know, we may even be searching in the wrong waters. These things take time. Fortunately, I am on sabbatical and this provides a convenient excuse to legitimize a long sea voyage. Perhaps we shall encounter something, perhaps not. I am content to wait and see."

"A most laudable attitude," said Devries. "Chances are, indeed, we will encounter nothing of any significance. However, one never knows until one goes and looks, eh?"

"And what about yourself, Dr. Delaney?" Verne said.

Finn shrugged. "If we do not find anything, Professor Cross and I will have wasted our time, so I prefer to remain optimistic. The university expects something for its money. I hope we won't have to disappoint them."

"How does Dr. Martinson regard this curious phenomenon?" said Verne.

"Dr. Martinson?" said Finn.

"Yes, surely, being from the University of Boston, you know him?"

"I'm afraid not," said Finn. "It's quite a large university, you know."

Verne frowned. "But Phillip Martinson is the chairman of the Department of Marine Biology!" he said. "How can you not know him? Surely, he must have conferred with you concerning this voyage!"

"Oh, *Phillip*!" Finn said, quickly. "Oh, yes, of course.

Forgive me, I tend to be a bit preoccupied on occasion. Yes, well, we spoke about it briefly and his attitude was much the same as Professor Priest's. Cautious optimism, you know.''

"I trust his leg is better," Verne said. "He was having difficulty with it when last I saw him. It must have healed by now."

"Oh, yes, Phillip is just fine," Finn said. "He bounds about the campus like an undergraduate."

Verne smiled. "I'm very pleased to hear that." The ship gave a lurch. "Well, I perceive we are getting under way. If you gentlemen, and lady, will excuse me, I think I will go up on deck and watch as we leave the harbor."

"Let's all go," said Devries. "It will be a while before we see land again."

As they filed out of the wardroom, Verne drew Finn aside momentarily, letting the others go before them.

"I just wanted to tell you, Doctor," he said, "how very pleased I was to hear Phillip Martinson is feeling so much better. Truly, it must have been an astonishing recovery. Doubtless, they'll be writing it up in the *Lancet* any day now."

"Oh?" said Finn, feeling suddenly unsure of his ground.

"Yes, quite," said Verne, smiling. "You see, Phillip Martinson has been confined to a wheelchair these past four years. He lost both his legs at Shiloh."

3

"I don't believe it," Finn said, throwing his cap down on the bunk. "We haven't even left the harbor yet and already I've blown my cover!"

"What happened?" Lucas said, frowning. "It was Verne, wasn't it? You slipped up."

"That's putting it mildly," said Finn. " 'How's Phillip's leg?' 'Oh, just fine, Mr. Verne, he's all healed up and running around campus like an undergraduate.' Me and my big mouth. Turns out Phillip Martinson lost both legs at the Battle of Shiloh."

"Oops," said Lucas.

"He hasn't told the others yet," Finn said. "He looked smug as hell about it, but he didn't pursue it. I wonder what he's thinking." He shook his head. "Damn. I told them it was a dumb idea to have us pose as university professors. And they had to pick well-known universities!"

"It was a calculated risk," said Lucas. "Samuelson, Devries and Vandenburg didn't know anyone from Maine or Boston. Nobody figured on Verne, though. He was a last-minute addition. Hell of a thing, running into him of all people."

"Well, I'm going to have to think of something to tell him," Finn said.

Lucas thought for a minute. "Why not pretend to be an undercover journalist?"

"That's not bad," said Finn. "Only why would a journalist need to go to such lengths just to get aboard? Why not simply come on board as a reporter?"

"Maybe because people, scientists especially, don't really act themselves when they know there's a reporter around taking everything down," said Lucas. "We already know how this bunch feels about reporters."

Finn nodded. "I like it. We'll go with it. I'll make Andre my assistant or something. We might as well hang on to your cover, so long as it's not blown. Just be careful what you say, especially around Verne. He's pretty sharp. Those others exist in that rarified atmosphere of academics, but Verne's a writer and writers watch everything obsessively."

"I'd say he was the least of our problems. I just keep wondering why there have been so many sightings in this fairly localized period as opposed to any other. It strongly suggests there's a special reason why that sub is here."

"Can you think of any particular thing about this time period that might attract them?" said Finn.

Lucas shook his head. "Hell, take your pick. Without anything positive to go on, we'd just be making wild guesses. This has to be the longest shot we've ever taken. That sub can translocate literally anywhere. This whole mission is nothing but a giant crap shoot."

"Well, we can always hope the Fate Factor intervenes," said Finn. "It would be nice to have temporal physics working for us for a change."

"Please," said Lucas. "I'd rather not discuss the Fate Factor so soon after that last mission." He touched his eyepatch.

"Sorry. That was insensitive of me."

There was a soft knock at the cabin door and Andre came in.

"The equipment's all secure," she said. "I've locked the cabin door, but it bothers me to leave it unattended."

"If we spend all our time watching it, that will only arouse curiosity," said Lucas. "The cabin's locked, the ordnance is packed away and locked. No one would know what the hell to do with it if they found it, anyway. Besides, I've got my trusty little alarm pager right here. It's as secure as it can be under the circumstances."

"Just the same," said Andre, "I don't think I'll be sleeping very well, alone in my cabin with a grenade launcher and ten warp grenades."

"You can always bring some strapping young sailor in there to keep you company," said Finn, grinning. "Just don't tell him what's underneath the bunk. That might kill all the romance."

"Or it might make things more interesting," she said with a smile.

"Well, first order of business is to check the ship out thoroughly and make note of all the crew stations," Lucas said. "We need to find a place we can fire the grenades from without being seen. If the sub is sighted, we'll have to move very fast. There will be a lot of excitement and that will work in our favor, because everyone will be watching the sub."

"Suppose we *are* seen?" Andre said.

"Then we'll just have to improvise," said Lucas. "The important thing is to destroy the sub and verify its destruction. Making sure nobody starts examining the warp grenades is the second priority. Making sure we get away safely only comes third. I don't think we'll be in any danger. At worst, Farragut will have us put in the brig, assuming there's a brig aboard this ship. If we get caught, they'll want to ask us lots of questions. So let's get our routine straight. Andre, since Finn just blew his cover—"

"*What?*"

"It's not serious. Verne caught him in a lie, so you're both undercover journalists now. Anyway, since you're both reporters, we can't exactly have you playing around with any scientific apparatus. I'll take over monitoring the SADD and radar and infrared gear."

"Just make sure none of the others gets too close a look at any of it," Finn said.

"No problem. I'm a professor, but I'm also something of a scientist and I've got ambition. I've been developing all this newfangled equipment and I'm very paranoid and possessive about it. Don't want anyone to steal my ideas. I may ruffle a few feathers, but these people will surely understand that."

"Good. That should work," said Finn.

"Andre," Lucas said, "you'll be in charge of the grenades. First sign of trouble, you clock out with them."

"What about you and Finn?"

"That'll depend on what the situation's going to be," said Lucas. "A warp grenade makes one hell of a depth charge. The only chance the sub's got of escaping complete destruction is to translocate before it goes off. One of us has to stay behind at least long enough to get a reading and make sure it's been destroyed. Since I'll be the one monitoring the instruments, I'm the logical candidate. Finn, once you've fired the grenade launcher, you clock out immediately. If for some reason that proves to be impossible, make sure you've fired your last grenade. Andre will be feeding them to you. No matter what, she *has* to clock out. I'll be scanning the instruments, so I won't be able to cover for her. You make sure she gets away, then if you can't clock out yourself, make sure the last grenade is fired and dump the launcher overboard."

"What about the instruments?" said Finn. "We can't let them get their hands on those."

"Better the instruments than the ordnance," said Lucas. "We'll take it step-by-step. I will already have established that it's experimental gear of my own design and they'll have no reason to tie me in with you. In all the excitement, I'll be able to get my readings. If they're positive, then we're home free. I can either toss them overboard when I'm done or clock out with them or just finish out the trip as Professor Priest. On the other hand, it might all go smoothly. We sight the sub, sink same, and Andre clocks out with all the gear. We report she fell overboard in all the fuss, very tragic, then wait until the ship makes port and simply walk off like the others."

"Sounds too damned easy," Finn said, scowling.

"The hard part's going to be getting lucky enough to encounter the sub," said Lucas. "And nailing it before it translocates. Any way you look at it, if we manage to get that lucky, the rest *is* easy."

"Yeah, famous last words," said Finn.

"That's okay," said Lucas. "You just keep thinking about what can go wrong. That way we'll be able to anticipate things better. The only—"

He broke off as the alarm pager went off.

"*Shit!* Someone's broken into Andre's cabin!"

They brust out of their cabin and ran down the companionway, covering the short distance to Andre's cabin in a moment. The door was closed, but it was unlocked and Andre had not left it that way. Finn reached into the waistband of his trousers and pulled out a small revolver, a Colt baby Patterson .28 caliber percussion pistol. Not as lethal as a laser, but far more suited to the time. He glanced at Lucas. Lucas nodded. He reached out, opened the door quickly, and stepped out of the way while Finn went in low, in case whoever was inside was armed.

Jules Verne was sitting on the bunk. He had opened the locks on their portmanteau and traveling chest and he had removed the ordnance cases. They were lying on the floor in front of him while he sat hunched over, in a posture similar to Rodin's Thinker. He did not look up as they came in.

"You know," he said, "I shall be forever grateful to that convict who taught me the trick of picking locks. I knew the skill would come in handy someday. Still, I was unable to get very far with these," he indicated the fastenings on the ordnance cases. "Most unusual design. Quite fascinating."

Lucas softly closed the door. "What is the meaning of this, Mr. Verne?" he said, tensely.

The writer was oblivious to the gun Finn held pointed at him. He kept staring at the ordnance cases.

"Fascinating," he said. "Absolutely fascinating. I have never before encountered a material even remotely like this. It appears to be of a high molecular weight, containing some manner of synthetic substance as its essential ingredient, possibly derived from a natural substance by some form of chemical treatment. Shaped by flow, undoubtedly, through the application of heat and pressure? Molded or cast. Yes, a laminate of some sort, no?"

"Mr. Verne," said Finn, "in case it has escaped your notice, I'm pointing a gun at you."

"Yes, well, *mon ami*, either you are going to shoot me or

you are not. The matter rests entirely in your hands. There is
not much I can do about it, in either case."

Finn glanced at Lucas helplessly. Lucas only shrugged.
Andre sat down on the bunk beside Verne.

"Is it your habit to break into a lady's room and search
through her belongings, sir?" she said, putting just the right
touch of indignation in her voice. "That is not the way a
gentleman behaves."

"I am not a gentleman, *ma chìre*," he said. "I am a novelist. Besides, no offense intended, but you are hardly what one
would call a lady. One glance at your shoulders and your
arms, to say nothing of the way you walk, and an astute
observer would instantly perceive you have not had an ounce
of pampering in your entire life. As for your compatriot, he
looks far more like a strongman than a university professor.
And I already know that he is not that. The question is, what
are you?"

"Very well, Mr. Verne," said Finn, putting the Colt away.
"I see we are going to have to be forthright with you. I hope
we can count on you not to give us away. The fact is, we are
reporters—"

"Oh, nonsense," Verne said, impatiently. He tapped the
ordnance cases. "Then how would you explain these?"

"Those are cases containing photographic equipment,"
Finn began, but Verne interrupted him.

"You are lying, sir. Perhaps you would care to open them?
I would like to see this photographic equipment."

"All right, look," Delaney said. "We don't have to explain
anything to you. You broke in here like a common thief."

"Then call Commander Farragut and demand I be ar-
rested," Verne said.

The three of them exchanged glances. "I think we've got a
problem," Andre said.

Verne leaned back against the bulkhead, crossed his legs
and lit a cigarette that he took out of a small, thin silver case.
He watched them with curiosity.

"Well, Mr. Verne," said Lucas, "now that you know we
are not what we say we are, the question is, what are you going
to do about it?"

"I honestly do not know," said Verne. "You three intrigue

me. Your intentions do not seem to be criminal, else you would have overpowered me and thrown me overboard. An accident. Such things occur. But you are not going to do that, I perceive, so we are at an impasse. You can kill me, but you seem reluctant to do so. I can expose you for the frauds you are, but I have no reason to. At least not at the moment. Aboard this ship, there is hardly any chance of your escape. So what do we do now, my friends?"

Finn looked at Lucas. "Do you believe this guy?"

"He's got nerve, I'll give him that," said Lucas.

"What is in those cases?" Verne said.

"That, Mr. Verne," said Andre, "is none of your business."

"Well, if whatever you have in there is any danger to this ship, since I am *on* this ship, I would say it is very much my business. However, let us see what we can infer. You have boarded this ship under false pretenses. Your intentions may or may not be criminal, though I am disposed to think they are not, else you would have handled my intrusion far more drastically. Obviously, the entire matter centers upon this expedition. You are clearly not what you claim to be. You, sir," he said, looking at Delaney, "have the appearance of a ruffian, yet I perceive you are an educated man. You," he glanced at Lucas, "have quite a military bearing and I doubt you lost your eye as a result of some disease or accident. You also limp, albeit very slightly, so I surmise you have seen some fairly recent military action. In the civil war, perhaps. As for you, my dear," he glanced at Andre, "you intrigue me most of all. Although you hide it well, your physical development is striking for a woman and there is something about your speech that is most interesting. I detect an accent, only the barest trace, something most people would not notice, yet I cannot put my finger upon it. I was initially disposed to think you were French, but you are not French. And then there is the curious matter of these cases, made of some sort of unique material and fastened by locks which seem to operate neither by key nor by combination. Astonishing. Truly astonishing. What can we infer from all of this?"

"Mr. Verne," said Andre, "you are far too perceptive for your own good."

"And then there is the matter of your timely arrival, prepared to deal with an intruder. You *knew* that I—or that someone—was in here, yet I made no noise breaking in and I did not set off any audible alarm. However, an alarm there must have been."

He got up quickly and walked over to the cabin door. Delaney grabbed him by the arm. "That will do, Verne."

"Should I cry out?" said Verne.

Finn took a deep breath. "Damn you." He let him go.

Verne bent down over the door latch, checking it and the area around it carefully. "Aha!" he said. "What have we here?"

He removed a small jackknife from his pocket, opened it, and used the blade to pry the small sensor loose.

"*Mon Dieu!* So small!"

"Finn, stop him!" Andre said.

"*How?*" said Delancy.

"Finn! An Irish name," said Verne. "Am I to suppose that Delaney is your real name, then?"

"Yes, they are our real names," said Finn, wryly.

"Well then, Finn, my friend," said Verne, showing him the sensor, "perhaps you could enlighten me as to what this is?"

"You're doing so damn well, you tell me."

"What logic tells me it must be, it cannot be," said Verne. "And yet, I can think of no other explanation. It *is* an alarm device of some sort, is it not? A miniature transmitter, but on such a scale! It is not possible. Yet, what else can it be? Such sophistication is unheard of."

"Mr. Verne," said Lucas, "you have inadvertently uncovered a top secret government mission. What you are holding is a highly classified piece of equipment. I must ask you to return it to me. This is a most delicate situation and you have seriously compromised us. If I cannot be satisfied that you can be trusted to remain silent about all of this, I'm afraid we shall be forced to do something very drastic."

Verne stared at him thoughtfully for a moment, then handed over the tiny sensor.

"Yes," he said, "yes, indeed. That you are agents of some sort, that I can believe. But there is much here that strains credulity. You may trust me to keep all this to myself, at least for the time being. I would not wish to force you into doing something very drastic, as you put it.'' He pursed his lips and stroked his beard. "But you have given me a great deal to think about. A very great deal, indeed. I shall have to sleep on it. Good night to you.''

He opened the door and walked out as casually as if he had been paying them a quiet social visit.

Finn exhaled heavily and turned to Lucas. "You were saying that he was the least of our problems?'' he said. He held up his thumb and forefinger, about a quarter of an inch apart. "He's *that* far from figuring out the truth.''

Lucas shook his head. "No, that's impossible.''

"Is it?'' Finn said. "You watch.''

"He's puzzled, true,'' said Lucas, "but there's just no way he'll ever guess we're from a future time. It would be too mind-boggling a concept for him.''

"Only you're forgetting one thing,'' said Finn. "This is the man who invented science fiction.''

Lucas bit his lower lip.

"What are we going to do?'' said Andre.

None of them had an answer.

4

An entire week passed with no sight of Jules Verne. He remained closeted in his cabin, pleading seasickness. His meals were brought in to him, but he ate extremely sparingly, if at all. The ship's doctor was sent in to see him and he announced the author did, indeed, appear to be suffering from nothing more serious than seasickness, claiming dizziness, nausea and an upset stomach. It would pass, the doctor said, there was no cause for concern. The three commandos, however, were very much concerned.

Time passed slowly aboard the ship as it steamed across the Atlantic, and they were not troubled by storms. Finn, Lucas and Andre had plenty of time and opportunity to examine the ship, observe the routine of its crew and pick put several likely places from which they might be able to launch their grenades unobserved if the submarine were sighted.

The three scientists proved to be no problem. Vandenburg was surly and morose by disposition, preferring to keep to himself and socialize to some limited extent only during mealtimes. The remainder of the time he spent reading, having brought several suitcases full of books along with him on the voyage. Samuelson and Devries were both considerably more gregarious, with Devries always wanting to discuss some scientific topic or another, which discussions were facilitated by the

45

implant programming the commandos went through in preparation for their mission. Still, Devries's expertise was so eclectic, they had to plead ignorance on several occasions when his discourse became far too esoteric for them. On such occasions, Devries was more than happy to quickly change the subject away from science to such fields as literature, theater, history and philosophy. He was one of those people who seemed to be able to talk about almost anything with authority and he dearly loved to talk, which did not endear him to Ned Land, who quickly grew bored listening to him go on and on. Samuelson turned out to be a chess fanatic, which gave him common ground with Lucas. They spent long hours playing, and discussing the finer points of the game.

Finn and Ned Land got along famously. One of Land's favorite pastimes was arm wrestling and, given his prodigious strength, he rarely lost. His harpooner's reflexes also gave him an edge in that regard, but in Finn Delaney, he met his match. The first time he challenged him, after having already bested the entire crew, it had been with a good deal of levity.

"Come on, then, Doctor, you're a stout fellow, let's see what you're made of."

Finn had accepted readily enough and a small group gathered round to see the "professor" get his comeuppance. The two men propped their elbows up on a keg, braced themselves and, at a signal from one of the onlookers, went to. Land's eyes widened in surprise immediately when he felt a strength opposing his that was equal to his own.

"Eh! Professor! That's some arm you've got there!"

Both men strained, hands locked, neither able to gain an advantage over the other. The crowd of onlookers grew and soon sailors were shouting encouragement and placing bets. It went on for almost four minutes, both men red-faced and sweaty, breathless from their exertions, until finally Land slowly started to give, fighting every last inch of the way. When Finn put him down at last, there was a mighty cheer and Land cheered loudest of all. He leaped up and clasped Finn in a bear hug, kissing both his cheeks and lifting him into the air. From that moment on, Land treated him like a brother.

Lucas kept monitoring the sea with his instruments every chance he got, closing them up immediately whenever anyone came near, acting suspicious and indignant whenever anyone questioned him about what he was doing. Since he only seemed to act so unreasonably when so occupied and was otherwise quite sociable, they soon left him alone at his task, writing it off to his scientific jealousy and insecurity.

For the first few days at sea, Andre was left pretty much to her own devices. Samuelson seemed somewhat misogynistic, Devries did not seem to feel women had much to contribute to intellectual discussion—in this, being typical of the men of his day—and Vandenburg was downright misanthropic. That left only Verne, who had removed himself from their company, and the officers and crew of the *Abraham Lincoln* who, like Ned Land, treated her with polite circumspection until one day one of the bolder sailors pinched her backside. Andre turned around and flattened him, to the amazement of his fellow crew members and Ned Land, who had witnessed the act. Thereafter, the crew of the *Abraham Lincoln* gave her a wide berth, but Land began to follow her around like a lovesick schoolboy, pathetically and endearingly trying to court her, as if he had never had anything to do with women before and didn't quite know how to go about it.

For her part, Andre found him to be quite attractive with his flaxen blond hair, sparkling blue eyes, wide smile and cleft chin, but his manner mystified her.

"What the hell's the matter with him?" she asked Finn one night. "God knows, I've dropped enough hints. If I was any more direct, I'd scare him off and ruin my chances. You men are so damned stupid, it's a wonder women ever manage to get laid!"

"Hey, I resent that!" Finn protested, laughing.

"Oh, you know what I mean. How the hell am I supposed to deal with a 19th-century male?"

"You should talk," said Finn. "You're a 12th-century female."

"With 27th-century sensibilities," she said. "Still, even in the 12th century, we were more direct than this! I like him. He's handsome, he's charming, he's fun, he's rough-edged and he has a terrific body. But he's so goddamn *dense*! What am I supposed to do, fall overboard?"

Finn began to laugh again, then saw the expression that suddenly appeared upon her face. "Oh, now *wait* a minute!"

"It's perfect! Why didn't I think of it before?"

"You can't be serious! That water's cold. By the time the ship could turn around—"

"It doesn't have to turn around! Not if we time it just right."

"*We?*"

"That's right, you're going to help me."

"Hey, get your own guys."

"Finn, dammit, you help me with this or I'll bust your jaw!"

"Boy, you're really nasty when you're in heat, you know that?"

A moment later, as he was picking himself up off the floor, he shook his head and said, "Okay, okay, I'll help you. But I hope you know what you're doing."

They timed it with excruciating precision. They took up their positions with Andre up forward and Finn roughly amidships. At the proper moment, Andre "slipped" and plunged over the side with a piercing scream loud enough to be heard in the Canary Islands. Instantly Land was diving over the side after her, hitting the water scant seconds after she did. Finn was ready with the rope and life preserver, tossing it to Land on cue. The ship was steaming along at a leisurely pace and there was plenty of time for them to be pulled aboard with the aid of several crewmen who instantly leaped to Delaney's aid. As Land picked her up in his arms, both of them shivering and streaming water down onto the deck, she threw her arms around his neck and said, "Oh, Ned! You saved my life! My hero!" And kissed him.

Lucas came running up to Finn, having heard all the commotion.

"What the hell happened?" he demanded.

"Excuse me," Finn said, brushing him aside. "I've got to go throw up."

They were eighteen days out when a knock came at Finn and Lucas's cabin door at about midnight. Finn opened the door to admit a haggard-looking Verne.

"I must speak with you," the author said, entering the cabin.

Lucas sat up in his bunk. "Are you all right, Mr. Verne?"

Verne waved his hand irritably. "I am *not* all right," he said. "Oh, I am occasionally seasick on an ocean voyage, but that is of no consequence. I have been for the past two weeks the victim of acute anxiety. I must ask you gentlemen to open those cases for me. I simply *must!*"

"Mr. Verne," Lucas began, "we've been through that. We simply cannot—"

"Then you must decide what sort of drastic thing it is you want to do about me," he said, visibly agitated. "For if I am not permitted to see what is inside those cases, I will go to Commander Farragut and tell him what I know."

"Mr. Verne," said Lucas softly, "we can't allow you to do that."

"That curious alarm device of yours," said Verne, "has left me almost completely bereft of sleep. I am on the verge of complete nervous collapse. I must know the nature of its operation, gentlemen!"

"Mr. Verne," said Finn, "Lucas explained to you. This is a top secret government—"

"Do you take me for a fool?" Verne almost shouted. "I *wanted* to believe you! I wanted for there to be some sort of sane, rational explanation, but there *isn't* one. You're lying to me. I know it beyond a question of a doubt. Even given all the resources of the American government or any other highly industrialized state, such a device could not possibly have been manufactured! *It contravenes known science.* It exists, yet it cannot exist. You understand, gentlemen, I am no scientist, but I keep abreast of new developments. I read voraciously; I am not an unversed layman. I do have some understanding of these things. The technology simply does not exist to manufacture such a thing! The scale of miniaturization is beyond *any* comprehension. There is no known power source which could be made small enough for such a device. There must be circuits, yet for someone to make circuits of such infinitesimal size, they would have to be able to dance upon the head of a pin! I must know how it was done. I must know what sort of process made those cases. I must know how those locks upon those cases operate when there are no apparent workings within them. I must know how these things were done. I must know *where* they were done. And I must know . . ."

He sat there, staring at them wildly.

"*Mon Dieu*, dare I say it?"

"Go on, Mr. Verne," said Finn.

In a voice that was almost a whisper, Verne said, "I must know *when*."

"Jackpot," Finn said.

Lucas gave him a tight-lipped look.

"I *am* right, am I not?" said Verne, softly. "I felt certain I was going mad. Or perhaps I am already mad. Please, gentlemen, I beg you, for the sake of my sanity, you *must* tell me!"

"Mr. Verne, Jules," said Lucas, "before this discussion goes any further, you must understand one thing. When I spoke of a top secret mission, I was not lying. If I tell you what you want to know, you must swear it will go no further than the confines of this room. Thousands upon thousands of lives could depend upon it."

Verne licked his lips and took a deep breath. "And if I do not swear so?"

"Then Finn and I will have to figure out some way to make certain you *cannot* tell anyone. We do not wish to harm you. We do not wish to harm anyone on board this ship. Chances are no one will believe you anyway, but we can't risk having our belongings searched. Please, Mr. Verne."

"All right," he said. "Conditionally, I will so swear. The condition is I cannot stand by and allow any wrongdoing. If that is what you intend, you shall have to kill me, for I will do everything within my power to stop you."

"I can accept that," Lucas said. "The answer, as you must already have surmised, is yes. We are not of this time."

Verne shut his eyes. "I knew it," he said. "I did not believe it was possible, but it was the only explanation that made any sort of sense. Both of you, and Miss Cross, as well—"

"Are from the 27th century," said Lucas.

Verne gasped. "The 27th . . . but . . . that is over seven hundred years in the future!"

"That's quite correct," said Finn.

"Travel through time," said Verne, awestruck. "I had thought about it from time to time—" he chuckled. "From time to time. Ironic choice of words, *n'est-ce pas*?" He stared at them both with wonder. "I had often thought of writing a story about it, but it seemed too incredible, too much of a fantasy for my sort of work. I always sought to strive for some believability and so I dismissed the notion. Yet . . . there are a thousand things I wish to ask you and I do not know where to begin! Yes, yes, of course I do. The most obvious questions is, why are you here? It is something about this creature, is it not? This must be like some sort of archaeology for you—but no. You said thousands upon thousands of lives could depend upon it. Surely an aquatic mammal could not threaten—no, naturally not, if it is so important, then . . ."

The sound of the forecastle gun was heard and there was shouting up on deck. Andre burst into the cabin. "It's Ned! He's sighted it! They've opened fire and—" She saw Verne and brought herself up short.

"Get the ordnance!" Lucas said. "*Move!*"

"What is it? What's—the creature!" Verne jumped to his feet as Finn and Andre both bolted out the door. Lucas put his palm up against Verne's chest and shoved him hard. He fell back against the bulkhead. Lucas grabbed his equipment and moved toward the door.

"I'm sorry, Jules," he said. "I can't explain now and you'd just get in the way."

He closed the door and locked it.

The torpedo struck amidships and the explosion rocked the *Abraham Lincoln*, blowing the steamer in two, obliterating men and metal alike as it shattered the ship's spine, sending a great gout of flame and smoke leaping high into the air to illuminate the night sky. Finn reached the deck with Andre right behind him and the shock of the explosion flung him over the rail into the sea. He never felt it when he hit the water.

"Finn! Finn, come on, wake up! Snap out of it, I'm getting tired."

"Andre?"

"Can you swim? Are you all right?"

Delaney began to tread water as Andre released him. He coughed as seawater sloshed into his mouth. "How long have I been out?"

"Don't know," said Andre. "Seemed like forever." She gasped, gulping in air. "The ship went down. I dove in after you when you went over. I think some boats got away, but there was a lot of noise . . . boilers blew . . . I screamed myself hoarse, but no one heard me."

"Lucas?"

"I don't know," she said.

"Damn."

"We're going to have to clock out, Finn. I can't stay afloat much longer. Holding you exhausted me."

"You're right," he said. "There's nothing else to do. We—"

"*Ha-llooo!*"

"Son of a bitch!" said Finn. "Someone's out there!"

"*Finn! Andre! Ha-llooo!*"

"That's Lucas! *Here! Over here!*"

They couldn't see a thing. The moon was full, but a thick fog had rolled in and visibility was practically nil.

"*Keep shouting so we can find you!*" Lucas cried. "*You sound very close!*"

"*God damn it, hurry up!*" yelled Andre. "*The water's freezing!*"

They heard Priest let out a whoop. "*Hang on, Andre! We're coming!*"

They shouted back and forth for a few moments, and then the boat came drifting out of the fog with Lucas standing up in the prow, peering intently into the water. He spotted them and within seconds, they were being pulled over the side. Verne was at the oars and Devries lay in the bottom of the boat, unconscious.

"I was beginning to think you drowned," said Lucas.

"I almost did," said Finn, gasping for breath. "Andre kept me afloat."

"I saw you both go over," Lucas said. "You can thank Jules here for the boat. I think maybe one or two others got away, as well, but we lost them in the fog. There was a rush for the lifeboats when the boilers blew and most of them were caught in the explosion. This one was literally blown off the ship and Jules swam for it. We managed to pull Devries out, but he's in pretty bad shape. We looked for other survivors, but with the ship going down so fast and the fire and the fog . . ." His voice trailed off.

"How the hell did you get out of the cabin?" Finn said, looking at Verne.

The author grinned weakly. "I have some slight skill with a lockpick," he said. "In all the excitement, you seemed to have forgotten that." His clothing was completely soaked and he was shivering in the cold night air. The heavy fog wasn't making things any easier.

"Christ, it all happened so fast," said Finn.

Andre flopped down in the bottom of the boat. "Ned spotted it first," she said. "He'd been keeping his eyes peeled for it ever since Farragut announced that reward for whoever saw it first. Several of the men were cleaning the forecastle gun and they were able to bring it into action almost immediately. I think they had time for two shots, three at the very most."

"Can we do anything about Devries?" said Finn.

Lucas shook his head. "I think he's got internal injuries. He's hanging on, but we haven't got anything aboard the boat to help him with. We don't even have any fresh water."

"Speaking of water," Andre said, "has anyone noticed this boat is leaking?"

They all exchanged glances. They were all thinking the same thing. The three of them could escape by clocking out, but that would still leave Verne and Devries. They couldn't simply abandon them.

"Quiet," said Verne. "Do you hear something?"

They fell silent, listening.

Lucas frowned. "No, I—"

"Listen!"

This time, they heard it. Somewhere, off in the mist, someone was singing.

"So I grabbed 'er and I kissed 'er, bent 'er down across me knee,

And I said to 'er, me bonny, this is how it's going to be,
If you want to love a sailor man, then best learn to be true,
For if you dally round behind his back, he'll beat you black
    and blue—"

"It's Ned!" said Andre.

"So I struck 'er on the bottom, kept it up til she cried, 'Hold!'
She gazed up at me so tearfully, yet saucy and so bold,
Says she, 'In ports across the sea, I know you wasn't true,
So if you love those foreign wenches, I'll go down for half
    your crew.' "

"Ned!" shouted Andre, leaning out over the side of the
boat and trying to see through the fog.

The singing stopped. "Andre? Is that you?"

"Keep singing, Ned!" cried Finn. "We'll row toward the
sound of your voice!"

"Put your back to it, my lad!" Land shouted, then began
singing once again, louder than before and with considerable
gusto.

"So I slapped that wench upon 'er bum and threw 'er to the
    floor,
Looked down at 'er and hated 'er, the bloody little whore,
I said it was all done with, that her words made up my mind,
And I told her I was leavin', I was finished with 'er kind.

"She looked up at me with fury and came at me with a blade,
I was faced with the most fiery wench the good Lord ever
    made,
I twisted round and felt that deadly steel scrape my side,
And I knew if I lived through it I would take 'er for my
    bride."

"Jesus fucking Christ," said Finn.

It loomed before them, shrouded in the mist, its teardrop-
shaped hull like a steel island rising out of the waves. They
could see the huge conning tower with its winglike sailplanes

and tall periscopes, the flattened top portion of the deck with ominous round hatches, beneath which lurked ballistic missiles in their silos.

"What in the name of God is that?" Verne whispered, awestruck. "What is that?"

"A submarine," said Lucas.

Land stood upon the deck, gazing out into the fog. When he spotted them, he waved.

"I've found your sea monster, Jules!" he shouted. "Come, have a look!"

"Finn, the sail!" said Lucas, grabbing his arm and pointing.

Delaney looked where he was pointing and saw a figure standing up on the bridge at the top of the conning tower. At the same moment, a hatch opened in the boat and uniformed men came streaming out, carrying automatic weapons. Land put up a struggle, but they overpowered him. A stream of bullets from an automatic rifle stitched the water close beside their boat.

One of the sailors barked out a command in Russian and waved them in.

"I think we're being invited on board," said Lucas.

"We must go," said Verne. "We cannot abandon Ned."

"I have no intention of abandoning Ned, Jules," Lucas said. "We came here looking for that submarine. Well, now we've found it."

Under the watchful eyes of the Soviet sailors, they came on board and, one at a time, went down the hatch.

They were taken to a cabin which slept six, with the bunks built into the bulkheads in tiers of three. By each row of bunks there were lockers and the cabin was equipped with a table, bolted down, as well as chairs. The bunks were close together, giving hardly any headroom, though there was plenty of space for a man of six feet to stretch out. Each bunk was equipped with a fluorescent light for reading and with a stereo headset. Moments after they were brought in, a crewman entered with coffee and a change of clothing for them, jumpsuits like those the others wore.

"Looks like we've got officers' quarters," Finn said. He

opened the door to the cabin and was not surprised to see an armed guard confronting him. "Well, they're willing to give us some privacy, but it seems we're not to be allowed the run of the ship."

"Boat," said Lucas. "A submarine is called a boat."

"One this size ought to be called a ship," said Finn. He began to strip off his wet clothes.

Verne, still in something like a state of shock, caught him by the arm. "What are you doing?" he said.

"Taking off my wet clothes, what does it look like I'm doing?" Finn said.

"But, my good man, have you forgotten? There is a woman present . . ." His voice trailed off as he saw that Andre had stripped down to the buff and was stepping into one of the jumpsuits. He gaped at her, then quickly turned his head. *"Mon Dieu!"*

The diving Klaxon sounded and Verne jerked as if stung. "What on earth was that?" he said, alarmed.

"Unless I miss my guess," said Lucas, "it is the signal the submarine is about to dive."

The submarine tilted as it began its descent and both Verne and Land, not knowing what to expect, were thrown off-balance. Lucas sat down at the table and caught the tray with the coffee cups. It had started to slide.

"I suggest we all drink some of this coffee," he said. "You, especially, Jules. You're shivering like an epileptic."

"I cannot cease marveling at this!" said Verne, sitting down at the table. "The water outside is freezing, yet it is as warm in here as on a summer's day. What a superb accomplishment this vessel is! I must know more about it. What is its power source? How is the air stored for us to breathe? How—"

"I'd leave all those questions for later if I were you, and get out of those wet clothes," said Finn. "Andre, turn your head so Jules doesn't die of embarrassment."

"What I can't figure is how this submarine boat managed to sink our ship," said Land. "It ain't likely that it rammed us, because of the explosion. But how could they have fired when they were under the water?"

"It's called a torpedo, Ned," said Lucas.

"What, you mean a mine?" said Land.

"No, this is a different sort of device," said Lucas. "It's fired from a tube within this boat while—"

"Yes, of course!" said Verne, interrupting him, carried away by his own enthusiasm. "The self-propelled torpedo! Built by the Englishman, Robert Whitehead. I have read of it. Whitehead worked from a design by the Austrian naval officer, Giovanni Luppis. But the Whitehead-Luppis torpedo is still only an experimental stage device. It is 14 feet long and 14 inches in diameter, as I recall, weighing some 300 pounds and carrying 18 pounds of dynamite in its nose. It is powered by a compressed-air engine which turns a small propeller and impels it at a speed of 6 knots for a maximum range of 700 yards."

"By Heaven, does this man know everything?" said Land.

"Admittedly, I do have a certain eclectic expertise in various fields," said Verne, "but I am a mere dabbler in such matters, a dilettante. The fact is, my friends, I have recently been giving a great deal of consideration to writing a novel, one of my *voyages extraordinaires*, about a submarine vessel much like this one. I have been doing a considerable amount of research to that end, but never did I dream I would actually find myself aboard such a craft! To think of the book I shall be able to write after this experience!"

"Assuming we survive it," Andre said. "And assuming you don't catch pneumonia from standing around with your pants down around your legs."

"*Sacre bleu!*" Verne flushed a deep crimson and quickly pulled his soaking trousers back up. Finn laughed and tossed him one of the jumpsuits.

"Try one of these," he said.

"I promise not to look," said Andre, turning around.

Verne quickly removed his wet clothing and slipped into the jumpsuit.

"So that's what happened to the *Scotia*," Land said. "She was sunk by one of them torpedo devices." He shook his head. "What ship would stand a chance 'gainst a vessel with such weapons?"

"I'm afraid this submarine is equipped with weapons far

more deadly," Lucas said. "We were very fortunate. The *Abraham Lincoln* might just as easily have been obliterated without a trace in less than an instant."

Land frowned. "How is it that you know these things, Professor?"

"Because he is not a professor, Mr. Land," said a deep voice from behind them. The door had opened silently without their noticing it. In the doorway, flanked by two men with drawn automatic pistols, stood a tall, heavily muscled man with raven-black hair lightly streaked with white and unusually bright, emerald-green eyes. His face would have possessed a classic, almost Byronic beauty were it not for the knife scar which ran from beneath his left eye in a straight line across his cheekbone to just above the corner of his mouth. His features were Slavic; a high forehead, blade-straight nose and a prominent jawline with a square chin. His posture was elegant; ramrod straight, yet somehow languid. He was dressed in a tailored naval uniform of dark blue cotton with gold captain's bands upon the sleeves of his coat and shoulderboards. The insignia was incongruously British. The coat had double rows of heavy brass buttons and, in a quite unmilitary touch, he had a deep-purple silk handkerchief neatly folded in the left-hand breast pocket. The handkerchief matched the purple ascot tie held down with a diamond stickpin. That pin was his sole adornment with the exception of a large ruby worn on the left hand.

Andre caught her breath. "*Drakov!*"

"It's so nice to be remembered, Miss Cross," he said with a smile. "And Mr. Delaney and Mr. Priest, as well. Quite a reunion. I had an intuition we might meet again. Tell me, is my father well?"

"He's better than he would be if he knew you were behind this," said Finn.

"Would one of you mind explaining what the devil this is all about?" said Land.

"Certainly," said Drakov. "If someone would be so kind as to introduce us, sir, I would be happy to oblige."

"Nikolai Drakov, Ned Land," said Lucas. "Ned is a harpooner by profession. Drakov's calling, Ned, would be a bit more difficult to explain. I'm not even sure I know what it is, but I can hazard a few guesses. At this point, calling him a pirate wouldn't be too far off the mark. And this is Mr. Jules Verne.''

Drakov looked surprised. ''Not the famous novelist, surely?''

Verne smiled slightly and inclined his head.

''Well, this is indeed an honor,'' Drakov said. ''I am among your most devoted readers, sir. In fact, I have renamed this submarine in honor of your own creation. I bid you welcome aboard the *Nautilus*.''

Verne looked puzzled. ''But I have never written—''

''Ah, but you shall, Mr. Verne,'' said Drakov, with a smile. ''You shall.''

''Well, whoever in blazes you might be,'' said Land, ''you've a lot to answer for. I have—''

''I answer to no one, Mr. Land,'' said Drakov, curtly. ''This vessel is mine and aboard it, I am the sole authority. This is my world and you exist in it at my discretion. I could just as easily have submerged while you sat upon my deck, braying like a drunken dockworker. If you cannot behave in a more civilized manner, I will have you placed in a torpedo tube and ejected from my ship.''

Land swore softly in French.

''You are quite correct, Mr. Land,'' said Drakov, tersely. ''I am, literally, a bastard. And fluent in French, as well. You have now been cautioned twice. Your next transgression shall be your last.''

Land remained silent, glowering at him.

''You must forgive Ned, Captain Drakov,'' Verne said, anxious to placate their host. ''His belligerence is . . . well, after all, sir, you did sink our ship.''

''Only after I was fired upon, Mr. Verne,'' said Drakov. ''Or do you not regard that as sufficient provocation?''

The author cleared his throat uneasily. ''Yes, well, to be sure, you have a point, sir. However, we . . . that is, Commander Farragut and his crew had no idea it was a vessel they were firing upon. They were—''

''Yes, yes, I know,'' said Drakov, impatiently. ''They were

hunting a sea monster of some sort. I do try to remain *au courant*, Mr. Verne. I was well aware of the *Abraham Lincoln*'s mission.''

Verne's eyes grew wide. ''Then you deliberately—''

''I did nothing of the sort, if I may anticipate you,'' said Drakov. ''Nothing would have pleased me more than to avoid your ship entirely. However, I am Fate's cats-paw. A living paradox. The forces which move me are not always under my control. As you can see, Fate has reunited me with three old adversaries.'' He swept his arm out to indicate Finn, Andre and Lucas.

''Which brings up the subject of what you're going to do about us,'' Finn said.

''I haven't yet decided,'' Drakov said. ''I could have you killed, of course.''

''No!'' said Verne. ''Surely, a man of your accomplishment—''

''Would be more than justified, under the circumstances,'' Drakov said. ''They were sent to destroy me. There is more involved here than even your imagination could encompass. But we can pursue that another time. Right now, I must decide what to do about the five of you.''

''Five?'' said Verne.

''Yes, regrettably, your injured companion died moments ago. My medical officer could do nothing for him.''

''Did he even try?'' said Andre.

Drakov fixed her with a piercing glare. ''I told you once before, Miss Cross. Whatever else I may be, I am not a barbarian. I could, for example, easily have destroyed the lifeboats from the *Abraham Lincoln*, yet I did not. Your Commander Farrgut will live to be an admiral. I regret the loss of life, but they brought it on themselves.''

''What about the *Scotia*?'' Land said. ''Or do you regard that as an impertinent question?''

''The *Scotia* was a munitions ship,'' said Drakov. ''She was carrying supplies of war. Sending her to the bottom was an humanitarian act.''

Verne started to speak, then thought better of it. Land's reply was cut off by Lucas, who reached out and squeezed his upper arm in warning.

"Do we at least get to find out why you took this sub before you kill us?" Lucas asked.

"I did not say I would kill you, only that I could," said Drakov. "You see, I am giving you more consideration than you would have given me. There are other choices. I could compel your obedience in the same way I have the Soviet sailors'. I would prefer not to have to do that. Fate has delivered you into my hands and until I know the reason, I will not act hastily. If you will agree to be bound by the conventions of prisoners of war, I will allow you the run of the ship so long as you do not interfere with me or with my crew. The first hostile act by any one of you will instantly result in the death of all. Your signal implants will be removed and you will surrender your warp discs to me, of course."

"And if we don't accept those terms?" said Lucas.

"I should think them to be very reasonable, all things considered," Drakov said. "If you find you cannot accept them, you are free to clock out. Having gone to so much trouble to find me, I can see where you might be reluctant to do so until you have at least deduced my plans. Also, you would be forced to leave Mr. Land and Mr. Verne behind. Mr. Land I could certainly do without, but I would be loathe to deprive myself of Mr. Verne's company. That leaves you with three other choices. Death, re-education, or being left locked in this cabin until I decide what else to do with you. So, which is it to be?"

"How do you know you can trust us?" said Delaney.

"You, Mr. Delaney, I know I cannot trust. However, you are vastly outnumbered and unarmed. Moreover, you will all be responsible for each other's lives. I do not regard you as a threat, merely as a potential for annoyance."

"All right," said Lucas. "We'll accept your terms."

"Good," said Drakov. "You will give Sasha your warp discs, please. Mess will be served in the wardroom in one hour. I would be pleased if you would join me." With a curt nod of his head, he departed.

"*Merde*," said Land. "I understand none of this. What's this about your being adversaries? How do you know this man?"

Lucas sighed. "Ned, you're going to think you've fallen

into a nest of raving lunatics after you've heard my explanation, but there's no way around it. You're going to have to know exactly what this is all about if we're going to get out of this, so here goes. Brace yourself . . ."

5 ———————————

Land wouldn't have any of it. If he was unwilling to accept Verne's theory that a gigantic narwhal could exist, he wasn't about to listen to any nonsense about time travel. He was not a scientist. He wasn't even literate. Unlike Verne, he couldn't look about him and realize the brilliant feat of engineering that was a nuclear submarine could not possibly have been accomplished in the 19th century. If an Englishman and an Austrian could devise a self-propelled torpedo, why then it made perfect sense to him that Drakov could construct a submarine. Lucas tried explaining to him gradually and patiently, with Land listening attentively at first, then scowling and squirming in his chair, then interrupting angrily to demand Lucas stop treating him like a fool and tell him the truth and finally threatening to bust his skull. Exasperated, Lucas was about to try another tack when Finn put a hand on his shoulder and took over.

"All right, Ned, we'll tell you the truth. It's clear you're nobody's fool. The fact is, Drakov was a brilliant scientist, a professor on the faculty of Miskatonic University, where Lucas and I were teaching courses in Creative Apathy and Rubber Physics. Andre, here, was a graduate student at Miskatonic at the time, taking her degree in Electronic Onanism. Drakov managed to convince the university officials he could prove a theory first advanced by the eminent acrocephalic, Dr.

Nicholas Gambrinous, namely, that interlocutory foreplay, properly applied, could achieve a state of labial penetration of normally recalcitrant subjects. To this end, he was awarded financial backing in the form of a grant and he proceeded to set up his laboratory, staffed with young graduate assistants eager to help in his experiments. Lucas, Andre and myself were working on a competitive project, and we were able to convince the university its funds would be better spent in supporting our research, instead. Drakov lost the funding for his project and left the university, vowing to revenge himself upon us. And there you have it.''

Verne sat staring at Finn, stunned into speechlessness. Land grunted, then looked at Lucas and said, ''Now why couldn't you say so in the first place? That makes a lot more sense than that other nonsense you were spouting.''

''It *does*?'' said Lucas.

''Just because I never went to a fancy university, don't think I'm a fool,'' he said.

''Of course not,'' Lucas said.

Verne made a whimpering sound.

''You all right, Jules?'' Land said, concerned.

''Oh, yes, quite, quite,'' Verne said, not daring to look him in the face. He cleared his throat several times. ''I must have caught a bit of a chill, that's all.''

They were escorted to the wardroom at the appointed time and entered to find most of the crew, save those on duty, already sitting down to dinner. Neither Verne nor Land had any reference for the scene they were confronted with, but for Lucas, Finn and Andre, it was not at all what they expected. On one level, there was an atmosphere of order to the mess. The men sat at their tables, dining in a reasonably quiet manner, enjoying the food provided by the huge stores of a nuclear submarine. Yet, on the surface, an element of the surreal had intruded. The bulkheads of the wardroom were obscured almost entirely by fabulous Chinese and Persian tapestries and the tables were set with fine china and real silver on ornate cloths. Wine was in evidence, as well as vodka, beer, rum and even mulled ale. Chamber music filled the wardroom.

As for the crew, the spartan Soviet military veneer had

slipped considerably. Beards and moustaches were in evidence, some quite elaborate. Hair was longer. A few of the men wore earrings. Many of the jumpsuits bore marks of individual ornamentation; gold brooches and jeweled clasps, silver pins and hammered bracelets, emerald and ruby necklaces of inestimable worth worn over the shoulders as aguillettes. Some of the men had their sleeves rolled up or cut off entirely, exposing intricate tattoos, blazing with color. It was a bizarre combination of a medieval feast and a pirates' mess. The only element lacking was a cadre of buxom serving wenches.

They were conducted to the captain's table and Drakov rose to greet them. Four men were seated at the table with him and they rose to their feet as well.

"Gentlemen, and lady, please be seated," Drakov said, indicating the places set for them. He had changed his jacket for a 17th-century British naval admiral's coat, festooned with gold braid, heavy gold epaulets upon the shoulders. Lace showed at his throat and cuffs. "Allow me to introduce you to my senior officers."

They sat down and Drakov turned to the man on his immediate right, a thin, dark-eyed, evil-faced Sicilian with coarse black hair and the manner of a Medici poisoner. "This is Santos Benedetto, whose name will be known to you three 'academicians.' Santos, aside from myself, is the last surviving member of the Timekeepers. After our last meeting, in Zenda Castle, I encountered Santos in one of our old rendezvous places. He helped me to begin this venture."

Benedetto gave them a dark stare and nodded. He wore 27th-century black base fatigues and a warp disc on his left wrist.

"Santos knows you three only too well," said Drakov, smiling. Then he introduced Verne and Land to his second-in-command. "The gentleman beside Santos is Barry Martingale, late of the 20th-century American Special Forces. When I met Sgt. Martingale, he was pursuing a career as a mercenary soldier and being terribly underpaid. I offered to remedy that situation and he graciously accepted."

The beefy, sandy-haired Martingale twitched his lips in what might have been a smile and said, "How do?" His muscular frame was sheathed in khaki—sharply creased trousers and an African bush jacket. He had a pencil-thin moustache, a square chin and foggy gray eyes.

"The man on my left," said Drakov, "is General Count Grigori von Kampf, late of the famed Imperial Black Hussars of Czar Alexander. Count Grigori comes of a colorful lineage. His father was a Russian aristocrat and his mother a Kirghiz Gypsy. We are old acquaintances and I could not embark upon my venture without him."

Count Grigori was huge, with shoulders like a Goliath and a chest like a wine cask. A former cavalry officer, it was a wonder a horse could have been found anywhere large enough to support him. His hands were easily twice the size of Finn Delaney's, and Delaney was not small. The lower half of Count Grigori's face was hidden by a square, luxuriant beard and large handlebar moustaches curled out from beneath his nose. His hair, both on his head and on his face, was gray and curly and his eyes looked Oriental, dark as anthracite. He still wore the uniform of an officer in the Black Hussars, a jet black tunic with ornate buttons and a stiff, high collar.

"*Otchen priyatno,*" he said, his voice a basso profundo.

"He says he's very pleased to meet you," Drakov translated. "Count Grigori has received the benefit of implant education, but he refuses to speak English. He considers it a barbarian tongue. He is, however, perfectly willing to converse in French, as well as Russian."

Drakov turned to the last man. "And this is Toshiro Kamakura, Shiro, as we call him." The tiny Japanese gave a little bow. He looked like a boy in his early teens, but his eyes were infinitely old. It was impossible to guess his age. "Shiro's father was assassinated along with his wife for a transgression against the Yakuza, of which he was a member. Shiro survived by running away with his sister. He could not save both her and his parents, you see. To atone for the shame of running away, Shiro cut off the little finger on his left hand. To prevent himself from ever revealing where he had hidden his sister, he cut out his tongue. He then systematically tracked down each of his parents' killers and dispatched them, quite efficiently and brutally. He was only fourteen at the time. He is seventeen now. I know what it means to grow up an orphan.

When I found Shiro, I took him in and educated him, so he could write and tell me where his sister was. She is now being well taken care of. Shiro is my most loyal and trusted aide. Do not let his youth deceive you. He is quite ruthless. I advise you to be polite to him."

Shiro studied each of them in turn, gazing at them long and hard with an unblinking stare. His slight frame, his long, straight black hair hanging to his shoulders and his delicate features gave him an androgynous aspect, but those eyes were chilling. When he looked at Lucas, Priest suppressed an urge to glance away from that ophidian gaze. This child prevailed over Yakuza assassins, Lucas thought. Quite a group Drakov had gathered.

Finn echoed his sentiments aloud. "Looks like you've found a hell of a crew, Drakov." He glanced around at the others, then at the Soviet submariners. "However, discipline seems a little lax."

"On the contrary," Drakov said. "These men are more efficient now than they were under their previous commander. They are more efficient because they have more freedom, because their initiative is rewarded and they are happier."

"Thanks to re-education conditioning," said Andre.

"Not entirely," said Drakov. "It is true most of them needed to be, shall we say, deprogrammed from a lifetime of a different sort of conditioning, but you might be surprised to learn that a great many of them, far more than I expected, went along with me quite willingly. After all, I offered them far greater opportunities. Do not be misled by their appearance. There is a great deal more to military efficiency than uniformity, precision drill and polish. Look at history. The mighty empire of Rome fell to wild barbarians. The greatest armies in the world crumbled before the onslaught of Genghis Khan. Ragtag armies of colonials prevailed over the dress parade regimentation of the British." He smiled. "My men may look somewhat piratical, but they know what they're about."

They were served their food and Verne gasped at the sumptuous repast. Roast beef, baked potatoes, yams, corn, cranberry sauce, ragout of pork, fruit preserves, fresh baked bread and steaming coffee.

"Amazing!" Verne exclaimed. "I cannot believe these miracles I am assaulted with! However can you keep such food supplies fresh, Captain?"

"Freezing and refrigeration, Mr. Verne," said Drakov. "This submarine is well stocked with food supplies. On board at present, we have some four thousand pounds of beef, two thousand of chicken, fourteen hundred of pork loin and one thousand of ham. We carry roughly three thousand pounds of sugar, twelve thousand pounds of coffee, one hundred fifty pounds of tea, eight hundred pounds of butter, twenty-two hundred of flour and some six hundred dozen eggs. There is also a considerable quantity of wine, vodka, whiskey, beer and ale on board, though my crew does not overindulge. I allow them all they wish to drink, but the penalty for being drunk on duty or incapacitated by the aftereffects of drink is twenty lashes, which Shiro administers quite adroitly. In addition to our supplies, we look to the sea for sustenance. Those are dolphins' livers in that 'pork' ragout you are devouring, and that which you assume to be fruit preserves is derived from sea anemones."

Land stopped spreading the preserves on his bread and looked at it with horror.

"Your vessel is a marvel, Captain," Verne said. "I have a thousand questions to ask of you."

"I have a few questions myself," said Lucas.

"Yours shall have to wait, Mr. Priest," said Drakov. "Mr. Verne, kindly ask anything you wish."

Verne was flustered. "I don't know where to start! I want to know everything!"

"And so you shall," said Drakov. "This submarine is constructed of titanium, with double hulls, and it displaces almost twenty thousand tons. It is some five hundred sixty feet long and its hull diameter is forty-two feet. It is capable of attaining speeds over sixty knots."

"Impossible!" said Land.

"I assure you, Mr. Land, it is not only possible, it is effortless," said Drakov. "We submerge by means of employing water as ballast, held in tanks between the hulls. Wings or diving planes, such as those you saw on the sail, enable us to dive or to ascend. Two rudders, one above the propellers, one below, control direction. We are equipped with two periscopes which can be raised when near the surface to allow us to observe without being seen and we are capable of going more than four hundred thousand miles without refueling, which would be sixteen trips around the equator.''

"How can that be?" said Verne. "How can you maintain an air supply allowing a trip of such duration? What manner of propulsion could achieve such a feat?"

"The *Nautilus* manufactures its own oxygen from seawater," Drakov said. "Unwanted gases such as carbon dioxide and carbon monoxide are disposed of overboard. As for our propulsion, Mr. Verne, our engines are steam turbines driven by the power of the universe, a power humanity will not discover in this century."

"I've not heard such nonsense in my life," said Land.

"Then how do you explain where you find yourself, Mr. Land?" said Drakov.

"What is this power of the universe?" said Verne. He had forgotten his meal.

"It is called nuclear fission, Mr. Verne," said Drakov. "The sun is powered by a nuclear reaction process called fusion. Nuclear fusion powers stars. Nuclear fission is similar, in a manner of speaking. It is the process by which the atom is split."

"But . . . that's contrary to the laws of physics!" Verne said. "There is no power on earth which can split the atom!"

"Say rather that such power has not been discovered in your time," said Drakov. "Even the men whose work led to the discovery believed as you do. Einstein, Planck, Bohr, Fermi, even they were not sure it was possible. Or, should I say, none of them *will be* sure it is possible? For that time has not yet come. Please, Mr. Verne, do eat. Your food is growing cold."

Verne started to pick at his food. His hand was shaking. For Land, it was all incomprehensible. For Lucas, Finn and Andre, it was all familiar, yet frightening. They had become part of a temporal contamination which seemed to be beyond their ability to adjust. They could only sit and listen in mute fascination as a man born in the 19th century, but educated in the 27th, explained the concept of nuclear energy to an author who had foreseen—or would he foresee as a result of what was now happening?—the very vessel they now sailed in beneath the sea.

"Mr. Verne," said Drakov, "you are a man of imagination to whom science is an avocation. Perhaps you will better understand when I explain to you how this discovery came about. Within a few short years, within your own lifetime, Mr. Verne, the first of two discoveries which will change the world will be made. On the eighth of November, in 1895, at the Julius-Maximilian University of Würzburg, Professor Wilhelm Konrad Roentgen will discover X rays. He will be experimenting with a glass tube through which he will pass gas and an electric current. He will cover the tube with dark paper and turn on the voltage, sending glowing gas streaming through the tube. In the darkened room, light will not come through, being blocked off by the paper, but Professor Roentgen will observe a small glow coming from a table upon which a plate of barium platinocyanide crystals was kept. Upon turning off his voltage, he will observe this glow die out. Puzzled by this phenomenon, he will continue to experiment until he concludes that some unknown ray was being produced in his glass tube, one capable of passing through the dark paper and causing the fluorescence in the crystals. Not knowing the cause or nature of this phenomenon, he will call it an X ray.

"Further experimentation will lead him to discover these X rays produce an effect upon a photographic plate and that the rays are stopped by bones, but not by flesh. The result will be X ray photography, which will aid in diagnosis and revolutionize medical science. Physicians will be able to see inside the body prior to surgery. A man named Thomas Edison will build a device called an X ray fluoroscope, consisting of an X ray tube and a screen covered with crystals of barium platinocyanide. Upon striking the screen, the X rays will produce light visible to the naked eye. Any portion of the body placed between the X ray tube and the screen will produce an outline of the bones and organs within. Unfortunately, it will take time before the hazards of the X ray will be understood.

"Researchers who will repeatedly expose themselves to X rays will sustain severe burns and if this practice is continued, as it shall be, it will result in death. It will be discovered that exposure to X rays over a prolonged period can cause harm to the eyes, loss of hair, ulceration, inhibition of bone growth, sterility and damage to the blood cells. Men will learn that all living tissue can be destroyed if exposed to a sufficient amount of radiation, a term which will be strange to you, but I will endeavor to explain. You may have noticed that everyone aboard this ship wears a small glass cylinder containing a photographic film, something invented after the photographic plate. This device is called a dosimeter. Its purpose is to measure the amount of radiation one is exposed to."

"You mean there is danger to us now?" said Verne.

"There is no cause for alarm. You will understand more presently. For now, let us return to the discovery of X rays, which will lead to the additional discovery that penetrating rays are also given off by certain crystals of an element known as uranium. In studying this phenomenon, Pierre and Marie Curie will give it a name—radioactivity.

"The Curies will embark upon research in an attempt to isolate the substance in uranium responsible for this phenomenon. In processing uranium ore, they will discover an element called radium. Pierre Curie will die upon being struck by a carriage in the street, but both his wife, Marie, and their daughter, Irene, who will carry on the work, will perish from exposure to radiation.

"Extensive scientific inquiry into the nature of this thing called radiation will establish the nature of a radioactive substance—its atoms are unstable. They disintegrate and become another element. Uranium becomes thorium. Thorium turns to radium. Radium becomes a gas called radon and so forth. This is known as nuclear disintegration and it results in the release of rays, or particles. The amount of time it takes for such a substance to decay in this manner to one half of its initial amount is called one half-life. Radon has a half-life of approximately four days. Certain types of uranium, on the other hand, can have a half-life of four and one half billion years. The shorter the half-life, the more atoms disintegrate per second.

"I mentioned two significant discoveries. The first will be that an element can be made radioactive. The second will come with the splitting of the atom. In 1932, an Englishman named Sir James Chadwick will discover a particle called a neutron. In 1934, Irene Curie and her husband, Frederic Joliot, will experiment with polonium and aluminum in their study of neutrons. They will discover that when alpha particles—a type of radiation—released from the polonium strike the aluminum, neutrons will be released, as well as electrons. Further, they will discover that the aluminum will continue to emit electrons for a short while after the polonium has been removed. In other words, they will find that an element which is not ordinarily radioactive can be made so artificially. When they bombard the aluminum with alpha particles, they will transform its atoms into the radioactive element radiophosphorous and this will be the first creation of artificially produced radioactive isotopes. You will find much of this unfamiliar and confusing, Mr. Verne, but there are books in the library we have aboard that explain all this in far greater detail. For our purposes now, I am simplifying as much as possible.

"These neutrons easily penetrate solid substances," Drakov went on. "In the year 1938, two Germans named Otto Hahn and Fritz Strassmann will bombard uranium with neutrons. They will be astonished to find this experiment produce three light elements named barium, lanthanum and cerium. It will make no sense to them. They will realize these elements could only have come from the uranium, but this transmutation would be against everything known in science. They will see the evidence before their eyes, but be reluctant to challenge the authority of eminent physicists such as Albert Einstein, Max Planck, Niels Bohr and Enrico Fermi. They will report their discovery, but refrain from making any conclusions about it, stressing they might have made errors in their observations.

"News of this discovery will cause Bohr and Fermi to realize these men had succeeded in splitting the uranium atom. Nuclear fission. Bohr and Fermi will also realize that nuclear fission might involve a chain reaction, in other words, one split atom of uranium would release two neutrons, which would split two more atoms, releasing four neutrons, splitting four more atoms and releasing eight neutrons and so on, in geometric progression, releasing fabulous amounts of energy in an infinitesimal space of time.

"Albert Einstein will have enabled us to understand all this with a formula which will revolutionize science. In the year 1905, Einstein will make history when he writes the simple equation, $E = MC^2$. Translated, it means energy equals mass multiplied by the square of the speed of light. The neutron, the sub-atomic particle with no electrical charge, strikes a large uranium nucleus, causing it to split. The 'debris' of this split is neutrons and lighter nuclei. What is left after the nucleus splits weighs less than the original. The mass which is lost is converted into energy via Einstein's formula. This debris shatters other nuclei in a self-sustaining process called a chain reaction and all that is required to produce this is a sufficient quantity of uranium, below which this process will not be self-sustaining. This quantity is known as a critical mass.

"On the basis of Einstein's formula, it can be calculated that one-thirtieth of a gram of water converted into pure energy would yield enough heat to turn a thousand tons of water into steam. A device which facilitates this process is called a nuclear reactor and it is that which drives the *Nautilus*.

"A uranium core—fuel rods—can be thought of as the firebox of your coal-fired steam engines. Nuclear fission produces heat. The steam from the heart of the *Nautilus* is taken to the engine room in two large, insulated pipes leading to four turbines, two turbo-generators and the auxiliary steam line. Again, I use terms you are unfamiliar with, but it suffices to say that this steam produces the power we require, then enters the condensers, having done its work, and in the form of water is pumped back into the steam generators, where it is heated once again by the pressurized water in what is called the primary loop of the reactor. The water in the primary loop is kept under very great pressure, so it cannot turn to steam. In this manner, we have a propulsion system in which no combustion is required. Coolant pumps circulate the water, drive motors raise and lower the fuel rods, controlling the reactor. The fuel rods will last for several years and when they are depleted, I have ways of getting more. Extreme precautions must be observed to ensure there is no leakage anywhere within the system, for such leakage would not only result in loss of pressure, but in radioactive contamination. That is the reason for the dosimeters, Mr. Verne, to monitor radioactive exposure.

"Yet, lest you should think this new fire of Prometheus is an inestimable boon to mankind—which it is—atomic energy has its darker side, and you will find that aboard the *Nautilus*, as well. The energy obtained by the fission of any given amount of uranium, released at an uncontrolled rate as an explosive, is millions of times more powerful than dynamite.

"You may have noticed large, round hatches in the deck of the *Nautilus* when you came aboard. Beneath each is a missile kept in a compartment called a silo. Think of these missiles as being rockets, if you will, of a very advanced nature. Each of these missiles carries fourteen atomic warheads, only one of which would be more than sufficient to level a city the size of Paris. From aboard this submarine, even while submerged, I can fire my missiles at any spot upon the globe. So, as you can see, I have at my command both the benevolent nature of atomic power and its destructive capability, which is the greatest the world has ever seen."

"You neglected to mention how you came by it," said Finn.

"Yes," said Drakov. "In that sense, Mr. Priest was quite correct in his earlier assessment of me. I am a pirate. I stole this vessel."

"But . . . for what purpose?" Verne said, his voice barely above a whisper.

"I told you, Mr. Verne, I am Fate's cats-paw. I am but following my destiny. Your three friends here are soldiers from a future time. At some later point, perhaps, you might wish to ask them the nature of their duties and why those duties have become necessary. Oh, I beg your pardon. *Will become* necessary. That which I explained to you just now heralded the dawn of a new age for mankind in the 20th century. The age of atomic power. It enabled mankind to reach farther than ever before, widening the horizons of science. Yet, as ever, mankind's grasp exceeds its reach. I told you I am a living paradox. Allow me to explain.

"Mr. Land earlier called me a bastard in his anger and he was quite correct. I am. My father, as it happens, is a man well known to Mr. Priest, Mr. Delaney and Miss Cross. His name is Forrester and he is their commander. As they have traveled to this time, so Colonel Forrester traveled to the time of my mother, where he seduced her and begat me. I am a man who should never have been born, Mr. Verne. At the time my father impregnated my mother, he himself would not have been born for hundreds of years. An impossibility, you say. Yet, here I am. A man who should not exist, brought into being by Fate to bring about an end to that which cannot exist, but does. There is an order to the universe and in the time from which these three soldiers came, mankind has disturbed that order. It has taken me a great many years, Mr. Verne, for I am far older than you think I am, to understand the purpose behind my existence. I was born to set things right, to restore order to the universe. And you, Mr. Verne, shall see it done. You shall be my Boswell. I could not have asked for a better man. But there is still much remaining to be done, many preparations needing to be made, before I can undertake the task Fate has set before me. You will learn things you have not dreamed of, see wonders beyond even your not inconsiderable imagination. My fate will forever alter yours. You have, indeed, a *voyage extraordinaire* ahead of you. And now, if you good people will excuse me, I will take leave of your company. I have matters to attend to.''

Drakov rose, followed by Shiro, and left the wardroom.

Verne gulped down some wine. "My head is swimming," he said. "A power that could level Paris! Rays, particles, unheard of elements, I must see this library he spoke of!"

"I would be pleased to show it to you, Mr. Verne," Count Grigori said in French. "Come."

They left together, the author dwarfed by the gargantuan von Kampf.

"How does he fit through the hatchways?" Andre said.

"With a certain amount of difficulty," Benedetto said, smiling a vulpine grin.

"We know why the others are in this with him," Finn said to Martingale. "What's in it for you?"

"I thought he made that clear," drawled Martingale. "Money."

"Just money?" Lucas said, wryly.

"There are easier ways of making money than being a

soldier," Martingale said. "I'm sure you know that. But it's all I know. It's what I do best. Besides, how many mercenaries can claim to have served in action across the boundaries of time? I wouldn't trade this for the world, Priest. It's one hell of a kick. See you round."

He got up and sauntered out of the wardroom, carrying a whiskey bottle with him.

"A kick," said Lucas. He glanced at Benedetto, who sat sipping wine and smoking a cigarette. "You know Drakov's insane, don't you?"

Benedetto shrugged. "I am not a judgmental individual. Who is to say what is sanity and what is not? I prefer to deal in the hard sciences and leave metaphysics to besotted Irish philosophers such as Finn Delaney." He glanced at Finn and raised his wineglass in a toast.

"You haven't changed at all, Santos," said Delaney. "You're still a pretentious asshole."

"My, my, such invective," Benedetto said. "And here I am trying so hard to be civil."

"Where did all this come from?" Lucas said, indicating the tapestries around them. "The jewelry some of these men are wearing looks almost priceless. You and Drakov indulging in some temporal piracy?"

"Only in a manner of speaking," Benedetto said. "Any military or even quasi-military unit requires funding. We have been amassing a treasury. A little from this time period, a little from that, it gradually multiplies. The sea is quite munificent. We have the richest shipwrecks of history at our disposal."

"You're equipped for salvage?" Finn said.

"Not in the manner you suggest," said Benedetto. "We have individual diving apparatus on board, suits equipped with hemosponges which act as gills, deriving oxygen from seawater. A bit of future technology that quite impresses our crew. I never go out, myself. It unsettles me. But the Russians rather enjoy it. They compete fiercely for the privilege. They are allowed to keep a portion of what is discovered for themselves and they often bring back a few delicacies to dress up the table. We have lobsters aboard the size of German Shepherds. Crabs that could easily crush a femur in their pincers. They find it great sport to collect such things."

"Where do we fit in?" said Andre.

"Your status, it would appear, is that of uninvited guests," said Benedetto. "You are not entirely unwelcome, however. Martingale does not like anyone, but I am happy for your presence. It gives me stimulating company. I find these Russians tiresome. Very boring fellows. No *brio* whatsoever. Especially our Count Grigori. A very moody fellow. I much prefer your companionship."

"You can joke, Santos, but we're going to stop you somehow," Finn said.

"What?" said Benedetto, with a feigned look of outrage. "After you gave your word to the good captain?"

"Don't be a fool."

Benedetto chuckled. "Finn, I bear you no hard feelings. No ill will whatsoever. We have always been upon opposing sides. I respect you for your accomplishments and for who you are. It was no easy feat to overcome the Timekeepers. I suspect, also, that you bear me a certain grudging respect, as well. Because of this, I would advise you strongly not to attempt anything against Nikolai Drakov. Your chances for success this time are quite small. I would hate to see you fall into the clutches of that little Oriental savage, Shiro. He frightens even me. Martingale and von Kampf are no less deadly, in their way, but Shiro is fanatically devoted to Nikolai and he is utterly ruthless. Look closely into that young boy's eyes and you will see snakes writhing."

"What's Drakov up to, Santos?" Lucas said.

"I do not know."

"Come on."

"Honestly," said Benedetto. "Look, I make no bones about what I am. I may have once been an idealist, such as Nikolai, but there is little that separates me from someone such as Martingale nowadays. I am, by profession, a terrorist. When I started with the Timekeepers, I was just an underpaid researcher, a re-education specialist. A somewhat glorified psychotherapist. I was embittered, vulnerable to seduction. Falcon convinced me to join in the grand cause against the war machine and I enlisted, burning with the fires of enlightenment. But Falcon is no more and I have seen far too much, done far too much to allow myself to remain deluded. Whatever ethics I may once have had, I lost along the way. The trouble with my former profession, you see, is one knows far too much, especially about oneself. Self-analysis becomes a disease. I know at heart, I am sociopathic. I know I have precious little in the way of scruples. I am an unprincipled blackguard, a killer, a morally bankrupt human being. Does that concern me? Not overmuch. I have managed to achieve a level of comfort in my acceptance of what I have become. It makes life easier that way, prevents one from getting ulcers.

"When you and your compatriots in Temporal Intelligence broke the organization of the Timekeepers, I fled for my life. I became separated from the others, to which I doubtless owe my survival, and I spent my days constantly looking over my shoulder, waiting to be caught. It was not much fun. Being with the Timekeepers had been stimulating. It was like a game. You against us. We kept telling ourselves that right was on our side and so we would prevail. Utter nonsense, of course. For a time, we did not know each other. Then, gradually, you learned a little about us, we learned more about you, we each compiled our dossiers and it was almost like a friendly rivalry."

"I don't think I would go that far," said Andre.

"Yes, well, it is all a matter of perception, isn't it? By then, I had long since stopped taking the whole thing very seriously. But when it ended, I was left, for a time, alone. I was surprised to discover I did not function well alone. The comforting mechanisms of the Timekeepers were denied me. There were no longer any plots to hatch, no longer any confused, idealistic, radical young women to divert one's attention in delightful ways. There was no money. I was, in short, out of a job. I was immeasurably relieved when Drakov found me and told me he was going to begin again, with a new, more vital organization. It was something familiar. And I had nothing else to do."

"You expect us to believe Drakov doesn't even tell his own second-in-command what his plans are?" Andre said.

"I do not *expect* you to believe anything," said Benedetto. "I have given you answers to your questions to the best of my ability. Believe them or not, as you choose. For myself, I am content to go along for the adventure. I live comfortably, eat well, enjoy my liberties in ports of call through all of time—though we do not actually make port, of course—and upon occasion my particular talents are found useful. I ask for nothing more.''

"I misjudged you, Santos," Lucas said. "I thought you were a fanatic, but you're just a decadent fool. Martingale may not be any better, but at least he's a professional. You're not even that. You're just going through the motions."

"I will tell you a secret, Priest," said Benedetto. "That is all life is, going through the motions. I prefer to go through the motions with at least a modicum of style. Nikolai is certain to cause some sort of cataclysm and when he does, life will be more interesting. I have no doubt you will do your utmost to prevent whatever he has planned and watching you try will be interesting, as well. In the last analysis, the greatest sin is boredom and I refuse to be bored." He smiled. "So by all means, interest me. Only wait until tomorrow, at least. Right now, this wine has made me sleepy."

"Is everyone aboard this blasted ship insane?" said Land.

"I'm beginning to think so, Ned," said Lucas. "I'm beginning to think so."

6 _____

After eating, they toured the Soviet *Vostochnaya Slava*, renamed the *Nautilus* by Drakov. It was a huge vessel, aptly deserving of its original name, which translated to "Glory of the East." Walking through it gave them the feeling of being inside the works of some giant machine, which in fact they were. Though very spacious, the submarine had been designed in typical Soviet utilitarian fashion, with minimum concessions to creature comforts. The crew members slept in nine-man rooms equipped with small tables and chairs, but the reading lights and stereo headsets were the sole touches of luxury. Everywhere were pipes and dials, gauges, wheels, control panels and watertight hatches. Everything was painted Soviet military gray. Despite the dosimeters worn by each member of the crew—Drakov had seen to it that dosimeters were given to his "guests," as well—the men aboard the submarine were shielded from the reactor by layers of water, lead and fuel oil, receiving less radiation than would a person on the surface on a sunny day. If any malfunction occurred with the reactor, control rods would automatically slide into position between the plates of uranium and shut it down. The submarine would then operate on its auxiliary diesel engines. There were laundry facilities on board, as well as a nucleonics lab, a fully equipped machine shop, a photo darkroom and a library with close to one thousand books. They looked into the library briefly and saw Verne, oblivious to their presence, surrounded by books, reading with the intensity of an archival researcher who had struck the mother lode, several dictionaries open by his side.

The crew of Drakov's *Nautilus* numbered one hundred twenty men, excluding themselves. They had learned of a number of casualties reducing the original complement. The Russian captain and several of his officers, as well as enlisted men, had not survived the change in command. Some had died during re-education, others had been killed trying to resist. Their guide upon the tour of the submarine, a young Soviet submariner named Sasha, answered all their questions frankly. He told them all members of the crew, with the exception of Drakov and his "officers," as well as the ship's doctor and its cooks, stood two four-hour watches each day in addition to work they had to perform off watch time.

Everywhere they went, they were carefully observed by members of the crew, but no one except Sasha spoke to them. There was no noise except for the hum of the ventilation system and the occasional gurgle of oil coming from the hydraulics, sounds which they quickly became accustomed to and ceased to hear. In the engine room, it was quite a different story. Crew members sat at their stations amid complex instruments and the noise of pumps, generators, turbines and reduction gears. The rapidly spinning propeller shafts turning at hundreds of revolutions per minute seemed not to move at all, except for a slight blur as they revolved. The control room of the sub resembled a bridge on a starship, with a semicircular central control station and a console holding banks of instruments. The helmsman controlled the planes on the submarine's sail for depth and handled the rudder to maintain course. The stern planesman trimmed the up and down angle of the sub by means of the stern planes, located forward of the propellers. The diving officer kept his eyes on gauges and dials on a large panel before him, monitoring the sub's depth, rate of dive during descent, the amount of roll the vessel was subjected to and gave orders to the planesmen. The chief of the watch was in charge of the water ballast, shifting it from one tank to another, depending upon requirements. The quartermaster of the watch was the submarine's navigator; the radioman had little to do save monitor transmissions and the engineering officer supervised the dozen men who operated the propulsion plant.

They cruised at a depth of two hundred feet, maintaining a speed of thirty knots, none of the power driving the *Nautilus* being wasted in turbulence. At their depth, pressure negated turbulence. The submarine experienced reduced resistance to forward motion at depth. There was no propeller slippage and speed was easier to achieve and maintain than on the surface. Except when the decks tilted during a dive or an ascent, there was no sensation of movement whatsoever. In answer to a question from Finn, Sasha told them, in English, that despite carrying a crew of over one hundred, the submarine could be operated by as few as a dozen men in an emergency. He was very proud of his ship—he used the term "boat," a direct translation from the Russian *podvodnaya lodka*, meaning submarine boat—and he was proud of his command of English. His military bearing was at curious odds with his appearance. He had started to grow his hair long and was doing his best to grow a beard. He wore a gold circle in his left ear and the cutoff sleeves of his jumpsuit revealed recent tattoos executed in an intricate, Oriental style with vivid reds, yellows, oranges and blues. A Chinese dragon covered his entire upper arm on the left side and his right arm was graced with a nude, almond-eyed woman whose hair fanned out to frame her entire body. The workmanship was exquisite.

"Shiro worked three hours on her," he said, smiling. "I wonder if his sister looks at all like this. If so, I must somehow arrange to meet her one day."

"I wonder if the little heathen would do one for me," said Land.

"I am certain he would, if you were to ask," said Sasha. "It seems to give him great pleasure, though it is hard to tell, he always looks so serious."

"What do you think of all this, Sasha?" Lucas said.

The young Russian frowned. "All this?"

"Being a member of the Soviet Navy one day and a time pirate the next," said Lucas.

Sasha smiled. "Time pirate. I like the sound of that. It is what we do, pirate time. How should I feel about it? I have been re-educated. I am, of course, aware of my previous loyalties, but they no longer matter. This is a new life. I am a new person. Captain Drakov has been very good to us. Mr. Benedetto has explained how he could have obliterated all our memories of what we were, but the captain would not allow that. He did not wish to rob us of our souls. He did not wish to make puppets of us."

"Didn't he?" said Finn.

"You met him; you saw what he is like," said Sasha. "He is a great man, destined for great things. We are all a part of something much more important now."

"And what would that be?" Andre said.

"You should ask the captain," Sasha replied evasively.

"He didn't want to rob you of your souls," said Finn, "but he robbed you of the ability of making choices for yourselves."

"That is not true," said Sasha. "He helped us see to make the correct choices. And there are those among us who did not require re-educating. They were able to see clearly for themselves."

"Which of the crew would those be?" Lucas said.

"Only the captain and Mr. Benedetto would know that," said Sasha. "We were not told, so we would not feel inferior to those of our shipmates who were more perceptive than we."

"Are you sure that's the reason?" Finn said.

"Of course."

"Very egalitarian of the captain," Finn said, wryly.

Back in their cabin, Land stretched out upon one of the lower bunks and put his hands behind his head. "Maybe I'm starting to lose my mind, too," he said, "or else this vessel truly is from some future time. I've never seen the like of it."

"When you have exhausted all the possible explanations, Ned," said Lucas, "consider the impossible. Try to imagine what it would have been like for a primitive caveman from the dawn of time to stand upon the decks of an iron steamship. If you can picture that, then put yourself in that caveman's place and you will begin to understand what has happened to you."

"This story Drakov told, about being able to destroy a city the size of Paris with but one of his explosives, can it be true?"

"Regrettably, Ned, it's only too true."

"*Merde*," said Land. "A man with such power, he could bring the nations of the world to their knees."

"Conceivably," said Lucas, "but I don't think that's what he intends."

"Why not?" said Land. "How could any man resist such a temptation?"

"In this time, with this submarine, Drakov could easily make himself the ruler of the world," said Lucas. "However, doing something like that would make him too obvious a target for others like ourselves. He has to remain hidden. He has to keep moving. He has become the object of an unprecedented hunt, Ned. And there are weapons in the future far more terrible than those he has on board. What makes him safe is his mobility, not only through the oceans of the world, but through all of time, as well. We found him only with the greatest luck. Or perhaps he found us. Maybe he really is the tool of destiny."

"You don't believe that, surely?" Land said.

Lucas grinned. "I'm not even sure I believe in belief."

"The trouble is," said Andre, "there seems to be no way we can stop him short of sabotaging this submarine, somehow. Only how to do it and survive?"

"Where in our orders does it say we're supposed to survive?" said Finn. "Maybe another team will get a crack at him. If they don't botch the job like we did, then our worries will be over. Permanently."

"What do we do meanwhile?" she said.

Lucas shrugged. "We wait."

"If this fellow is truly so dangerous," said Land, "why not just do away with him? Kill Drakov and this Benedetto, and the others will lack for leadership."

"The only problem with that idea," Lucas said, "is Drakov's promise to kill us all if any one of our group stepped out of line. The three of us would be perfectly willing to accept that risk, but what about yourself and Verne?"

Land shrugged. "For my part, the risk don't bother me a great lot. But do you think he would kill Verne? He seemed quite taken with him."

"That may be true," said Finn, "but if Drakov's killed, who'll protect Verne from the others?"

"Yes, that is true," said Land. "We can't decide without asking him. Maybe we'll have a chance to kill this madman and escape. This boat must surface sometime."

There was a knock at their door and it opened, admitting Benedetto. He took one step into the cabin and looked around at them, shaking his head.

"If you are intent upon hatching plots," he said, "at least have the brains to do it in a manner that you cannot be overheard. This cabin is monitored, you know. It would not have gone well for you if someone else had overheard you, rather than myself. If you must have private discussions, I would suggest the engine room. It is rather noisy there. Of course, the crew will wonder what you are talking about and they will report it to the captain. If I were you, I wouldn't bother. And I wouldn't waste my time trying to incite any of these Russians to mutiny, either. It would be pointless. Now, if you don't mind, I would really like to get some sleep. Do try not to stay up late. We will keep military hours aboard. Good night to you."

He closed the door.

"There goes a most strange man," said Land. "What do you make of him?"

Lucas shook his head. "Damned if I know, Ned. I'm starting to think you were right all along and everyone on board is crazy."

"Interesting he should have us monitored, though," said Andre. "It does tell us one thing we needed to know."

"What might that be?" said Land.

"He's vulnerable," said Andre. "Let's sleep on it."

Verne did not return to the cabin at all that night. They encountered him at breakfast, looking haggard, but with a wild light in his eyes.

"I am going to spend all of my time in this ship's library!" he said. "I did not sleep at all last night. There is so much to learn. That library is a treasure trove! Books on science, history, novels and texts, in Russian, French, German and English, all published years from now! I have been trying to understand this atomic energy more completely. This Einstein was a genius! Or, I should say, I suppose, he will be a genius.

One could read his work for *years* and still not comprehend it all. What an amazing stroke of luck to find myself aboard this submarine boat! What a fantastic opportunity!''

"You are about to be given yet another fantastic opportunity, Mr. Verne," said Drakov, coming to the table with his inevitable escort. "I trust you all slept well?"

Only Verne replied. "I could not sleep a wink, Captain Drakov. I found myself unable to resist your fabulous store of books."

"Then you must force yourself to rest immediately after breakfast, sir," said Drakov. "You will need all your energy for what is to come. Are you up to a stroll upon the ocean bottom?"

Verne looked alarmed, as did Land.

"Never fear," said Drakov, smiling. "It is not my intention to drown you. I assure you that you will be able to accompany me on a submarine excursion in complete safety."

"But . . . how is this possible?" said Verne.

"You shall see," said Drakov. "Shortly after breakfast, we will be making temporal transition. The diving Klaxon will sound, followed immediately by the chimes used to signal a missile alert. Since this submarine was not equipped with a special signal for time travel, we must improvise and use a combination of those two. At that point, I would advise you to go to your cabin and lie down. The effects of traveling through time can be mildly unpleasant, but no more so than those of drinking too much wine. The effect will not last long."

"Traveling through time!" said Verne, in awe. "But . . . to where?"

Our destination will be the deep water off the Florida Keys, in the 18th century," said Drakov.

"The 18th century!" said Land.

"Quite correct. We are going on an expedition to recover undersea treasure."

Land's eyes lit up. "Treasure? What sort of treasure? Gold?"

"That and much more," said Drakov. He drank his coffee, watching them with amusement. "We can expect for there to be quite a horde aboard a sunken Spanish galleon."

"A Spanish galleon!" said Ned.

"Part of a fleet," said Drakov. "Does the prospect interest you, Mr. Land?"

"You're going to attack this fleet?" said Andre.

"No, Miss Cross, I will not. I could easily destroy the entire armada if I chose it. However, the destruction of this fleet is a fact of history. I know you respect history," he added, with a smile.

"On the 15th of July, in the year 1733," he continued, "a hurricane of immense strength swept up from the Lesser Antilles, past the English Leeward Islands, heading toward the Florida Keys. In its wake, it left massive destruction on the islands of Marie Galante, Guadeloupe, Montserrat, Redonda, Nevis, St. Kitts, St. Eustatius and Saba. A Spanish treasure armada under the command of General Don Rodrigo de Torres y Morales had the misfortune to be caught in this terrible storm. Their ill luck and our good fortune.

"The armada sailed from the harbor of San Cristobal de la Habana on the morning of July 13. In all, twenty ships made up this fleet, escorting treasure back to Spain. It was composed of galleons, *naos* and smaller merchant vessels. Only one, the *Nuestra Señora del Rosario*, survived the storm. The others, the *Almiranta, El Infante*, the *San José*, the *Populo*, the *Lerri*, the *El Sueco de Arizon*, the *Capitana*, all perished, pounded into bits as they were driven on the reefs by the fierce winds.

"They were carrying a fortune in treasure valued at over twelve million pesos in gold and silver, as well as tobacco and spices, teas, ceramics, semi-precious stones and that was only the reported cargo. You can be certain there was contraband on board the ships, as well."

"Why contraband?" said Verne.

"Greed," said Drakov. "The King of Spain's treasuries were supplied by the wealth of the New World. All the treasure brought to Spain was taxed. The tax was known as the King's Fifth or the Royal Fifth. Smugglers went to great lengths to avoid paying this tax. Despite agents of the Board of Trade examining all cargo carefully, much was hidden from their eyes by clever sailors. The penalties were severe and informants were rewarded with a portion of the contraband recovered, so smuggling became quite an art. Treasure was hidden in barrels of spices and in bales of tobacco, among the ballast stones, anywhere one could think of secreting some gold or silver. There is no telling how much treasure might be aboard those ships. There were even incidents where entire ships were not listed on the manifests and hidden among the other vessels of large fleets.''

"How will you be able to obtain this treasure?" Land said.

"We will arrive upon the scene of the disaster after the Spaniards have completed what salvage operations they were able to employ," said Drakov. "This is not to say we shall arrive soon after the disaster itself. These salvage operations often went on for years. Considering what was at stake, ships which sank in coastal waters were eagerly sought after by freebooters who would immediately flock to the location if protective measures were not taken. In this particular case, the Spaniards were able to refloat several of the ships. Those which were too damaged to refloat were burned to the water line, the better to enable divers to swim down directly into the cargo holds and to aid in hiding the locations of the wrecks. A great deal of the treasure was recovered, but there was much left to interest future treasure hunters in the coming centuries. It would be years before the wrecks were thoroughly picked clean, years before the invention of the magnetometer enabled hunters to find the treasure. Some of the wrecks would, in several generations, even become tourist attractions. But we are seeking one wreck in particular.''

"There was one ship," Drakov said, "a man-of-war named *La Floridana*, which sank completely in deep water. The Spaniards searched for her extensively, but no trace of her was ever found. *La Floridana* does not appear on any of the Spanish maps charting the locations of the wrecks, maps which despite their inaccuracies guided future treasure hunters. *La Floridana* is a mystery ship. Only she is not a mystery to me, for I have found her. She lies in the deep water off Key Largo, where the ocean currents buried her in sand, hiding her beneath the ocean bottom, safe from prying eyes. Only I have seen her prior to her burial. I have been there once before.''

"What will you do with this treasure, Captain?" Land said, already in the grip of gold fever.

"Sell it, Mr. Land," said Drakov. "What else does one do with gold and silver? I am a wealthy man already, but my venture has seriously depleted my reserves and I must augment my treasury. We have the advantage not only of clocking back to a time before *La Floridana* was buried in the ocean floor, but of clocking forward to a time when the worth of what is aboard her will have increased a thousandfold. You may join us on our salvage operation, if you wish. A good worker is always welcome and you will be allowed to keep a part of what you find."

"How much of a part?" Land immediately asked.

Drakov chuckled. "Enough, Mr. Land. Enough to satisfy even a man of your voracious appetite. What is to be found aboard *La Floridana* is but a minuscule portion of what is available to us beneath the sea. There can be times when life is hard for us, but there are also times when we live very well indeed. We can pick and choose those times."

"What are you doing, Drakov?" Finn said. "Recruiting?"

"And why not? Mr. Land is aboard my submarine already. Why not as a productive member of the crew instead of as awkward supercargo?" Drakov shrugged. "There is always room for more in my organization. It is something worth considering." He turned to Ned. "There is no need to give your answer now, Mr. Land. There is ample time. Once you have experienced fully the sort of life we lead, then you can decide. I wish your choice to be an informed one."

"And what about the others?" Land said. "You make the same offer to them?"

"No, Mr. Land," said Drakov. "I have too much respect for them to think they would ever be disloyal to their commander. Their duty is to stop me, to kill me if they can. It is up to me to make certain they do not have that opportunity. It's really all quite simple. We understand each other. I cannot tempt them with treasure. But you, Mr. Land, I have a feeling you might be tempted."

Back in their cabin, they searched for three hours without finding the bug. Land lay silently in his bunk, eyes open and staring. Verne was in the library once again. They finally gave up and went to the engine room, where their presence caused suspicious glances, but nothing more.

"This is ridiculous," Finn said into Lucas's ear. "We're not getting anywhere."

Lucas leaned close to Finn. "We have to find that monitoring device. We can't even take the chance of talking among ourselves until we do."

"We looked everywhere," said Finn.

"We must have missed something," Andre said. "Think."

"I'm more concerned about that warp disc," Lucas said. "It's got to be somewhere aboard this sub."

"What about Drakov's cabin?" Andre said.

"Good a place to look as any," Lucas replied, "but it seems a little obvious."

"The problem is not in finding it, but what to do about it when we do," said Finn. "If we sabotage it, they'll know immediately. And it won't be any trouble for them to clock out to wherever they've got the rest of the shipment hidden and get another one."

"That is a problem," said Lucas. "Everyone on board's got warp discs. Even if we manage to sabotage the sub, they can all clock out to God knows where. Drakov's got us and he knows it."

"Only what's he going to do with us?" said Andre.

Count Grigori entered the engine room and stood there, his huge arms folded across his chest.

"I think the conference is over," Lucas said.

They walked past him out into the companionway. He said nothing to them. They found Verne in the library, reading avidly.

"You'd better do as Drakov suggested, Jules," said Lucas. "You need to get some rest."

"How can I rest?" said Verne, indicating the books around him. "There is enough here to keep dozens of scholars busy for decades. I cannot waste a moment of such an opportunity."

"Jules," said Andre, "transition can be difficult, especially when you've never experienced it before. Please."

Verne sighed. "Very well, if you insist. I am beginning to feel a bit weary."

Finn glanced at Lucas. "You think he'd have the library bugged, as well?"

"Bugged?" said Verne.

Lucas explained. "Drakov has planted a listening device somewhere in our cabin."

"Ah, I see," said Verne. "And you have been unable to locate it?"

"We've searched everywhere," said Andre.

"You are quite certain?" Verne said.

Lucas shrugged. "I can't think of anywhere else to look."

"This device," said Verne, "it could be quite small, no? Like your alarm device back on the ship?"

"Yes, it probably would be," Lucas said.

"But you have taken that into consideration and still been unsuccessful?"

They nodded.

Verne scratched his chin, thoughtfully. "It is certain he did not expect us to be aboard," he said. "If such a device was installed in the cabin, it must have been done after we arrived."

"That would pose no problem," Finn said. "They've had ample opportunity."

"Yes, yes, but I am thinking you would know what to look for and still you have not found it," Verne said.

"Don't concern yourself, Jules," said Lucas, putting a hand on the writer's shoulder. "If we couldn't find it, I doubt you could."

Verne looked up at him from where he sat and smiled. "I must seem quite primitive to you three," he said.

"I didn't mean it that way," Lucas said quickly. "It's only that—"

Verne reached out and unclipped the dosimeter from the belt of Lucas's jumpsuit. He looked at it thoughtfully for a moment, then held it up. Lucas frowned, then understanding dawned.

He took the dosimeter from Verne and examined it closely. Then he showed it to Finn and Andre. They immediately checked theirs, as well. Each contained a listening device.

"I apologize, Jules," said Lucas. "I didn't mean to be insulting. You're quite welcome to search for the listening device, if you want to. But it's probably a waste of time. Even if we found it, they'd only install another one and hide it more cleverly the second time."

Verne looked puzzled for a moment, then he understood. "Well, you are quite right, *mon ami*. We are, after all, uninvited guests aboard this vessel. One can hardly blame the captain for wishing to be cautious. I will put the matter from my mind and get some rest, as you suggest."

When the diving Klaxon and the missile chimes sounded one after the other, Verne tensed and clenched his fists; he went rigid in his bunk and glanced with alarm at the others. Land was also in his bunk, but Lucas, Finn and Andre sat at the table, playing cards with a deck they borrowed from one of the crewmen.

"It will be all right, Jules," Finn said. "Try to relax."

"Relax?" said Verne. "Relax? I am about to travel to another time and you want me to relax? Should you not lie down as well?"

Lucas smiled. "We've done this many, many times before, Jules. We're accustomed to it."

"What am I to expect?" said Verne. "How will it feel? *Mon Dieu*, I should have rested more. I am not well. My nerves . . . I am dizzy and my stomach—"

Abruptly, he retched.

Aghast, he stared at the mess he had made upon the cabin floor and wiped his mouth with the back of his hand. "How disgraceful!" he said. "How terribly embarrassing! I am so very sorry, my friends—"

"Nothing to be embarrassed about," said Finn. "It's one of those aftereffects Drakov warned you about. It happens even to seasoned veterans of time travel. You'll be feeling better shortly."

Verne stared at him. "You mean . . . that was it? It is over?"

"That was it," said Finn.

"But . . . but nothing happened!"

"You mean you didn't notice anything happen," Lucas said. "It would have been much more dramatic if you had been wearing an individual warp disc and clocked from one location to another, but since it was the submarine that made transition and we are inside the submarine, you haven't noticed anything change. And, in that sense, nothing has.''

"Can't a man get a bit of sleep around here?" Land said, turning over in his bunk.

"Ned!" said Verne. "I cannot believe it! You slept through it!"

"Slept through what?" said Land.

"We have traveled through time, Ned!"

Land grimaced. "Yes, from the moment before to this one. Stop talking nonsense."

"How do you feel, Ned?" said Lucas, glancing at his cards.

"My stomach aches from that miserable food we're served on board," said Land. "No doubt I've been poisoned by squid preserves or seaweed spinach."

Finn chuckled. "Go back to sleep, Ned."

There was a knock at their door and Sasha entered. "The captain desires your presence in the control room," he said. "There is something he wishes you to see."

7

Drakov stood at the periscope. He took his face away from it and looked at them as they came in. There was a grim expression on his face.

"We have arrived in the year 1739," he said, "in time to witness a sea battle."

"We're going to surface?" Land said.

"No, Mr. Land. However, you will be able to see through here." Drakov indicated the periscope. "If you are familiar with your history, you will know that England is involved in a war with Spain. We are at present in the Caribbean and above us a Spanish ship is being attacked by an English privateer. Would you care to see this sterling example of humanity at its worst?"

They took turns looking through the periscope. The two ships, oblivious of the submarine's presence close beneath the surface, were drifting closer and closer, exchanging cannon fire. The smaller ship, the English privateer, was coming up on the Spaniard's stern so as to prevent a broadside. The English captain was moving in at a slight angle from the rear, his cannoneers blazing away at the masts of the Spanish ship. As Verne looked through the periscope, he saw one of the masts shot away, the debris falling to the deck of the crippled Spanish ship. He called out to the others what was happening, then let Andre take a turn.

"Has the Spaniard struck his colors?" Drakov asked.

"No," said Andre.

"Then it will be bloody," Drakov said. "They will continue to pound away at each other until they are close enough for the British seamen to swarm over the bulwarks of the Spaniard. They will do each other in with muskets, pistols, cutlasses and knives, the decks running red with blood until one or the other prevails. And for what? What will have been won? This war will spread through Europe and become the War of the Austrian Succession. Then, in a few short years, the Seven Years War, followed by the War of American Independence, then the French Revolution, then Napoleon. It never ends. It never ends."

Drakov picked up a phone.

"Tubes forward," he said. "Prepare to fire two mark fifty torpedos. This is no drill. Repeat, this is no drill."

"Drakov, don't!" said Lucas, stepping forward, but instantly he was grabbed from behind by the burly von Kampf.

Verne stared at Drakov. "*Why*?" he said.

Drakov had a slightly glazed look in his eyes. "If they want war, then I shall give them war," he said. "Sound general quarters."

The alarm for battle stations came on throughout the ship.

"Tubes are flooded, Captain. The outer doors are open."

"Feed your range and bearing to the torpedo room, Chief," said Drakov.

"Drakov," said Finn. "What's the point?"

Drakov did not respond.

"Set!" said the chief.

"Fire one," said Drakov.

The chief punched the firing button, keeping his gaze on the indicator lights. The torpedo left the flooded tube under its own power.

"First torpedo under way, Captain."

"Fire two," said Drakov. His gaze was unfocused.

Verne stood at the periscope. They all waited tensely.

"Directly on target, sir," the chief said.

Verne gasped as both ships exploded in geysers of flame and debris.

"Direct hits!" the chief said.

Drakov walked out of the control room.

"Captain?" the chief said.

Drakov paused in the hatchway. "Oh," he said, sounding faintly puzzled. "Secure from general quarters."

They suited up in the wardroom. There was no need to use escape hatches to get out of the sub when they could simply clock down to the ocean floor directly below. On the floor of the wardroom, Benedetto had placed a programmed R-30 warp disc. It would generate a field large enough to enable anyone standing within a thirty-foot circumference of it to be teleported to the wreck of the *La Floridana*. Everything had been cleared away and they stood ready in their bright orange diving suits and weighted boots. The packs containing the oxygen-manufacturing hemosponge apparatus were attached to their backs. Crewmen helped them on with their diving helmets. The helmets made them look as if they were spacemen. Wide faceplaces curved around the front and built-in lights were set into the helmet crowns. The party would consist of twenty divers. A number of the divers carried spearguns, several others carried various tools. All save Lucas, Finn, Andre, Land and Verne were equipped with underwater pistols which fired needle darts by compressed air.

Verne was nervous. "What will happen if I become ill again?" he said, sweat beading on his forehead. "If I should become ill inside my helmet . . ."

"Possible," said Drakov, "but unlikely, Mr. Verne. The effects are nowhere near as strong with a short teleportation as with a temporal transition. However, in the event you do become ill, it will be necessary for you to return to the *Nautilus*. I think you will be quite safe. You haven't eaten anything since transition, have you?"

Verne shook his head.

"Was that a yes or a no?" said Drakov, coming close to look inside Verne's faceplate.

"No," said Verne.

"Good. Then if you all are ready, we will proceed."

Drakov crouched down and activated the warp disc. It began to glow faintly around its perimeter, then the glow brightened quickly and they were standing on the ocean floor.

Verne reached out and grabbed Drakov's arm.

"Nothing to be frightened of," said Drakov. "Can you hear me?"

"Y-yes," said Verne, softly. He swallowed hard. "I—I am not certain I can move, Captain."

Drakov's chuckle sounded in their helmets. "It's simple, Mr. Verne. You put one foot in front of the other. Come."

"Mother of God," whispered Land. He bent backward slightly, looking up at the *Nautilus*, which hovered above them like a giant whale.

"Beautiful, is it not?" said Drakov. "I never cease to marvel at it. A tranquil, deep-blue stillness. The water filters out the warm colors at this depth. Only the cool blue remains." He swept his arm out, indicating submerged reefs. "Coral. The tiny architects of the sea. Slaving away for centuries, building their magnificent castles. Next to their graceful spires, even the grandeur of Mad Ludwig's castle in Bavaria pales into insignificance."

The other members of the party had moved on ahead, their lights beaming out before them. Schools of fish surrounded them, darting past like underwater fireflies. Vegetation undulated all around them, like a dancing forest.

"Keep together," Drakov said. "This world is beautiful, but it is not without its hazards. Fortunately, we are well-protected from most of them. Coral is razor sharp and a certain type, called fire coral, can raise welts upon bare skin. Our suits will protect us from that, as they will from the spines of sea urchins and the stinging threads of the jellyfish known as the Portuguese man-of-war. However, we must be on the watch for sharks, which are ever unpredictable. They exist only to devour and their jaws are immensely powerful. Likewise the barracuda—a fish which is considerably smaller, but no less deadly. Mr. Land, as a seaman, you are familiar with these creatures, I trust?"

"I am, Captain."

"In that case, you will be responsible for pointing them out to your friends in the event we should encounter them. Sometimes they will only circle round, investigating. Other times, both shark and barracuda will attack with incredible ferocity. They are quite deserving of respect."

"I, too, am familiar with the appearance of these creatures, Captain," Verne said, "though I have never actually encountered them. I have heard one should make violent waving or splashing motions to frighten off a shark."

"I, too, have read that, Mr. Verne. However, practical experience has taught me one is just as liable to attract a shark with such motions as to frighten it away. Very little is known about these creatures. The only advice I can give you is to try not to appear as if you might be food."

"And how does one do that?" said Andre.

"Your guess is as good as mine," said Drakov. "Another creature to be wary of is the moray eel. It is rare to encounter one swimming in the open. They prefer to hide in dark places, such as caves and nooks within the coral or in the wrecks of ships. They will dart very quickly out of such hiding places, usually keeping a portion of their snakelike bodies hidden and fastened onto the nearest handy appendage. So please, try to refrain from groping around in spots where they might lie in wait. Some of them grow to be quite large and the larger ones may be able to penetrate the suits. Regardless of their size, they are universally tenacious. Should one grab hold of you, try not to panic. Call out for aid at once and one of us will come. Above all, remember that sharks are attracted by blood. Should the integrity of your suits be broken and you begin to bleed, it is imperative you return to the *Nautilus* at once. Again, do not attempt returning on your own. Call one of us to aid you. Any questions?"

"Yes," said Andre. "What do we do if a shark attacks?"

"Try your very best not to make it angry," Drakov said.

They moved on, walking like ballet dancers in slow motion across the sloping underwater ridge. Overhead, a giant manta ray "flew" past, its huge wings rippling gracefully. The jagged peaks of coral all around them teemed with life. Bright flashes of movement made the coral seem to gleam as tiny fish darted in and out of the numerous crevices. The sandy bottom they walked on sloped into a valley and fell off to greater depths beyond.

Drakov pointed. "There she lies," he said. "*La Floridana* in her watery grave."

It was a large wreck. Pieces of the ship were scattered all

over the slope. Broken, ribbed sections of the hull brought to mind the picked-clean carcass of some giant underwater mammal. One broken section of mast stuck up at an odd angle, the other masts had been sheared off. A large mound of ballast stones from the ruptured hull looked like a convict's rock pile, encrusted with vegetation, coral and shellfish. A large lobster scuttled across it. The crew of the *Nautilus* were already at work, two of them manning a portable airlift which had been clocked down from the submarine. Lightweight and powerful, the airlift was a compressor and a pipe with a diameter of twelve inches, steel teeth around its mouth for cutting through the sea grass. There was a valve upon the pipe for diverting the suction into the sea. In this way, the suction action could be stopped and a clogged pipe would not become buoyant and start to rise.

"Treasure hunting is hard work," said Drakov, as they stood on a small rise watching the divers move around the wreck. "Much of it is done by hand. In order to check for hidden contraband, the ballast must be sorted through, stone by stone. It is a task which must be done slowly and carefully, or the stones which make up the mound could shift and trap a diver, even crush him."

"What are they doing with that pipe?" said Verne.

"The airlift is the principal means of liberating loose items from the sea bottom," Drakov said. "Other tools used are handpicks, spades and prybars. The men you see there are at work enlarging that opening in the hull. It will enable them to get inside the cargo hold, a task made easier by the position of the wreck."

One of the divers came into view, brandishing a skull. Another found a cutlass. There were many cannonballs, ceramic pieces, shards of china and porcelain. The undiscovered wreck still contained all the cargo it had gone down with. Drakov was after the gold.

"Our ability to arrive upon the scene not long after the ship went down makes our task a great deal easier," said Drakov. "There is still a ship to search through and there are still wooden chests to be found. A ship which has been underwater for a considerable length of time falls prey to the teredo, a voracious parasite also known as shipworm. The wood is eaten away and the vessel slowly disintegrates. Wood weakened by the worms breaks off and is carried away by the current or buried beneath the sand. Only mahogany and the larger, heavier pieces of timber survive for any great length of time. Iron falls prey to oxidation. Silver turns black with sulphate. Brass turns green and as corrosion sets in, metallic pieces become encrusted with coral and start to resemble stone. In time, the only things remaining to guide the treasure hunter are rotted sections of the hull and piles of ballast stones. The death of *La Floridana* is a fact, but we have come upon her corpse before it has totally decayed. Look there, already she has started giving up her riches."

As he pointed, they saw two men bringing out a large wooden chest. They set it down upon the sea floor and began to hammer away at it with their picks, freeing the hasp from the rotting wood. Moments later, it was open, revealing a fortune in silver tarnished by the sea. As they approached to look closer, they saw the chest was full of irregularly shaped slivers, green with the action of the seawater on the copper used in the alloy as a hardening agent.

"Pieces of eight," said Drakov, taking several and passing them out for the others to examine. "So called because each is worth eight *reals*. Colonial treasure hunters called them 'cobs' because of their irregular shape, which is the result of their being chiseled off a block of silver prior to stamping."

"There must be hundreds of them in that chest!" said Land.

One of the divers was heard over their helmets, speaking to Drakov. There was a quick exchange of Russian, then Drakov said, "I am told there are several more such chests within the hold."

Land needed no more encouragement. He immediately joined the divers at their task of clearing the chests out of the hold. Finn, Lucas and Andre were content to watch, while Verne remained close to Drakov, peppering him with questions, turning ceaselessly in all directions to observe everything about the undersea world he found himself in. Their presence attracted several groupers, which swam about goggle-eyed, curious about the alien intruders. Finn made friends with one, discovering that it like being petted.

As the divers worked, *La Floridana* steadily disgorged her treasure. Hundreds of pounds of pieces of eight in wooden chests and sacks made of burlap; bar silver; gold doubloons or escudos; silver wedges weighing about four pounds each; silver and gold statues, rings, pendants, necklaces and crosses. They found gold ingots and an entire chest of gold imperials. They discovered several boxes containing jewelry set with emeralds and rubies, some of the stones the size of eyeballs. One diver spotted the ship's anchor some distance away, wedged in a coral reef. The ship's captain had thrown it out in a last desperate attempt to save his vessel from destruction, but it had struck on the submerged reef and the ship turned, foundering.

They went over to look at the anchor. It was huge. Standing, it would have towered over them. Already, the coral was encrusting it. Verne, interested to chip off some to study back aboard the sub, borrowed a handpick from the diver. Some of the coral came away, but a flash of brightness was also revealed. Verne chipped away some more, then the diver took the pick away from him and started chipping at the anchor in earnest. It was gold.

"Congratulations, Mr. Verne," said Drakov, examining the results. "You have inadvertently uncovered a most audacious smuggling attempt. They made the anchor out of gold and then painted it over. You have discovered a fortune."

Land swore, furious at not having found it himself, thereby earning a portion of the profits they would realize from its sale.

"Take heart, Mr. Land," said Drakov. "You have already assisted in recovering much treasure. Your share will not be inconsiderable."

Land turned away, then turned back quickly and gave Drakov a hard shove. With an exclamation, Drakov fell back, just in time to avoid being struck by a fifteen-foot shark that came diving down at them like a juggernaut. The shark seized upon the other diver and they heard him scream over their helmets as its jaws fastened upon him. A mist of blood filled the water as the shark thrashed, holding the diver in its jaws. Drakov fired his underwater pistol. The needle darts penetrated the shark's tough hide and it was paralyzed in seconds. It began to sink to the ocean floor, the diver still held in its jaws. Drakov bent down to check the man.

"He's finished," he said. "The blood will soon bring others. We must leave at once."

He gave quick orders over the headset in his helmet and the divers began taking the treasure they had recovered back to the point at which they had clocked in. There were already other sharks arriving, drawn by the scent of blood, when they activated the warp disc and teleported back aboard the *Nautilus*.

When his helmet was removed, Drakov turned to Ned Land and said, "I neglected to thank you, Mr. Land. You saved my life."

Land grunted.

"You will not find me unappreciative," said Drakov. "But we can discuss that later. Right now, we are all tired and I suggest we retire to our cabins for some well-deserved rest. We've had a good day's work."

Back in their cabin, Lucas took all the dosimeters containing the listening devices and carefully wrapped them up and muffled them beneath one of the bunks. Verne's exhaustion had finally made him fall asleep and he was stretched out in his bunk, snoring quietly.

"It looks as though you've made your decision, Ned," said Finn.

Land looked at him blankly.

"That shark might neatly have solved our problem," Finn explained. "But it would have meant a lost opportunity for you."

Land understood. He shook his head. "I've decided nothing," he said. "There may be riches to be found in this life, but what sort of life is it for a man, spending his days locked in an iron barrel at the bottom of the ocean? It's not natural. I do not know why I saved him from that shark. I didn't think. I only acted."

"Finn isn't blaming you, Ned," said Lucas. "Are you?"

"I don't know," Finn said, sourly. "Maybe I am."

"Drakov's death wouldn't have helped us recover the stolen shipment of warp discs," Andre said. "And it would not have solved the problem of this submarine."

"That's true enough," said Lucas. "We'll be lucky if we can find the warp disc that clocks this sub. It's probably no more than twelve inches in diameter and cleverly camouflaged. Besides, as we've already discussed, taking that disc out of commission won't prevent them from replacing it by having someone clock out and get another one. There's no way I can think of for us to knock out every warp disc on this sub. We'd have to take on the entire crew."

"That leaves us only one option," Finn said. "We have to destroy the sub."

"They must have an arms locker somewhere aboard," said Andre. "They may have warp grenades in there."

Lucas massaged his temples. "Even if we could gain access to their arms locker, I don't much fancy blowing myself away with this sub. If there isn't any other choice, well, that's what we'll have to do. In that case, I don't see any reason why all of us should die. Maybe we can overpower several of the crewmen at the right moment and relieve them of their discs. Then the others could clock out and whichever one of us remains to blow up the sub might have a chance to make it. But it would be a hell of a long shot."

"Andre's right, though," Finn said. "We can't just leave an entire shipment of warp discs lying around for anyone to find. Drakov must have a base of operations somewhere. We have to find out where."

Andre smiled. "Think he'll tell us if we ask him nicely?"

"No, but perhaps he'll show us. It stands to reason he has a base. He'd need a submarine tender, at the very least. Before he puts his plan into effect, whatever his plan is, I think he'll touch base."

"Yes, but suppose he kills us before then?" said Lucas.

"Not much we can do about that, is there?" Andre said. "He's liable to do just about anything. The man is insane."

"Maybe that works for us," Finn said. "If I were in his place, I would have killed us right off. This living paradox, instrument of Fate thing has really got a hold of him. Maybe we can play on that somehow."

"Suppose I were to decide to join him?" Land said.

They all turned to look at him.

"What I mean is," Land said, "I've seen the treasure. My greed's been awakened. I saved his life. What if I were to go to him and tell him, in secret, I've decided to accept his offer? I would say I overheard you three making plans and I will maybe pass on some of those plans to him. I'll tell him I am afraid you three will spoil my chances of being a rich man. I will secretly become a part of his crew, but stay with you so I can spy on you and keep him informed, and watch out for my own interests. He might take me into his confidence and I might learn something of use. How does it sound?"

Lucas looked at Land with new respect. "It sounds good, Ned. Damn good."

"Maybe too good," Finn said. "How do we know that's not exactly what you'll do? Spy on us for him?"

Land was on his feet in an instant and in the next instant, Finn was on the floor. Land had his fists up.

"Get up," he said. "Get up and fight!"

Finn sat up slowly, rubbing his jaw. "Not me," he said. "You hit too hard." He grinned. "I'm sorry, Ned. I had to do that. I'm the suspicious sort. I believe you."

Land glowered at him. "How do *I* know that?" he said.

"*Touché*," said Finn. "I'll tell you how you know that. Because you hit me, that's why."

Land frowned. "That makes no sense at all."

"It makes a great deal of sense," said Finn. "If you were planning to double-cross us, I don't think you would have hit me. You wouldn't have reacted that way. You would have reacted with outrage at the suggestion, but then you would have tried your utmost to convince us you were sincere. A man who's planning treachery would act deviously. He'd play up to those he's planning to betray, not attack them."

Land scowled. "I think you are a devious man yourself, *mon ami*."

"You're right," said Finn. "That's why I've lived so long."

"The next chance you get, Ned," Lucas said, "approach Drakov. Tell him you overhead us planning to break into his cabin to search for something called a warp disc. You won't know what that is, of course, but you'll tell him because you are afraid our efforts might ruin your chances of sharing in the treasure, maybe even get you killed."

Land nodded. "But suppose my doing that gets *you* killed?" he said.

Lucas shrugged. "That's just a chance we'll have to take."

The atmosphere at mess that night was jubilant. They might have expected otherwise, with the death of a member of the crew, but life went on. Treasure had been found and wine flowed freely. No one mentioned the man who had died.

Drakov was last to arrive, as usual, with the ever-present cadre of Shiro, Martingale, von Kampf and Benedetto in his wake. They had seen little of von Kampf and virtually nothing of Martingale. Land inquired of Drakov if he would ask Shiro to tattoo him and was invited to come to Drakov's cabin after mess, where Shiro kept his inks and needles.

"I will do better than that, Mr. Land," said Drakov. "Tattooing is a pleasant diversion for Shiro, but not much of a diversion for yourself. Thus far, you have only tasted of our life beneath the sea. In a short while, you will see how we recreate, as well."

"We're making port?" said Land.

"In a way," said Drakov. "It is past time for my men to enjoy some liberty. The company of men is pleasurable, but somewhat limiting. I like to keep my crew happy."

"Does that mean women?" Land said.

Andre gave him a wry look.

"It does, indeed, Mr. Land," said Drakov. He turned to the commandos. "You may have noticed Mr. Martingale's absence of late. He has been upon an errand for me. I am pleased to report matters are well in hand. Before too long, I shall be ready and you will know my plans in full at that time. I have decided to make good use of you."

"With or without our consent?" said Lucas.

"Oh, you will give your consent," said Drakov. "I feel sure of that. And you will be pleased to learn you will survive. At least, if you follow my directions."

"And if we don't?" said Finn.

"I think you will."

"Why don't you stop playing games and tell us what's on your mind?" said Finn.

"I'm disappointed that you have not deduced it," Drakov

said. "Where is your imagination? I am in command of an underwater, mobile, virtually undetectable strategic missile base. What use might I make of it?"

"If you believe you can get away with international blackmail, Drakov, you're madder than I thought," said Finn.

Shiro started to rise, but Drakov quickly motioned him back down.

"Please, Mr. Delaney," he said, "Shiro is quite sensitive about the manner in which I am addressed. I would advise you not to provoke him. You would be no match for him. As for your suggestion, I thought you would give me credit for more imagination than that. In point of fact, I could easily get away with international blackmail, though I—but no. I will let you contemplate it further. It amuses me. At any rate, you will all know soon enough. For now, you may prepare to leave the *Nautilus* for a short time. We can hardly put into Barataria in a nuclear submarine. For that purpose, we require another type of ship."

"Barataria?" said Land. "The name rings a bell. Where have I heard it before?"

"It should be well familiar to a seaman, Mr. Land," said Drakov, "even one such as yourself, who has worked out of New England and Canada. You will have heard stories of Barataria, perhaps during your boyhood. There are several places we visit for recreation and Barataria Bay is one of them, a particular favorite with my men. In the year 1807, Barataria came into prominence as an island smuggling base. It is located at the mouth of a bay in the bayou country at the gulf near New Orleans. In many ways, Barataria was a tiny nation unto itself, a haven for pirates and smugglers where the law did not reach, at least for many years. The man who ruled this pirate island is one you will undoubtedly have heard of. He was one of the last freebooters, a legendary figure among corsairs. His name was Captain Jean Lafitte."

8 _____

Benedetto came to their cabin after transition was completed and announced they were surfacing. "The captain requests the pleasure of your company on deck," he said, with a mock bow.

"Have we got a choice?" said Finn.

Benedetto grinned and stood aside, holding the door open for them. They climbed up through the hatchway and stepped onto the outer deck of the *Nautilus*, into the open air for the first time since they came aboard. The warm wind was the first thing they noticed. The second thing was a sight which brought them up short. Several hundred yards away, sailing toward them, was a long, clipper-bowed schooner with tall masts and a sleek, low hull. It was a lovely ship with graceful lines, its wooden hull painted white. As it came about, its sails luffing, its crew prepared to bring her alongside.

"Beautiful, isn't she?" said Drakov. "My prize possession, the *Valkyrie*. Everything I learned in my youth as a ship's captain in the Pribilofs, I used in building her. We shall be going aboard while the *Nautilus* submerges and awaits our return."

"Who's sailing her?" said Lucas.

"And where did she come from?" said Drakov, smiling. "Isn't that what you really want to know? For now, I will tell you only that she is a time ship, like the *Nautilus*. Mr. Martingale has arranged for her arrival at these temporal coordinates. We are now in the Gulf of Mexico, in the year 1812. As to where she came from, as you have surmised, I have a base of operations where she is berthed when I am not using her. You will forgive me if I do not tell you where or *when* it is located. You will see it for yourself before very long. Then you will be able to fully appreciate the extent of my resources. The *Valkyrie*'s crew are people I have carefully selected, from various nations and time periods. I have created my organization in the mold of the Timekeepers, only I have made it a great deal more clandestine and efficient. We are all united in one cause. Temporal corsairs or, as you would put it, time pirates." He grinned. "Thus far, Mr. Priest, you have seen only the tip of the iceberg. I want you to see it all."

"We're to be your messengers, is that it?" Finn said. "That's why you've been flexing your muscles for us. We're supposed to be suitably impressed, so we can tell Forrester how formidable you are when you send us back to him with your demands, right?"

"Rather crudely phrased," said Drakov, "but you're quite correct. I want my father to have a clear understanding of my strength, of what I have accomplished. A father should be proud of his son."

"You expect him to buckle under?" Finn said.

Drakov chuckled. "If the choice were his, I am certain he would not, regardless of the cost. But the choice is not his. Is it?"

The *Valkyrie* came alongside and lines were tossed to the men aboard the *Nautilus*. The crew of the submarine secured the lines to cleats built into the deck. The exchange of crews began. Several of the men sailing the *Valkyrie* remained on board. Drakov explained they would stand watch upon the ship while the crew of the submarine enjoyed their liberty among the smugglers and corsairs of Barataria. The rest of the *Valkyrie*'s crew boarded the submarine. They were a colorful group, dressed according to period in loose-fitting cotton shirts, leather vests, sea boots and striped breeches. They were Blacks and Asians, Europeans, Scandinavians, Hispanics, a melting pot of nationalities and races, all rough-looking, all in excellent physical condition. They moved quickly, with military precision.

"This is looking worse and worse," Finn said to Lucas.

Lucas nodded. If, as Drakov boasted, they had only seen the tip of the iceberg, then it was already more than they could handle. They needed help badly, only there was no way to summon help. Even if they could, by the time it arrived, Drakov would be long gone, to another century. Drakov knew there was nothing they could do and his confidence was galling.

"You will, of course, accompany us," said Drakov. "I would hate to be deprived of your company. Besides, I think you'll find Lafitte a fascinating man."

"He was a pretty fascinating child," Finn said.

Drakov looked at him with surprise. "You encountered Jean Lafitte as a child? How?"

"It was during an adjustment mission in Paris," Lucas said. "He was only about twelve years old at the time."

"How extraordinary!" said Drakov. "This could prove to be a problem if he remembers you."

"He shouldn't," Finn said. "He became involved in our adjustment mission and it was necessary to condition him to forget his part in it."

"Then there should be no problem," Drakov said. "I will be very interested in discussing this with you later. Jean must indeed have been a fascinating young man."

"That's an understatement if I ever heard one," Finn said. "He was scary enough as a kid. I can imagine what he must be like as an adult."

They went aboard the *Valkyrie*, where a change in clothing was awaiting them below decks. The crew of the *Nautilus* had already changed into period costume prior to boarding, so they had the privacy of one of the cabins to themselves. Drakov took Verne to his own stateroom to share a glass of port. He seemed especially anxious to please the author, no doubt to ingratiate himself with his future biographer.

In the cabin below, they sorted through clothing to find garments which would fit them. Andre put on a blousy white cotton shirt that laced up at the neck, a black leather vest with gold trim which hung down to her hips and high black sea boots over tight-fitting white breeches. Finn found a similar shirt sized to his proportions, striped breeches and a red brocade vest. Lucas wore a white shirt, a lightweight coat in navy blue with brass buttons and black breeches. They had worn more unusual garb before, but Finn could not resist the comment that Andre would probably need her knife and cutlass to keep the men of Barataria at bay.

Lucas examined his own sword. "Arrogant of him to allow us these," he said. "Of course, the others all had pistols, did you notice?"

Ned Land looked completely in his element in the pirate clothing. His short-sleeved shirt revealed his new tattoo, with which he was quite pleased. Shiro had adorned him with a shark upon his upper arm, to commemorate his having saved Drakov's life.

"I've had a chance to speak with Drakov," Ned said. "He's being careful, but I think I've convinced him of how bad I want to join his crew."

"Did you tell him we were planning to search his cabin?" Lucas said.

Land nodded. "He just laughed. He told me not to concern myself, but to keep him informed."

"Well, if the disc isn't in his cabin, it could be in any of a hundred places aboard that sub," said Finn. "Maybe we should try searching the reactor room, only how are we going to manage that with crewmen constantly stationed there?"

"We'd better try searching Drakov's cabin anyway," said Lucas, "just to give Ned's story credibility."

Martingale entered the cabin, surprising them. For a big man he moved so silently. "If you're going to try searching Drakov's cabin," he said, "make sure Shiro doesn't catch you at it. Grigori's dangerous enough, but when it comes to protecting Drakov, Shiro can be difficult to control."

They stared at him. "I guess you got an earful," Finn said in disgust.

"I guess I did," Martingale drawled, giving them a half smile. "Drakov wants you people up on top soon as you're changed, so he can brief you on Lafitte. Verne's already up there with him, looking like some damn silly New Orleans dandy in a long green coat and pantaloons. Drakov wanted to make sure he looked all right, which is just as well. I'm not sure where he stands. I wasn't too sure about the Canuck, either, until what I just heard. Here, take this.''

He handed Lucas a small plastic box.

Lucas frowned. ''Martingale, what's this—''

''Open it.''

He opened the box and removed a tiny plastic envelope. ''A plastiskin graft? I don't get it. What did you mean just now when you said—''

''I'm in the Underground, soldier,'' said Martingale. ''Have been for about ten years now. I deserted during an arbitration conflict in 20th-century Southeast Asia. Drakov has the Underground worried, too. I'll explain more later, when I get the chance. Right now I want you to slap that graft on. Under the arm's a good place.''

''Just hold on a second, Martingale,'' said Finn. ''You—''

''I haven't got time to get into this right now,'' said Martingale. ''I need to get topside before Drakov starts wondering what's taking me so long. There's a particle level device molded into that graft. It's a little like a warp disc, only different. Don't ask me to explain, it's too damn complicated. If you want to stop Drakov, you'll have to trust me. Our best chance lies with the Doctor.''

''Who?''

''Later. Slap the graft on and get up on deck.''

''Wait a minute,'' Finn said, but Martingale left without another word.

''What was he talking about?'' said Land. ''Who's the Doctor?''

''I haven't the faintest idea,'' said Finn. He glanced at Lucas. ''You think he's on the level about being Temporal Underground?''

''I don't know,'' said Lucas. ''How would a 20th-century mercenary know about the Underground?''

''Maybe he wouldn't,'' said Andre. ''That doesn't mean Drakov couldn't have told him.''

''Let me see that,'' Finn said.

Lucas handed him the envelope.

''What's this Under ground?'' said Land.

"It would take too long to explain now, Ned," said Lucas. "It'll have to wait."

"It looks like a perfectly ordinary graft patch from a field medical kit," said Andre.

"With something like a warp disc in it, only on the particle level," Finn said. "Really? There's no such thing as a warp disc that small. I don't buy it."

"There's only one way to find out," Lucas said, reaching for the envelope.

Finn gave it to him. "You're going to chance it? It's not smart."

Lucas shrugged. "What do we have to lose? If Martingale's not lying, I can't afford not to chance it. Things can't get much worse."

"The last time you said that, things got a whole lot worse," said Finn. "What if it's a bug?"

"I'll risk it," Lucas said. "We can always cut it off. What's a little pain?"

He ripped open the envelope and carefully removed the graft patch. Using two fingers, he spread the exceedingly thin square of plastiskin on the palm of his right hand. On contact with the skin, it began to grow warm. He put his hand inside his shirt and pressed the graft patch against the skin of his underarm. As it started to adhere, he smoothed it out with his fingers, spreading the softened patch evenly as it became part of his skin.

"It's *hot*," he said. "They aren't supposed to get that hot." He bit his lower lip. "Jesus, it's really starting to burn!"

Finn came over to him quickly, pulled off his coat and raised his shirt. "Lift your arm," he said. He examined the skin there closely. "It's taken. I can't see it anymore. The skin's red in that area, but that's normal."

"Are you all right?" said Andre.

"I think so," Lucas said. "It's fading now. But it feels strange. A tingling sensation, like tiny needlepricks. It's not supposed to do that, either."

Land stood by, his brow furrowed with concern, wishing he could understand what was going on.

"Well, whatever it is, it's part of me now," said Lucas.

"I don't like it," Finn said. "I'm going to get that bastard

Martingale and make him tell us—"

"It's too late now," said Lucas. "One way or another, we'll find out what it's all about eventually. What the hell, we're not paid to play it safe. Let's get topside before Drakov starts getting nervous."

"Ah, there you are," said Drakov, when they joined him on deck. "I was about to send Martingale back down to see what was keeping you."

"Finn had some trouble finding clothes to fit," said Lucas.

"You look splendid," Drakov said. "The very image of corsairs. That is what you are, by the way. Corsairs, or privateers. I should caution you not to use the term 'pirate' in the presence of Lafitte. He has a nasty temper. He makes a great point of the fact his ships sail under letters of marque, with the official standing of privateers. It may be a small distinction, which he interprets rather loosely, but it is important to him."

"What are we supposed to do in Barataria?" said Andre.

"Anything you like," said Drakov. "You may even attempt to escape if you should choose to. No one will stop you. But you won't do that. That would be dereliction of duty, wouldn't it?" He gave them a mocking look. "Besides, without your warp discs, your chances of making it to the mainland would be very poor. Barataria Bay is located at the mouth of the Mississippi Delta, in marsh country. The coast of Louisiana is a vast, wet plain composed of hundreds of bayous, swampland veined with winding streams and overgrown with vegetation. You could easily become lost in it forever."

"But Lafitte and his men know their way around?" said Land.

"Lafitte could find his way through the bayous blindfolded," Drakov said. "He makes his headquarters on Grand Terre Island. He leads a commune of *contrebandiers*, smugglers who enjoy the sanction of the New Orleans citizenry by providing them with cheap, duty-free goods, especially Negroes. They are called Negroes in this time period, where racial distinctions are so fine. New Orleans is predominantly French, though quite cosmopolitan. The people of the bayou country are largely Creole, of Spanish-French ancestry. There is also a racial category known as quadroon, descendents of white fathers and black mothers. Such distinctions are important here.

"Lafitte is extremely wealthy. He has made much of his fortune smuggling slaves. Due to the ban on slave importation, there is a shortage. Lafitte takes advantage of it by raiding Spanish ships and bringing their slave cargoes to America, to sell. He has vast connections in this market, reaching as far as Memphis, where his principal buyers are the Bowie brothers. In Barataria, he is the law. It is a kingdom unto itself. Smugglers and corsairs are always made welcome."

"How do you tie in with him?" said Lucas.

"He knows me as Captain Drako, an Italian navigator who led a mutiny aboard a Balkan trader, stole the ship and embarked for the Caribbean or the Indies, as they call the area, to pursue a career as a corsair. Since that time, I have moved up in the world, obtaining this wonderful ship by means of my profits. This story explains the accents of my crew and why some of them speak neither English nor French. We last visited Barataria a year or so ago, by the reckoning of this time. I will explain to him that you signed on with me in Martinique, Mr. Priest. Mr. Delaney, you will be an Irish seaman I encountered in my travels and Miss Cross, we shall make you a Frenchwoman from the seaport of Marseilles. It is important to establish the proper nationalities for you. Lafitte passionately hates the Spaniards. He hates the British only slightly less and they are at war with the United States at this time."

"Then there is danger of our encountering a hostile ship?" said Land.

"Some slight danger, perhaps," said Drakov, "but we are well armed and the *Valkyrie* can easily outsail any ship in the British navy. By the way, Mr. Land, we will devise no elaborate identity for you. A French-Canadian harpooner will be quite acceptable to Jean Lafitte."

"What about Jules?" said Land.

"I am the scion of a wealthy French family, recently rescued from a pirate who was holding me for ransom," Verne said. He seemed quite taken with the idea.

"How long will we be in Barataria?" said Finn.

"A few days, perhaps more," said Drakov. "Why so anxious, Mr. Delaney? We have not even arrived yet. Enjoy yourself. There will be plenty of reason for anxiety later on.''

The archipelago which separated the waters of Barataria
Bay from the Gulf of Mexico came into view late in the
afternoon. The low-lying islands were pointed out by Drakov
and he identified Grand Terre and Grand Island, the two
large islands lying close together. To the west was the island
Chênière Caminada.

A warm, orange-scented breeze reached them and they
could see the palm trees on the islands swaying gently. The
heat was oppressive, even with the sea breeze. Lucas took off
his coat. They dropped anchor in the security of the bay and
took the boats in, pulling past skiffs belonging to shrimp
fishermen, and houses, little more than cottages, erected upon
piles. The air had a piscatory taint to it which at times overpowered the smell of oranges and oleander. A number of
other ships were anchored nearby, ships belonging to the fleet
of Jean Lafitte. Drakov pointed out Lafitte's own ship, the
Jupiter, a clipper-built schooner with a sleek, black-painted
hull.

''It was built for speed,'' said Drakov, ''but my *Valkyrie*
can outsail her. Lafitte has several times offered me vast sums
of money for her.'' He laughed. ''He asked me to name my
price. Gold, silver, women, anything. But I will not sell. A
ship such as the *Valkyrie* in the hands of a man such as Jean
Lafitte would wreak havoc in the waters of the Caribbean.''

''What about a ship such as the *Nautilus* in the hands of a
man such as yourself?'' said Verne.

Drakov raised his eyebrows. ''Am I to take that as a rebuke,
Mr. Verne?''

''It was only a question,'' the author replied.

''To which you will soon receive an answer,'' Drakov said.
''First, however, we have business here.''

''Business?'' Lucas said. ''I thought it was recreation.''

''I meant that our business here was recreation, nothing
more,'' Drakov said, innocently.

There was a carriage waiting for them. The man driving the
carriage was small, with broad shoulders and light-brown hair
bleached lighter still by the sun. He was deeply tanned and
dressed in elegant, cream-colored trousers and a white shirt

open at the neck. He wore a lightweight green frock coat and a vest of yellow brocade. He greeted Drakov warmly in French.

"Ah, Captain Drako! Jean spied your ship while coming in from his veranda and immediately dispatched me to meet you. I trust your voyages have been prosperous?"

"You shall soon see for yourself," said Drakov. He turned to the others. "This is Captain Dominique Youx, Captain Lafitte's chief lieutenant. Under letters of marque from Carthagena, he has become known as the most formidable privateer in the Indies."

Youx flashed a wide, disarming smile. "One does one's best, eh? Come, Jean awaits."

They climbed into the carriage as Youx ascended to the driver's seat and urged the horses to a gentle trot. Drakov leaned close to the others, speaking so Youx would not hear.

"It is not generally known, nor will it be known until many years after Youx's death, that he is Lafitte's brother, Alexander. An older brother whose adventures necessitated an alias."

"I thought his brother was named Pierre," said Finn.

"That is another brother," Drakov said. "We may or may not see him. He spends much of his time in New Orleans. One side of his face has been affected by a stroke. Should we encounter him, try not to stare."

"That lying little bastard," Finn said. "In Paris, he told us Pierre was his only brother."

Drakov shrugged. "Lafitte has always been secretive about his past. Future biographers will disagree on many facts concerning him. Even in his own journal, when he writes it long after his retirement, Jean will be somewhat elusive. I have a copy of it aboard the *Nautilus*. He is a pivotal figure in history. His island will eventually be overrun by an American naval force, yet he will nevertheless go to the aid of General Andrew Jackson and help repel the British invasion of New Orleans. For this, he will receive a pardon from President Madison, but no recompense for his losses. Undaunted, he will establish another corsairs' base on Galveston, displacing a pirate named d'Avry, and go on as before. When he leaves Galveston, he will burn his colony and for years it will be believed that he has sailed off into the sunset, never to be seen or heard from again. In fact, he will take the name John Lafflin and settle in Charleston, South Carolina, where he will marry, father a son and pursue a career as a merchant and ship owner. In time, he will move to St. Louis, then to Europe, where he will meet two gentlemen named Marx and Engels, whose ideas will so appeal to him that he will finance the printing of the *Communist Manifesto*. He will bring copies of it back to America with him and even have one delivered to a congressman named Lincoln. He will die in Alton, Illinois, in the year 1854, having lived to the ripe old age of seventy-two."

"What are you talking about back there?" said Youx.

"I was telling my friends about your chief," said Drakov. "They are quite anxious to meet him."

"We are almost there," said Youx.

"Imagine," said Verne, "to know a man while he lives, and yet to know the date of his death and all that will happen in his future!"

"I have, of course, had the courtesy not to reveal any of this to him," said Drakov, in an amused tone. "I have no idea how he would take it."

"You seem to think pretty highly of him," Lucas said.

"He has become, in many ways, my role model, Mr. Priest," said Drakov. "A hero in a world in which, even in this time, heroes are becoming a dying breed. Lafitte is the last of the swashbucklers, the final gasp of the golden age of piracy."

"You will excuse my saying this, I hope," said Verne, "but I have some difficulty in comprehending what it is about a pirate that is in any way heroic."

"I will concede your point to a degree," said Drakov. "Most of them were barbarians, indeed. Men such as Francois Lolonois, Roche Brasiliano, Henry Morgan, Blackbeard, even women, such as Anne Bonny and Mary Read, were capable of unspeakable acts of cruelty. Yet, consider the cruelty of the times in which they lived. Few of their actions were more cruel than those practiced aboard Spanish and British ships. They were criminals, outcasts of society, but they were also free. They recognized no code of ethics other than their own, to which they rigidly adhered. They were dissatisfied with their world, so they made their own, upon the seas. I find heroism in that.''

''I find self-justification,'' said Andre.

''You would, Miss Cross,'' said Drakov. ''Condemnation is only to be expected when one flaunts the laws and conventions of society. The alien is not to be tolerated. Yet what if society is wrong? What is the individual of principle to do, go along with the wrongs and conform, thereby being accepted by society? Or choose the more difficult path of idealism and resist the society he feels is wrong?''

''Who's to say he's right?'' said Andre.

''A question such as that could lead to endless philosophical debate,'' said Drakov. ''Frankly, I am not in the mood. A free man is concerned with no one's judgment other than his own. He makes his own decisions and lives by the consequences.''

''Interesting,'' said Verne. ''There was a novel published this year—or rather, in the year 1866, since I am there no longer—by a Russian named Dostoyevski, in which a very similar argument is raised, that the superior man is above the law. Have you read *Crime and Punishment*, Captain Drakov?''

''Try to remember to address me as Captain Drako while we are here. And in reply to your question, yes, of course I have read it. A fascinating novel; the story of a self-deluded young man. However, I dispute your statement concerning the similarity. It is one thing to believe, as did Dostoyevski's protagonist, that a man of genius is above moral law. It is quite another to recognize the existence of non-subjective morality, base one's principles upon it and perceive society as having violated that morality. In that sense, I am not an outcast of society due to my beliefs. I have *never been* a part of society. I was born in the 19th century and my education was completed in the 27th century. In neither century did I belong. I was an outsider from birth, by virtue of my birth. No one can view society quite so clearly as an outsider, Mr. Verne. No one is or has ever been more of an outsider than myself.''

The carriage drove down a narrow path, past small cottages with no more than one or two rooms and windows with heavy blinds made of strips of wood which were favored over glass for protection from the storms that lashed the gulf. Orange groves and large oleander bushes were everywhere. Palm trees and vivid flowers gave the palmetto-thatched settlement a tropical flavor. It was a peaceful, lazy scene, one in which their conversation seemed incongruous.

Lafitte's house was a mansion, located near the warehouses where the slaves were kept. His home was on a rise, overlooking the sea, its brick walls covered with plaster mixed together with crushed oyster shells. There were two floors, with iron bars on the windows and a veranda circling the house on the second floor, creating a shaded area beneath. As they drove up, Lafitte stood on the veranda, hands on hips, looking down at them with a wide smile upon his face.

He was a tall, slim man in his late twenties, with black hair and long sideburns. His teeth were very white and his eyes were very dark, very striking. He was an elegant, handsome man. He called out to them in French, in a clear, strong, mellifluous voice.

"Drako! You scoundrel! Where have you been keeping yourself? Come in, come in, bring your friends and have a drink or two or ten."

The door was opened for them by a quadroon girl, one of the loveliest young women they had ever seen. She couldn't have been more than sixteen or seventeen years old. Her skin was light, almost golden-colored and her eyes were a deep, dark brown and very large. Her hair was a thick, luxuriant mass of dark curls. She curtsied as they entered.

Lafitte came down to greet them, dressed in a lightweight black suit and a black brocade vest with a white silk shirt. He moved gracefully and his carriage was that of a nobleman.

"Marie, some wine for our friends," he said. He came up to Drakov and embraced him.

"You look well, Jean."

"A year has not aged you at all," Lafitte said. "It is a mystery to me how you stay at sea so long, yet never grow very tanned or appear weathered. But then, you are a man of many mysteries, no? Tell me, have you reconsidered my offer?"

"Ever respectfully, I must still decline," said Drakov.

Lafitte shook his head. "Foolish man. You would prosper here in Barataria. Your ship would be the crown of our fleet."

"You mean of *your* fleet, Jean," said Drakov.

"I respect your independence. We will speak no more of it. For now, at any rate. You must introduce me to your friends."

Drakov performed the introductions. When he got to Andre, Lafitte looked at her admiringly, then bent down to kiss her hand. "A woman corsair! My respects, Ma'mselle. Anyone who can hold her own with Drako's crew of cutthroats is deserving of admiration. Wherever did your find her, Drako?"

"In Marseilles," said Drakov." Andre was in some slight legal difficulties at the time."

"You must tell me all about it later," Lafitte said. "Come, we will take our wine on the veranda, where we can enjoy the breeze."

Marie brought their wine to them and silently departed. Land couldn't take his eyes off her.

"It appears you have been captivated, Mr. Land," said Lafitte.

"Your pardon, sir," Land said, awkwardly, having been caught staring. "I meant no offense to your wife, sir."

Lafitte laughed. "*Wife?* She is my slave. You want her? I will sell her to you. But you will pay dearly."

Land was too flustered to reply.

"Your men will be welcome ashore, as always," Lafitte told Drakov, "however, I should caution you that Gambi is back. He and his crew have been a problem. I hope there will be no incidents."

"There won't be, so long as my men are not interfered with," Drakov said.

"I am growing weary of Gambi," Lafitte said. "He takes too much upon himself. We have enough problems already without him."

"What sort of problems?" Drakov said, sipping his wine.

"Oh, that idiot Claiborne," said Lafitte. "That fool of a governor who sits in his mansion on Toulouse Street and denounces me as a pirate to all and any who will listen. We must stop the smuggling, he says, over and over again. Stop the smuggling, indeed! He was only too happy to have *this* smuggler stop at his house and deliver goods to him on more than one occasion in the past. Now, he is a force for moral righteousness. The man is an insufferable ass. Do you know what he had the temerity to do? He posted a reward of five hundred dollars for my arrest! Can you imagine? I had the exact wording of the proclamation copied, substituting his name for mine, and I posted a reward for *his* arrest, only I offered fifteen hundred dollars. I sent him a challenge, offering my sword. Of course, I received no answer. Still, it caused some amusement in the city and the publicity is good for business."

"Have you had more trouble with the British?" Drakov said.

Lafitte sneered. "Those imperialist pigs! Only the Spaniards are worse. I hear they have secured Detroit. Rumors have them heading toward us. They will find a warm welcome."

The carriage returned with Dominique Youx and two men, who unloaded a chest and brought it into the house. Moments later, they had carried it up the stairs, grunting from the weight of it, and then out onto the veranda.

"Captain Drako comes bearing gifts, Jean," said Youx. He opened the chest, revealing part of the treasure they had recovered from the sunken *La Floridana*. It was filled with pieces of eight, which Drakov's crew had meticulously cleaned so they would not look as if they had been under water.

"Drako," said Lafitte, reprovingly, "there is no need of this."

"I know, Jean, but please accept the gift. Think of it as a token payment from my men for their entertainment."

"In that case, I must present you with a gift, as well," Lafitte said. "What will you have? Another ship, perhaps? We have recently brought in a prize, a Spaniard. She is only a merchantman, nothing like your *Valkyrie*, of course, but—"

"One ship is enough for me, my friend," said Drakov. "From you, I will accept only hospitality and nothing more."

"Well, then I must do something for your men, at least. Land, you like Marie? She's yours. I give her to you. *Marie*!"

Land was thunderstruck.

"Now, Jean—" Drakov began.

"No, no, it is all settled! I have spoken. Ah, Marie, meet your new master, Mr. Ned Land. I have made him a present of you."

Marie looked aghast. Her eyes filled with tears.

Drakov came to the rescue. "Jean, please, you will cause me problems if you do this. This girl is not made for a life at sea. If you give her to Land, it will only make the rest of my crew jealous."

"Then I will give each of them a woman," said Lafitte. "I have hundreds. Well, perhaps not hundreds, but certainly enough for each to take his pick."

"Just what I need," said Drakov. "A woman for every man aboard my ship."

Lafitte grimaced. "Yes, I suppose that would be a problem, wouldn't it?"

"She seems quite close to you, Captain Lafitte," said Land. "I wouldn't wish to cause her to be unhappy."

"Bah! Women attach themselves to men like barnacles. If a man gives them any regard, he'll have a devil of a time scraping them off. Very well, then. I shall think of something else. Never mind, Marie. It appears Mr. Land prefers for you to stay with me."

"Oh, thank you, Monsieur!" Marie said, standing on tiptoe to kiss Land upon the cheek.

"Go and thank him properly, at least," Lafitte said.

She took his hand and led the bewildered Land away.

"Are you as cavalier with everyone, Captain Lafitte?" said Verne, in a reproving tone. "Or only with your slaves?"

"Do I offend you, sir?" Lafitte said.

Drakov quickly intervened. "Mr. Verne, though something of an aristocrat in France, is nevertheless rather liberal in his ideas, Jean."

"Is it liberal to believe that people should not be considered property?" said Verne.

"Ah, yes, the Negro question," said Lafitte. "I perceive you subscribe to this anti-slavery idea, sir. I will tell you something, quite sincerely. In principle, I am not against it. However, allow me to point out that this idea, whatever its merits, is not a very popular one, certainly not at present, in this region. In the future, things may well change. I suspect they will. For now, it is the Negroes' misfortune to be slaves. This does not mean I mistreat them. As you have seen, Marie was quite reluctant to leave me. What is more, the slaves I bring to Barataria and sell in places such as Donaldsonville and Memphis are not Negroes I have captured and taken from their homeland. Those I take from Spanish ships bound for Havana and South America have already been thoroughly subdued and domesticated. There would be little point, assuming a great idealism on my part, in returning them to Africa. Such a voyage would be prohibitive and they would not survive, in any case. Africa is not a civilized country and their own tribes would doubtless kill them. If I were to set them free, where would I take them? Where could they enjoy such freedom? How would they survive? Or would you rather I leave them with the Spaniards, who are, I assure you, far less benevolent masters than they will find here? What would you have me do?''

"Your points are well taken, Captain," Verne said. "Nevertheless, and meaning no offense, I cannot help but feel pity toward young Marie."

Lafitte shook his head. "You know very little of our ways, Mr. Verne. I do not say this in rebuke, you understand. Allow me to explain. Marie is what we call a *griffe*, the daughter of a white man and a quadroon woman. Here in New Orleans, we frequently have quadroon balls, lavish affairs attended by all eligible quadroon women and most of the young New Orleans gentlemen. A quadroon is not considered a Negro, Mr. Verne. However, neither is a quadroon considered white. Their position in society is strictly defined. For years, the young men of this city have gone to the Quadroon Ballroom, as is the custom, in search of mistresses. Do not make the mistake of thinking we have made them prostitutes or whores. They are not that. Their best chance for a good life is to find a white man who will act as their protector and their mothers prepare them for this from childhood. A quadroon girl usually becomes the mistress of a young gentleman of means, who keeps her in a comfortable home or an apartment, cares for her, frequently has children by her. She lives a good life, devoted to one man, who provides for her in a manner that allows her to live quite comfortably. Sometimes this association is terminated when the young man marries, sometimes it continues. Quadroon men—free men of color, as we call them here—are not as fortunate. Sometimes their fathers provide an education for them, but more frequently they become laborers or musicians. They often marry former mistresses of white men and lead normal, happy lives. If they are light enough in color, they might leave New Orleans and travel far away, passing as white.

"Marie would have been a free woman of color in New Orleans and she would easily have found a wealthy man to provide for her. However, until I intervened, her destiny was to be a Spanish slave. She was in chains when I found her, though she was kept chained in the captain's cabin, rather than in the hold with the others, for reasons which seem quite obvious. She was born in Havana and she grew up a slave. The Spaniards *did* make a whore of her. She knew nothing else since the age of twelve. In New Orleans, she could have been free, only what would have been her opportunities? She had received no training in manners and social graces. She has no mother to take her to a quadroon ball. She had no home, no means of support. She would have fallen back on the only thing she knew and would have become a prostitute for certain. Nevertheless, I gave her that choice. It may not have been much of a choice, but it was all I could offer her. Freedom or being sold as a slave. She pleaded with me to keep her. She said she would serve me faithfully and keep me happy. Well, sir, I understood only too well what she meant. And I did not wish to put myself in the position of taking advantage of such a situation. That would have made me no different from the Spaniards."

"Yet you keep her as a slave," said Verne.

"I do," Lafitte said, "so other men will respect her as my property. Yet, I have trained her, taught her, treated her well and never bedded her."

"And offered her to Land," said Verne.

"As was my right," Lafitte said. "I offered her the choice of freedom or slavery." He shrugged. "She chose slavery."

Verne sighed and stared out at the setting sun. "You are a complicated man, Captain."

Dominique Youx joined them once again to tell Lafitte the men were arriving for the council.

"You will excuse me for a short while," Lafitte said, getting up. "Prior to your arrival, I called for a meeting of my captains. It is a matter of some importance. Please, the night is warm. Remain here for a while and I shall have supper brought to you. This should not take very long."

They waited on the veranda, watching the captains of Barataria arrive, many coming with members of their crews who remained outside, and they gorged themselves on the delicious Creole cuisine. Ned did not reappear, prompting Andre to observe that Marie must be giving him a truly proper thanks. Verne looked shocked.

Downstairs, shouts were heard, then the sounds of furniture overturning. They heard a door slam and looking out over the railing of the veranda, they saw a heavyset, swarthy-looking man leaving in a huff to join some of the men gathered on the beach.

"That's Gambi," Drakov said. "It appears he has walked out of the meeting. This may mean trouble."

The meeting broke up soon after that and Lafitte rejoined them, looking no different than before. Whatever had happened at the meeting seemed to have affected him little, if at all.

"We saw Gambi leaving in a rage," said Drakov, trying to draw him out. "If he is being difficult, perhaps I should send word to my men to steer clear of him and his crew during our stay."

Lafitte shrugged. "Gambi is his own worst enemy. His own greed and lack of self-control will do him in. He has never understood that we owe our existence here to the most precarious balance. As corsairs, we prey on Spanish and British shipping, indulge in a little smuggling, in short, provide goods and services in return for which we are left well enough alone. But Gambi is a stupid pig. Of late, too many ships have been disappearing in the gulf. American ships. I know for a fact Gambi has attacked at least one. Some of the others have started to follow his example. I have laid down the law. The American flag is to be respected. Anyone attacking a ship flying that flag will be expelled from Barataria at once. Gambi did not take that well."

"What about the others?" Drakov said.

"The others will fall in line, but they shall wait and see how I deal with Gambi first."

"And how will you deal with him?" said Verne.

"I will give him enough rope to hang himself with," Lafitte said. "Unless I am very much mistaken, he is about to start gathering that rope right now."

There was quite a bit of shouting coming from the direction of the beach. The sun had gone down and the men on the beach had lit fires. A large group of them were now advancing on Lafitte's mansion, carrying torches, shouting, being led by Gambi. Lafitte produced a clay pipe and casually began to fill it with tobacco.

"LAFITTE!"

The man shouting from below was not Gambi. He was a large, muscular seaman, dressed in a loose-fitting white shirt and loose white trousers. He was bald and bearded and he looked quite formidable as he stood in the glare of the torch-light, shaking his fist at those sitting up on the veranda.

Lafitte calmly lit his pipe.

"Jean Lafitte! You hear me?"

Lafitte did not respond.

"Listen to me, Jean Lafitte," the seaman shouted, taking out a pistol and brandishing it in the air. A chorus of shouts backed him up. Gambi stood to the side, his arms folded on his chest, watching the performance with approval. "We do not take orders from the likes of you, eh? Captain Gambi's crew only takes orders from Captain Gambi! Here is what I think of your orders . . ."

The seaman spat up at the veranda. Lafitte seemed to move lazily, but that was deceptive. He reached inside his jacket, pulled out a pistol, leveled it almost casually and fired. The shot startled them all. With an expression of surprise upon his face, the seaman pitched forward onto the sand, shot through the heart.

Lafitte stood slowly, the smoking gun still held in his hand, and leaned on the railing of the veranda, looking down at the assembled men. He said nothing. His eyes met Gambi's. With

a scowl, Gambi turned away and walked off into the darkness.
The remainder of the mob broke up.

"Now then," said Lafitte, turning around and putting the
pistol back into the holster hanging inside his jacket. "What
do you say to a game of poker?"

9

Fires burned on the beach. Men drank and sang, caroused with women, danced, fired guns off into the air and pummeled each other drunkenly. Many of Drakov's crewmen went into New Orleans with seamen from the other ships of Lafitte's fleet. Drakov went downstairs with Lafitte and Verne, to play cards with some of the other captains. Lucas, Finn and Andre had declined. Drakov didn't seem to care. Apparently, it made no difference to him whatsoever what they did. Land rejoined them shortly after the others had gone down to play cards. With some awkwardness, he pointedly explained that all he and Marie had done was talk. To do any more, he said, would have been taking advantage.

"I learned a bit that may be of interest," he said, as he filled his wine glass. "Drakov does not come here just so his crew can enjoy themselves. He buys slaves from Lafitte."

Lucas frowned. "*Slaves?* You're sure?"

"Marie told me," Land said. "She said that Negroes are being put aboard the *Valkyrie* even as we speak."

"How many?" Finn said.

"This time, he bought a hundred," Land said. "Last time, twice as many. She saw his men taking them from the warehouse. Grigori and Martingale, from what she said. She hasn't any idea where he takes them."

"Martingale," Andre said. "What's he doing, playing both ends against the middle?"

"I don't like him," Land said. "You said you would tell me of this Underground he claims to belong to."

"It's not easy to explain, Ned, but I'll try," said Lucas. "You remember when I tried telling you before about how people in the future travel back through time so they can fight their wars in the past?"

Land nodded, grimly. "I didn't want to hear. I thought you were making fun of me. After what I've seen, *mon ami*, I would no longer doubt a thing you tell me."

"Well, that'll make things easier," said Lucas, wryly. "The Underground is made up mostly of soldiers from the armies of the future. These soldiers have become deserters. Sometimes soldiers from the future become . . . well, lost, for lack of a better way of putting it. They become separated from their units. Sometimes they're found again. Sometimes not. Some of them become trapped in the past through no fault of their own, others become deserters. Many of them make contact with the Underground. Either they find the Underground or the Underground finds them. If they wish to return to their own time, the Underground helps them. But if they wish to desert, the Underground takes them in. It's a complex, loosely knit organization. They have methods of keeping in touch with one another, but they're spread out through all of time. Some of them, by choice, remain in one specific time period. Others travel a great deal, to any time they choose. We met one of them once. His name was Hunter. He was responsible for taking Andre from the time where she was born, 12th century England, to 17th century Paris, where our paths crossed again. Andre became one of us. Hunter, unfortunately, was killed by a member of the same group Drakov once belonged to."

"The Timekeepers," Land said.

Lucas nodded. "Hunter lived in 12th century England most of the time, but he could visit any other time, any other place, anytime he wanted to. The Underground is an illegal organization. Technically, they're criminals, but no one tries very hard to catch them."

Land frowned, concentrating. "Why?"

"Because, for one thing, it's very hard to do," said Lucas. "For another, they may be deserters, but they also serve a purpose. It's just as important to them that history not be interfered with as it is to us. They represent a certain danger, since they are people living in times where they do not belong, but they are very aware of the dangers and they take great care not to interfere. If any of them are ever caught, they are tried as criminals, but there are more important things to do than spend time actively looking for them."

Land shook his head. "I'm not sure I'm understanding you."

"What don't you understand?"

"Why should they care about preserving history? If they're criminals, deserters—"

"There are many reasons why people join the Underground," said Finn. "Some of them just couldn't take being soldiers anymore. Others became soldiers because they thought they'd find adventure, but what they found wasn't exactly what they had expected, so they deserted to find what they were looking for. Still others prefer living in the past, or in *a* past, to living in their own time. Just because they're in the Underground, that doesn't mean they're evil or criminals in the sense you mean. I liked Hunter a great deal. And he helped us that one time. He saved our lives."

"There's still more to it," Lucas said. "Suppose, Ned, you got on board a ship heading out of Boston on a whaling expedition. You don't really expect Boston to change very much in the time you'll be away. You come back and it's still the same old Boston, same old streets and houses, same people, nothing's really changed. But imagine you're in Boston right now and you decide to take a trip to Boston the way it will be three hundred years in the future. If you're in the Underground, that wouldn't be very different from going on your whaling expedition and then coming back. Boston three hundred years from now would still be familiar to you because you know its history. You've probably been there before. Only what would happen if someone like Drakov succeeded in altering the course of history somehow? Then the Boston you arrive in might not be the same place you expected you would find. It may no longer even be there. Some interference with the past may have caused a chain of events to take place which would result in a completely different future, a completely different world. In order for the people in the Underground to be able to exist, they need to protect the world they exist in. Do you understand?"

Land exhaled heavily. "I think so. If I'd not seen what I've seen, I'd say all this was mad."

"It *is* mad," Finn said. "But we've got to live with it."

"If I take your meaning," said Land, "these people in the Underground are like the gypsy-folks, except that they travel not only from place to place, but from one century to another?"

"That's it, exactly," Lucas said. "That's a very good way of putting it."

Land sighed. "Lord, what a life it must be! How many of them do you figure there be?"

"Nobody knows," said Finn. "Thousands."

"And there's no way to tell who they are?"

"Could you tell who *we* were, Ned?" said Lucas. "We're just people. Who'd suspect the truth? Who'd believe it? Even after all you'd seen, you didn't *want* to believe it. It sounds crazy."

Land stood up and leaned on the railing of the veranda, staring out to the sea, glinting in the moonlight. "Part of me keeps waiting to wake up and find all this is a dream," he said. "This beats any tall tale I ever heard. If I ever told anyone about this, I'd be put in a madhouse for sure. From now on, I don't think I will be so quick to not believe things. If someone tells me he saw a sea monster breathing fire, until I know better, I will think that there just may *be* a sea monster that breathes fire!" He looked down, then quickly leaned out over the railing and glanced from side to side. "Look here! There are no guards! Quick, now's our chance!"

He vaulted the railing.

"Ned!" shouted Lucas.

"Hell," said Finn, jumping to his feet. "We'd better catch him before he gets in trouble."

They jumped down to the ground, rolled, came up running and caught Land after a hard sprint of about seventy-five yards. Finn grabbed the harpooner and spun him around.

"Where the hell do you think you're going?" he said.

Land looked at him as if he had lost his senses. "What do you mean? This is our chance to get away!"

"And go *where*?" said Andre.

Land looked blank for a moment, then he snapped his fingers. "There are some of Drakov's crew about," he said. "A lot of them will be drunk. We can take them and steal those things they use for traveling through time! We'll find one, knock him senseless, then—"

"Ned, your heart's in the right place, but you haven't thought it through," said Lucas. "Besides, you really don't understand how it all works."

"But you said—"

"It wouldn't be much trouble to knock a couple of Drakov's crew out and take their warp discs," Lucas said. "You're right as far as that goes. But we can't get back aboard the submarine without knowing where it is. Even if we could, Drakov still has a crew aboard it and they looked pretty capable to me."

"Couldn't you go back to your own time and return with more of your people?" Land said. "You could take Drakov and his entire crew—"

"Again, not a bad idea," said Lucas, "but nothing short of an armed assault would take Drakov here on Barataria. Lafitte and his people would side with Drakov and fight the invasion. We can't touch Lafitte. The British will be moving on New Orleans before too long and without Lafitte and his men, General Jackson will lose the battle and history will be changed. Drakov's already interfered with history to a dangerous, perhaps even irreversible extent. You see, we're the ones concerned with preserving history. Drakov doesn't care. He has the advantage because of that and he knows it. There's no way to attack him here and at the same time guarantee that no one on Lafitte's side will be killed."

"But if you were to bring back ships," said Land, "like Drakov's ships travel through time, so could yours! You could—"

"We could, but it wouldn't do much good," said Finn. "Those ships would still have to find the *Nautilus*. The submarine is well-armed and difficult to detect. At first sign of pursuit, it could escape to another time. Remember that the *Nautilus*, the *Valkyrie*, Drakov and all his men can travel through time independently. They can all escape to his secret base and without knowing where it is or in which time period, there's no way we could follow.''

"Is there nothing we can do?" said Land. "If we can't act and if we have no weapons, then we're helpless!''

"Maybe not, Ned," Lucas said. "But we need to know more before we can act. When we began this, we thought it was just a matter of destroying the submarine, which is difficult enough. We need to know the full extent of Drakov's power. We need to know his plans. He knows we can't afford to try anything until we know where his base is. And when he takes us there, his guard will be up. But he may be overconfident. The thing to do now is find Martingale and make him tell us what is going on."

"How do you know you can trust him?" Land said.

"I don't," said Lucas. "I'm still worried about that graft patch he gave me. If it was a listening device, we'll know soon enough. I've got a lot of questions for Mr. Barry Martingale. If this is all part of a ruse by Drakov, I want to know *before* we reach his base."

They continued down the path, through the village, toward the boats. In the distance, they could still hear the sounds of revelry on the beach by Lafitte's house, but now the chirping of the crickets by the sides of the path was louder. As they neared the boats, still louder sounds reached them. Gunshots and men shouting. The sounds not of festivity, but of fighting.

"Come on!" said Lucas, breaking into a run.

The docks were the scene of a pitched battle. Terrified blacks ran past them, others cowered in the boats, still others lay dead among white bodies on the dock. Out on the water, several boats rowing out to the *Valkyrie* were being attacked by about ten pirogues, and the sounds of the blacks screaming and the shots fired back and forth carried across the bay. On the dock, Martingale was in the thick of it. He had emptied both his pistols and was flailing away with his sword, keeping a small group of men at bay. He was holding one in front of him, as a shield, his arm clamped tightly around the man's throat. The man he held was dead, shot several times by his own compatriots in an effort to shoot Martingale, who kept swinging the body around, trying to interpose it between himself and his attackers, able to do so only because he was on a narrow section of dock that would not allow him to be surrounded. Even so, he had been shot. They could see him bleeding from a crease in his scalp and there was blood on his exposed shoulder. It would be all over for him in another moment.

One of his attackers had gone into the water and swam out to the end of the dock, climbing up on it so he could get behind Martingale. Andre pulled out her knife and let fly. The blade whizzed past Martingale's left ear, missing him by inches, and embedded itself to the hilt in the swimmer's chest. He cried out and fell back into the water. Ned and Finn drew their swords and ran forward to help Martingale. As Andre charged the men who were attempting to shoot him down, Lucas threw his own dagger, wounding one of them in the shoulder. Then Andre was on them and Lucas followed on her heels, turning the tide of the fight.

The odds had evened out now. Land knocked one man into the water, charging him as he reloaded. Finn disarmed one man, ran another through with his sword and, seeing reinforcements arrive, Martingale dropped the corpse he had been using as a shield and joined them on the offensive. He fought in a style the pirates had never encountered before, saberfencing combined with martial arts. They were no match for trained commandos and, now that they no longer outnumbered their intended victim, they took flight.

Martingale took a deep breath as he watched them running off down the beach into the darkness. "Thanks," he said. "I thought I'd bought it for sure."

"See you've used a katana at one time," said Finn, remarking on his style with the sword. "What happened?"

Out on the water, the pirogues had seized the boats and were now pulling toward the *Valkyrie*, intent on boarding her.

"Gambi's men," said Martingale, ripping a section of cloth from the shirt of one of the dead men and using it to stanch the flow of blood from his shoulder. "They came at me so fast I didn't have a chance."

"Here, sit down," said Lucas. "Let me see that wound."

"I'll live," said Martingale. "I've had lots worse. Lucky for me those clowns couldn't shoot straight. Watch this, they're in for one hell of a surprise in those pirogues."

As the canoes drew closer to the *Valkyrie*, keeping spread out to minimize the effects of cannon fire if the ship opened up on them, there seemed to be no resistance from the ship. Then a sharp, bright beam of coherent light lanced out from the bow of the *Valkyrie* and hit one of the canoes. A second later, it was followed by a blast of white hot plasma as the auto-pulser, locked in by the laser-tracking circuit, systematically began to pick off the pirogues. One boat became awash in searing light, then it was gone, leaving nothing but smoke and some residual flaming plasma burning out upon the surface of the water. The screams of Gambi's men echoed across the bay; the remaining pirogues turned and pulled for their lives, but nothing could save them.

"If Gambi's lucky, he died out there," said Martingale. "Quicker and cleaner than what Lafitte will do to him if he survived. Guess he saw an opportunity to seize a ship and a nice cargo of slaves, to boot. Too bad he picked the wrong ship."

"That bullet's going to have to come out," said Lucas, examining Martingale's shoulder. "I can't do it here."

"We'll go out to the ship," said Martingale. "There are medical supplies aboard. Besides, someone's got to go out and get that boatload of blacks. It's drifting."

One of the other boats containing slaves had been hit by the auto-pulser from the ship. The remaining boat was slowly being carried away by the current, the blacks aboard howling in fear, not knowing what to do.

They helped Martingale into a boat and rowed out after the slaves. Martingale cursed. "We lost several men. Maybe von Kampf, too. Drakov's going to be furious. Our own fault. We should have been more careful, knowing Gambi was around."

"What are the slaves for?" Finn said. "Damn it, Martingale, you'd better start leveling with us right now."

"Same thing slaves have always been for," Martingale said. "Cheap labor. Drakov needs them at the base."

"Where *is* the base?" said Lucas.

"Small island off the coast of Papua, New Guinea, in the early 19th century," said Martingale. "Visitors are discouraged by the slaves Drakov buys from Lafitte. The area is known for having cannibals and even though Drakov's slaves aren't, they play the part real well."

"If you've known where it is all along, why haven't you done anything?" said Finn. "Why hasn't the Underground reported it to us?"

"It's not that simple," Martingale said. "The timing must be right. The Doctor will explain it all."

"That's another thing," said Lucas. "Who is the doctor?"

"His name is Dr. Robert Darkness," Martingale said. "He's the inventor of the warp grenade."

Martingale sat on the edge of the table while Lucas bandaged him. Two men stood guard on the deck of the *Valkyrie* while Count Grigori von Kampf, who had been slightly wounded in the battle of the boats, led the others in a search for the slaves who had escaped during the fight. Martingale had been wounded in several places. Two bullets had been lodged in his body and he had sustained several sword cuts, but he carried on as though such injuries were a part of his daily routine. While Lucas worked, only an occasional grimace or grunt from Martingale gave evidence of his feeling any pain.

"So the mysterious inventor of the warp grenade joined the Underground," said Finn. "Christ, no wonder they've classified everything about him, including his name."

Martingale shook his head. "You've got that wrong," he said. "Darkness isn't part of the Underground. He isn't part of *anything*. Years ago, he just split the scene. Took off for some remote corner of the galaxy. He's real strange, Delaney. All he ever wanted was to get as far away from people as it was possible to get, but he wanted it both ways. He wanted to be able to deal with people when he felt like it, only on his own terms."

"Sounds like what a lot of people want," said Andre.

"True," said Martingale, "only Darkness did it. He was working on temporal translocation around the same time Mensinger was, only he was going at it from another angle. He started out working on voice and image communication by tachyon radio transmission.''

"That isn't possible," said Finn.

"Hey, don't tell me, I'm no scientist," said Martingale. "Tell the Doctor. He's been doing it for years. What he came up with was a means of communication at a speed six hundred times faster than the speed of light. That still meant a delay in transmission, though. A five-second time lag over thirty-six hundred light seconds or a one-year delay in messages at a distance of six hundred light years. He wanted it to be instant. He got involved in some very obscure mathematics, working from the Georg Cantor theory of transfinite numbers. He discovered a solution. He found a way to make his tachyon beam move more quickly by sending it through an Einstein-Rosen Bridge. Instantaneous transmission. Going from Point A to Point B without having to cover the distance in between. Only he wasn't satisfied with just having achieved instant tachyon TV communication. He wanted to travel.''

"Wait a minute," Lucas said, pausing in his ministrations. "You're telling us he did all this *before* Mensinger invented the chronoplate?''

"I don't know if it was before or about the same time," said Martingale. "It was certainly before the chronoplate was perfected.''

"And no one *knew* about this?''

"How would anyone know unless Darkness told them?'' Martingale said. "He didn't give a damn. He just took off for deep space like some Flying Dutchman and started living life according to his own rules. But he still wanted to be able to keep in touch, so he started working on a process by which the human body could be turned into tachyons which would depart at 600 C along the direction of the tachyon beam through an Einstein-Rosen Bridge. His chief concern was that conversion to tachyons would violate the law of uncertainty.''

"How do you mean?'' said Finn.

"Well, the way he explained it to me was that if you take one hundred eighty pounds of human being and one hundred eighty pounds of bacteria and put them into a genetic blender, the result would be indistinguishable. His main concern was whether the RNA and DNA would reassemble themselves in the appropriate order at the appropriate time and place."

"Same thing Mensinger was worried about in terms of chronoplate transition," Finn said.

"Exactly. Because if they didn't, what might materialize would be a blob. He was also worried about the reassembly process itself, since there wouldn't be a receiver. He solved this by incorporating a timing mechanism into the tachyon conversion, which reassembled him at the moment of arrival based on time coordinates of transition. He focused the beam by means of gravitational lenses scattered throughout the galaxy. But while the uncertainty principle didn't trip the Doctor up, it didn't turn out as he imagined, that he had invented the ultimate form of transportation. Mensinger did that. Darkness discovered instead that the taching process was ultimately restrained by a little known law of physics, called the law of baryon conservation. While he arrived "in corpus," he was unable to move. He appeared much like a holographic projection or a distant ghost seen underwater. A figure frozen in time and trapped by the laws of the universe."

"You mean he's insubstantial?" Andre said.

"Well, no, though he *can* be, if he wants to. He can project an image of himself or actually tach himself, but he can't move from one spot. He's trying to work on a way to do more than talk and wave his arms and stare at people, but he hasn't got that one licked yet."

"Why can't he simply use a warp disc or even a chronoplate?" said Andre.

"Because his body has been tachyonized," said Martingale. "Something about the way the process has altered his subatomic structure won't let him clock. He can transmit objects, but he can't clock himself. It makes him angry as hell. Mensinger perfected the device that would allow him to do exactly what he wanted all along, only he can't use it. He said once that after twenty years of scientific research, consulting thousands of libraries on hundreds of worlds, he still can't duplicate the beaming process envisioned over one thousand years ago by some television writer. He hates that writer."

"Now let me get this straight," said Finn. "He can teleport, much the same way we can, only he does it through an

Einstein-Rosen Bridge via tachyon beam and he can't move once he gets there?''

"He can move some, but he can't leave the spot he materializes on," said Martingale. "Sort of like a hologram with substance. I wouldn't get too close to him if I were you. He may be a genius, but he's unbalanced, sort of. He just might grab you."

"And this guy is supposed to *help* us?" Andre said.

"That graft you gave me," Lucas said, "it's a device for him to home in on?"

"Essentially. I've got one, too. Don't ask me how it works, though. I haven't got the faintest notion. The Doctor comes up with stuff most scientists don't even understand. Like the warp grenade. He had a brainstorm one day and designed the thing, then didn't know what the hell to do with it. So he tached over to the Temporal Army Ordnance Chiefs and laid the plans on them. Just like that."

"Well, if it's all the same with you," said Lucas, "you can keep your little tachyon homing device or whatever, but I think I'd feel better getting rid of mine. Long as we have the medical kit here, we'll do a bit of minor surgery. Finn, give me a hand with the local."

"Don't waste your time," said Martingale. "You can't remove it."

"What do you mean, I can't?"

"You remember feeling a sort of burning, tingling sensation when you put it on?" said Martingale.

"Yes?"

"That was the device bonding itself to you."

"*What*?"

"It's fused with your atoms, chum. Become a part of your chemical essence. Unless you can figure out some way to get a body transplant, you're stuck with it, permanently."

"You mean anytime this spaced-out scientist wants to find me—"

"He finds you and pops in for a visit."

"You son of a bitch! Why didn't you *tell* me?"

"Because you wouldn't have done it if I had," said Martingale. "The Doctor told me to make sure one of you guys got terminaled. That's what he calls it. When Darkness says to do something, you do it. You don't argue with a guy who's liable to materialize a warp grenade between your legs and make it go boom.''

"That's just great," said Lucas. "I should have just let Gambi's men cut you to ribbons."

"Yeah, but then you wouldn't have received any answers."

"Well, the answers stink."

"Sorry. You should've thought up better questions. Look, the Doctor might be a little weird, but he knows what he's doing. Your superiors knew what they were up against and what the odds were. That's why they asked his help."

"The Referees are in contact with him?" Finn said.

"More like the other way around," said Martingale. "Nobody can contact the Doctor. Nobody knows where he is. It's how he likes it." Martingale put his shirt back on, being careful of his bandaged shoulder. "He does things his own way. I guess he decided to mobilize the Underground. He put the word out for us to try to infiltrate Drakov's group. Of course, we didn't know who they were then. It's sort of funny; Darkness makes your people so nervous, they've classified his existence, but we've known about him for years."

"So you're the only one who's managed to get close to Drakov?" Lucas said.

"There were several of us," said Martingale, "but I'm the only one who made it."

"How often do you see Dr. Darkness?" Andre said.

"He just shows up sometimes," said Martingale. "It's pretty spooky. He can move faster than light, but he can't move when he arrives. So he can sort of arrive without materializing completely. You can't see him. That's how he knows if I'm alone. It's an eerie feeling."

"If he can do all that, you'd think he'd be more involved in what's going on. Why hasn't he been?" said Andre.

"Why don't you ask him? Better yet, let Priest or Delaney ask him," Martingale said.

"Why?"

"The Doctor doesn't much like people," Martingale said, "but he doesn't like women, in particular. Now, unless there are any more important questions, I think we'd best be getting back. Drakov's going to want to know about what happened, if he hasn't heard already. I feel sorry for any of Gambi's crew left alive. If they have any sense, they've left Barataria. I sure as hell would, rather than face Lafitte.''

The men stood lined up on the beach in the early morning sunshine. The survivors of Captain Gambi's crew, and Gambi, himself, had been quickly rounded up. Lafitte's men had moved fast. Gambi's ship had been boarded soon after the fight and those aboard were taken. There had been no time for them to reorganize, no time to make good their escape. They stood uneasily on the sand, covered by the guns of Lafitte's men. Lafitte, still dressed in his black trousers, only without his vest and jacket, paced back and forth on the sand, his hair and white shirt ruffling in the breeze.

"Vincent, Vincent, Vincent," he said, approaching Gambi and shaking his head. He looked the swarthy Italian in the face and Gambi looked away. "You have been very troublesome to me. Very troublesome, indeed."

Gambi said nothing. Drakov stood to one side with the others, watching.

"I cannot afford to be lenient with you, Vincent," said Lafitte. "Do you know why? Because you are a stupid man and you would not understand. You would mistake lenience for weakness and that would only lead you to act foolishly again. I cannot have that. I cannot allow you to attack my guests with impunity. I cannot allow you to set yourself above my authority. You see that, don't you?"

"I have never acknowledged your authority," said Gambi, defiantly. "You have no right—"

"My strength gives me the right," Lafitte said, curtly. "You never should have come here, Vincent. You should have gone your own way instead of trying to challenge me. Now you have lost. It is not enough for me to confiscate your ship. I must confiscate your life, as well."

"So kill me, then," said Gambi, contemptuously. "You can be brave now, with all these guns at your back."

"Dominique," Lafitte said. "Give him your sword."

Youx stepped up to Gambi and gave his sword to him.

"I will give you a chance to acquit yourself with honor,"

said Lafitte. "Dominique, I charge you to carry out my orders. If Vincent should succeed in killing me, he and his crew go free. No one is to interfere. Understood?"

"Understood, Jean," said Dominique.

"He will keep my word," Lafitte said to Gambi. "Now, you wanted to challenge me, here is your chance. Make the most of it."

Gambi growled and charged.

Lafitte smoothly drew his sword and, in the same motion, beat down Gambi's blade and sidestepped the attack. He turned, moving lightly on his feet, one hand on his hip, the other holding the sword out before him, wrist circling slightly as he came back on guard. He looked bored.

"Come, Vincent, you will never win your freedom that way," he said. "A little more finesse, eh?"

Gambi swore and returned to the attack, moving more cautiously now that his first rush had failed. He attempted a cut at Lafitte's head, but Lafitte parried neatly, beat and riposted, slashing at Gambi's shoulder. A bright streak of red appeared through Gambi's shirt. They disengaged, circling each other on the sand as Gambi's men called out their encouragement to him. Gambi bent down quickly and scooped up a handful of sand, flinging it at Lafitte's face, but Lafitte read the move and ducked quickly to one side as Gambi moved in for a thrust.

Gambi recovered fast, but not before Lafitte opened up his cheek with a lightning slash across his face. Gambi howled and charged again, but Lafitte sidestepped him, playing him like a toreador plays a bull, working close to the body and using the barest minimum of motion. It was no contest. Gambi realized this and became desperate, flailing away madly with his saber and trying to put Lafitte on the defensive. Lafitte retreated smoothly, parrying each stroke and lunge, leading Gambi on, laughing and taunting him.

"Come, Vincent, come on, again, faster! Faster!"

Blade clanged against blade as Gambi desperately pressed his attack, sweat running down his face. His crew, thinking he was gaining the advantage, cheered him on, but then Lafitte stood his ground, his sword describing spare arabesques in the air as it darted in at Gambi, cutting, slashing, pricking, stinging like a persistent bee as Gambi started to retreat. Each disengage met with a counter disengage, each parry with a riposte, each lunge turned aside as Lafitte pressed on, driving Gambi back until finally he lost his footing and fell. Snarling, he reached behind his neck and pulled a dagger from the sheath hanging down his back. He hurled it at Lafitte, but in mid-air Lafitte's sword deflected it in an astonishing display of quick reactions. He stood, waiting for Gambi to get back to his feet.

"Enough of this," he said. "I'm done with indulging you. It's time for the coup de grace."

Gambi glanced around wildly, but there was no escape. With a scream, he lunged at Lafitte. Lafitte spun his blade, wrenching it out of his grasp and in the same motion, ran him through the chest. Gambi gasped, clutched at his chest and fell face down onto the sand. Lafitte looked down at him and sighed.

"Stupid man," he said. He glanced at Gambi's suddenly silent crew and then at Dominique.

"Kill them," he said, and walked into the house without looking back.

10

Lafitte seemed to have completely forgotten the morning's episode with Vincent Gambi by midday, when he announced he would be going into New Orleans to see his brother. He insisted Drakov come along, so they could dine together in the French Quarter. Together with Jules Verne and Dominique Youx, they left in the early afternoon. Land chose to remain behind, which surprised them, but his reasons became clear later on, when he was seen walking hand in hand with Marie toward the back end of the island. Grigori, anxious to be away from "the peasants," as he called Lafitte's men, went aboard the *Valkyrie* to make things ready for their departure, leaving Lucas, Finn and Andre alone with Martingale and Lafitte's servants in the house.

Before he left, Drakov took them aside and thanked them for saving Martingale's life. "His death would have been a great loss to me," Drakov said. "He's the best of my mercenaries. I have invested a great deal of time in training him. His adaptability to unusual situations is impressive. However, I must admit to being curious about why you interfered."

"It had less to do with Martingale and the odds against him than it did with the *Valkyrie*," said Lucas. "We've got enough to worry about with stopping you without having a time ship fall into the hands of a pirate like Gambi."

"As practical as ever, Mr. Priest," said Drakov, smiling.

"You still believe you can prevail. I admire that."

"I could do without your admiration," Lucas said.

"Pity," Drakov said. "I rather like you. You are a man of principles, a rarity in any time. Of all the men I've ever met, I respect you the most. Which is why I want to make certain we understand one another. You three are unquestionably the First Division's finest, which is why it would be fitting for my father to receive the news of his defeat from you. Tomorrow morning, we shall be leaving Barataria for my base. I fully expect you to attempt something. I would be disappointed in you if you did not. However, I will remind you that I am at war and that you three are prisoners of war. The battle for you is over. I will take special precautions to insure that you do not have any opportunity to cause trouble. When we arrive at my base, you will find yourself even more helpless than you have been up to now. If you find that idea intolerable, Mr. Priest, then I urge you to escape now, while you can. It will not be easy, but no one will pursue you and you may be able to make contact with someone in the Underground eventually. If not, there are worse times in which to be marooned. But I hope you will remain. If you do, you will become a part of history. I leave the choice to you."

After the others had left, they found Martingale on the veranda, being attended by two young women Lafitte assigned to him while he recovered from his injuries. He sat in a cane chair while the girls fanned him, poured him rum and fed him bits of sweetmeats with their fingers.

"You look like a dissolute Roman emperor," said Lucas.

Martingale grinned and sent the girls inside to bring more glasses and more rum.

"You seem to be bearing up remarkably well," said Andre. "Try not to strain yourself."

"The trouble with Lafitte is that he likes 'em too damn young," said Martingale. "What the hell have I got to say to a couple of sixteen- or seventeen-year-olds, fresh from the Gold Coast? They're babies. They don't know anything. Now you, on the other hand, you and I could probably find a thing or two to talk about."

"Right now I'll settle for talking about what we're going to do about this mess," said Andre.

"Have a seat," said Martingale. The slaves brought out the rum and glasses, then he sent them away while they talked.

"Lafitte certainly has a hard life," said Finn. "He's come a long way since he was a filthy little street urchin in Paris."

"He'll be on the way back down again before too long," said Martingale. "He's too visible, too famous. The secret of success is to keep your head down."

"You consider yourself successful, do you?" Andre said.

"I'm doing exactly what I want to do," said Martingale. "That's all being successful is. It's not about money or anything else. I say I'm in it for the money because that's something Drakov understands. He's got lots of it. People who have lots of money understand real well what it's about when someone comes to them wanting some of it. They can deal with it because they know the rules of that game. Drakov could never understand you like I do. He doesn't even understand the rules you operate under."

"What makes you think you do?" said Finn. "You opted out of the game, as you put it."

Martingale shook his head. "No, I didn't. I just changed the rules around a little, so they would suit me more. The game is still the same, in many respects. Not to get overly philosophical, but life's just a joke. You're born, you struggle, you learn, you grow, you accomplish, then you die. No matter what you manage to pull off, death is still the final reward. So it's a joke. No matter who you are or what you do, everyone gets paid off the same."

"That sounds pretty cynical to me," said Lucas.

"It happens to be true," said Martingale, "but it's a trap only if you accept it at face value. It's not the payoff that matters. That's where people go wrong. It's the work. I deserted the Temporal Corps and became a mercenary not because I wasn't happy with what I was doing, but because I wanted more control over it. The only real difference between us is that you have to serve the missions Forrester picks out for you. I get to pick my own. I can say no, and I do, frequently. I only fight the good fight."

"I see," said Finn. "Martingale only fights on the side of the angels, is that it?"

"You think that sounds corny?" Martingale said. He shook

his head. "It only sounds that way because people think idealism is corny. I'll tell you something, if six billion morons got together and decided that blue was purple, that's what the world would accept. But it wouldn't change the color, chum. Only the name. I'll tell you what's corny. We're sitting here in a sunlit veranda on an island in the Gulf of Mexico, waited on by slave girls, for God's sake, while out there somewhere is a nukie sub with enough death on board to wipe out half the globe. The guy who's got his finger on the button is in New Orleans, having dinner with a pirate chieftain and a science fiction writer while we're sitting here sipping rum punch. Now you tell me life's not a joke."

"Yes, but what's the punchline?" Finn said.

Martingale took a long drink. "You've got me there. Drakov won't tell anybody anything. He's all twisted up inside, but he's sure as hell organized. He has a knack for picking people and a knack for leading them, as well. He's recruited men from all different periods of history, all soldiers, all top professionals in their own way. He keeps them well in line and he's always got our buddy, Santos, to fall back on. One session with Benedetto and you're a good little soldier again, programmed for following orders unquestioningly."

"You don't have any idea at all what he's going to do?" said Andre.

"I assume it's going to be nuclear blackmail," said Martingale. "The same sort of thing the Timekeepers tried to do, only on a larger scale. But he's been set up to do that ever since we stole the sub. He's got something more complicated planned—"

"Wait a minute," said Lucas. "I knew there was something bothering me about all this. If the Referee Corps asked Dr. Darkness to help them with this, and you're working for him, how could you have been involved *before* the sub was stolen?"

"It had nothing to do with the sub, initially," said Martingale. "Darkness knew about the theft of the warp discs before your people did."

Finn frowned. "How?"

"Who do you think owns Amalgamated Techtronics?"

"*Darkness*?"

"You think a scientist can be bothered with manufactur-

ing?'' said Martingale. ''He needs someone to turn out the giz-
mos he invents. You'd be surprised at what he controls.''

''But Amalgamated Techtronics! That's one of the biggest
corporations in the whole—''

''So? What do you think, he gave the Temporal Corps the
warp grenade for nothing? When they found out about the
stolen shipment, they didn't dare report it until they'd had a
chance to tell the Doctor. They couldn't exactly call him. No
one knows where he is. He just sort of . . . appears from time
to time. Fortunately, he was due in to check on a shipment of
weapons prototypes they were building for him. It's a lucky
thing Drakov didn't steal those.''

''What sort of prototypes?'' said Lucas.

''Disruptors,'' Martingale said. ''The Temporal Corps
doesn't even know about them yet. You'd better hope they
work, because they're probably what we'll be using against
Drakov's base when the time comes.''

''What's a disruptor?'' Finn said. ''Or shouldn't I ask?''

''I haven't seen one yet,'' said Martingale, ''but they sound
impressive. It's a sort of warp gun. Its transponder taps into
the energy field of a neutron star by means of an Einstein-
Rosen Generator link. A limitless supply of ammunition in the
form of energy, leeched from a star through a time warp.
Sounds like a lovely little sidearm, doesn't it? You squeeze the
trigger and you get a stream of neutrons.''

''You're kidding,'' Finn said.

''Just the thing for plinking, eh?'' said Martingale, with a
grin. ''Bad analogy. There wouldn't be a 'plink.' The target
would be atomically disrupted. Disintegrated.''

''Jesus,'' Finn said. ''How the hell do you control a stream
of neutrons?''

''Very carefully, I should think,'' said Martingale. ''I sure
hope it works, otherwise we're liable to have a very interesting
experience.'' He chuckled. ''Sort of makes you want to think
about gun control, doesn't it? 'If warp guns are outlawed,
only outlaws will have warp guns.' Make a great T-shirt.''

''What about radiation?'' Lucas said.

''Most of it is supposed to be warped elsewhere, like with
the grenades,'' said Martingale. ''At least that's what the Doctor said. They haven't been tested fully yet.''

"And we're going to field-test them against Drakov's base?" said Andre.

"I'd say that's the least of our problems," Martingale said. "Drakov has set up an impressive organization. He used time fugues to do it. Before your people even learned he'd hijacked a Soviet sub, he'd done something like ten years worth of organizational work. He learned a lot from the Timekeepers. He has everyone divided into subgroups. There are the Russian sailors on the sub. Then there are the crew of the *Valkyrie*."

"Aren't they part of the base personnel?" said Lucas.

"Is that what Drakov told you? Don't you believe it. The *Valkyrie* hardly spends any time at the base. The crew has their own agenda, but I have no idea what it is. There's also the fact that the base is rarely at full strength. A lot of them are always clocked out somewhere, doing God knows what in some other time period. I don't know where. On top of that, there are the slaves Drakov got from Lafitte. They're used as labor and a sort of 'hostile native' security force. Very showy. He has them dress up in loincloths and feathers and war paint, playing cannibals. They do a good job of keeping the curious away. Drakov is a real stickler for security. He hasn't forgotten that the TIA managed to infiltrate the Timekeepers. No one is allowed to talk to anyone else about what they're supposed to be doing. I have no idea how much von Kampf knows. I've tried to pump him, but he won't talk. Santos doesn't know all the details or at least he pretends not to. He genuinely doesn't seem to care. He's a burnout. Maybe Shiro knows the whole story, because Drakov has practically adopted him, only Shiro can't talk and he's about as easy to approach as a king cobra."

"You said Drakov recruited people from different times," said Lucas. "How many? What kind of people?"

Martingale shrugged. "I don't know how many, exactly. At least several hundred. He's got Celts, Huns, Romans, Spartans, Indians, Afghanis, Samurai, a regular melting pot of human savagery, all working together as a unit."

"That's bad," said Finn.

"Not if the warp guns work out okay," said Martingale.

"That's not what I meant," said Finn. "Drakov is smart. He's set it up so that we not only have to neutralize him and his submarine, but we have to take out the *Valkyrie*, as well, plus the base and all his personnel. And if what you say is accurate, then none of them are ever all there at the same time. If that doesn't cheer you up, he's got a force of temporally displaced persons. You want to talk about what the odds are of their removal from their natural times not affecting history? The cumulative effect, at least, would be bound to show up somewhere in the timestream.''

''That's probably why he did it that way,'' Lucas said. ''Even if we can stop him from changing history, we're liable to change history ourselves by changing the history of the people whose history he's already changed.''

''You want to run that by me again?'' said Martingale.

''Better not,'' said Finn. ''It sounded confusing enough the first time. Martingale's right. The whole thing *is* a joke. No wonder Drakov isn't worried about us. We might as well just kick back and get drunk.''

''How did you manage to get on the inside?'' Lucas said.

''The Underground has something similar to a Code Red,'' said Martingale. ''We've all been on the watch for the surviving Timekeepers ever since we heard their leaders got away. Some of us almost got Falcon one time, but she slipped away. Well, now that she's dead, that leaves only two of the original group. Drakov and Benedetto. Santos is harmless by himself, but Drakov is another story. We always figured it would be Falcon who would start it up again. We got hold of their dossiers and circulated them through our network of contacts. We're not as well organized as the TIA, but we got the word out. We didn't want the Timekeepers starting up again any more than you did. They were scary enough the first time.''

''So you had the entire Underground on the watch for them?'' Andre said.

Martingale nodded. ''When Drakov started recruiting his mercenaries, one person got in and put the word out. We had no idea where he'd be recruiting or in what time periods, so everybody kept their ears open. I got a lead from a soldier who managed to get in and I clocked over to sign up, as well. We thought we'd try to get as many of our people on the inside as possible, find out what the story was, then contact the Temporal Corps. But we had some bad luck. First off, we were only able to get five people in. Drakov moved very fast. Of the network people, that is, the ones who have the homing grafts the Doctor can trace, I was the only one who got recruited. Stroke of luck there. But we failed to take an important thing into consideration. One of the people who got in was recruited in ancient Rome. Another in the 14th century, another in the 16th and so on. Drakov put most of the primitives through re-education, so they would be able to accept 27th-century science. We should have thought about that. Can you imagine trying to explain time travel to a Thuggee?''

"So you lost your people when they went through the conditioning process," Lucas said.

Martingale nodded. "They're now part of Drakov's loyal crew. I was the only one who didn't get brainwashed. I was put through Benedetto's little head game, too, but it didn't take for some reason. I had a real bad moment there.''

"It doesn't always work on everyone," said Finn. "Geniuses are supposed to be difficult to condition. So are hardcore sociopaths. But when it doesn't take, it usually results in a complete mindwipe.''

"I heard that," Martingale said. "The Doctor said the reason I survived it had something to do with my brain waves being altered somehow by the homing graft. He said he anticipated that when he designed it.''

"I can't wait to meet this guy," said Finn.

"You will. He's already overdue. He could pop in at any moment.''

"Why haven't you been able to get the word out about the location of the base?" said Lucas.

"Because for a long time, I didn't even know where it was," said Martingale. "You'll understand what I mean when you see it. Besides, I had no way of getting in touch with anybody. See, all of Drakov's people were issued warp discs, but nobody knows how to use them. I'm okay with a chronoplate, but there was no way I could take one with me. Too damn bulky. If I brought along a remote unit, it would have been turned up in a search. Drakov wants to be able to control his people's transitions.''

"You mean the destination coordinates are pre-set for them?" said Lucas.

"That's right. Take the submarine crew, for example. Should anything happen to the sub, their discs are pre-set to clock them back to the base. That way, at least, Drakov won't lose any personnel. That's if they react quickly enough. Ditto the crew of the *Valkyrie*. Anytime he sends people anywhere, they have to report to get their discs set for destination and return. They know how to activate them, but that's it. He provides the coordinates. He programs the discs. I never even saw a manual on these things. I never even heard of warp discs until Drakov gave me one. They're too damn new."

"Couldn't Darkness have shown you how to program them?" said Andre.

"Sure, if there was enough time," said Martingale. "Remember, he didn't invent them. He'd need time to scope one out first. It wouldn't have taken him long, since they work on principles he developed, but he couldn't be bothered with that. It was up to me, as the guy on the inside, to find out where the base was and tell him when he checked in with me. Then he could notify your people. Meanwhile, he's been trying to track down Drakov's other movements, in other time periods. And working on the warp guns."

"So you can't go anywhere Drakov doesn't want you to go," said Lucas.

"Not only that, but it took me a long time to work my way up in his organization," Martingale said. "And he still doesn't trust me all the way. I thought I'd died and gone to heaven when you three came aboard the sub, but I couldn't talk to you because I knew Drakov had your dosimeters bugged. He was worried you might try to sabotage the sub."

"Well, at least we can fix one problem right away," said Lucas. "We can show you how to program the warp disc. There should be enough time."

"You know, back when I was still in the Temporal Corps, I was just a grunt," said Martingale. "I don't know anything about temporal adjustments. You people are supposed to be the experts. What do you think of our chances?"

Lucas took a deep breath. "You sure you want to know?"

"That bad, huh?"

"Well, if we can get word to Plus Time about the location of the base and if the First Division can be mobilized quickly enough, then they're going to have to attack at exactly the right time. They'll have to hit hard and fast. How well defended is the base?''

"It's not a fortress, if that's what you mean," said Martingale. "The personnel are armed, but Drakov isn't set up to repel a large attack force. First off, he won't be expecting it and second, why fight when you can clock out?''

"So you're saying small arms, basically?''

"The sub would be the biggest threat," said Martingale. "The missiles will be my worry. There's a gray steel box in the control room which opens the firing circuits and arms the warheads. It's opened by two little silver keys. Drakov has one, on a chain around his neck. Shiro has the other one.''

"If we can prevent his firing the missiles and neutralize the sub, we may have a chance of getting out of this without serious damage to the timestream," Lucas said. "What about the base personnel? You said Drakov never taught them to program the warp discs. If they're already at the base, are their warp discs set for any other destination?''

Martingale smiled. "No. Drakov was very careful about that. Anytime someone's disc is programmed to clock out, it's preset for a round trip. Once they've returned to the base, the discs would have to be reprogrammed before they could clock anywhere else. Hot damn! His own paranoia about control is going to beat him. If the First Division hits the base hard and fast, there won't be any time to reprogram all the discs. They won't be able to escape. They'll be forced to stay and try to fight it out. If they see the odds are against them, most of them will probably surrender. Then, with the base secured, your people can just wait around and pick up the others as they clock back in. That hadn't occurred to me. But they'd have to come in real fast for it to work. And they'd be liable to sustain heavy casualties.''

"What's the layout of the base?" said Lucas.

"Remember I said once you'd seen it, you'd know how I didn't know where I was even when I was there? It's inside an extinct volcano. Unless you clock in, there are only two access points. Through the opening of the volcano or by way of an underground canal. I'd never been outside and I had no reference point for telling where I was.''

"How'd you finally figure it out?" said Finn.

Martingale grinned. "Quite literally, by the oldest method in the book. Drakov has books on sailing and navigation in the library. I learned how to take a sighting with a sextant."

"A sextant," Finn said, shaking his head with admiration. "I never would have thought of that. Not bad. That's what I call initiative."

"You say the slaves he bought from Lafitte are kept on the outside, like a local tribe of cannibals?" said Lucas.

"That's right."

"We don't want to have any of them killed," said Lucas. "What would be the chances of getting the attacking force clocked directly inside?"

"Very risky," Martingale said. "I can't supply any coordinates. There are several locations inside the base which are used for clocking people in. That's how I went there and back. But they're inside buildings. You can get the program for the one I've got preset in my own disc, but you can't use it to clock in a large body of men. A squad, maybe two, at most."

"At least that will get a squad or two on the inside," said Lucas. "The main force will have to come in through the opening."

"Airborne with floater-paks?" said Finn.

Lucas nodded. "That's what I was thinking. Unfortunately, that will give the people inside a point on which to concentrate their fire."

"It's a fairly large opening," said Martingale.

"Still, it'll leave the attacking force exposed unless they have an opportunity to attack at night. Timing is going to be critical. We have to catch the sub inside the base and keep it from clocking out."

"And the *Valkyrie*, as well," said Finn, "though she's nowhere near as important as the sub."

"I wish to hell I knew what Drakov's plan was," Lucas said, chewing on his knuckle. "I'm really bothered by those people he has clocking out to other time periods. What could they be doing?"

"If we can pass the location of the base on to the Doctor," Martingale said, "he could tach to Plus Time and let your people know. They could attack the base and try to get the information out of the people there. Then, by the time we arrive with the sub—''

"It might work, but it's too risky," said Lucas. "The submarine has to be the first priority. We only have two options there. Either we find a way to destroy it while we're on board, or we wait until we get to the base and catch the sub inside the base. Specifically, we've got to catch Drakov *outside* the sub. That's when the attack has to occur. So long as he's not aboard, he can't clock the sub out and he can't fire any missiles."

"Good point," said Martingale.

"What worries me the most," said Lucas, "is that once we get back aboard the sub, Drakov is going to have us watched constantly. He plans to send us back to Forrester with his ultimatum and that will leave only you at the base. We need for the attack to happen while we're still there."

"Don't forget Ned Land and Jules Verne," said Andre.

Lucas rubbed his temples. "Damn. I'm getting a killer headache. No matter how well we try to plan it, it will still result in temporal disruption. The only question is, how severe?"

"At least our chances now are better than they were before," said Finn. "Martingale here has done a good deal of the job."

"No, I've just done a small part," Martingale said. "The big part's coming up and that's going to be, you'll pardon the expression," he said, looking at Lucas, "your headache."

"Can you draw a layout of the base for us?" said Lucas.

"Come on inside. I'll get some paper and a quill."

"All right," said Martingale, using the quill to point out various points on the rough map he had drawn. "This part here at the bottom is a lake. It's deep and the underwater canal feeds into it at about this point, I think, I can't say exactly. Around here you have a sort of beach, maybe five hundred yards of it. The buildings on this side, on the lower slope, are quarters for the personnel. You'll note they're constructed on several levels. Walkways have been cut or built into the sides of the volcano here, here, here and here. You've got two Bailey bridges running across the lake to the other side, here and here, and cable span bridges going across, close to the side here. The buildings on this other side are larger, used for gatherings, storage, mess hall and kitchen, recreation and so forth. Drakov's quarters are this separate building over here, higher up and to the side of the cable span. It's built on a ledge, giving him a view over the entire base."

"It's pretty spread out," said Finn. "You know, I'm thinking the smartest thing for our guys to do would be to lob a warp grenade or two in once they've made sure the sub was there. From the outside, it would look like one hell of a volcanic explosion, I suppose. From the inside, well, I don't think we'd get much of a chance to see anything."

"I really hate to agree with you," said Martingale, "but that would be the best thing." He shrugged. "Who knows, there might be a chance for us to get out before the whole damn mountain gets nuked. What the hell, if I was Forrester, that's probably just what I'd do. Order a warp grenade strike."

"No," said Lucas. "That's the last thing he'd do. Even if the attacking force sustains heavy casualties, it's better than a warp grenade strike. We've got to try and take as many of Drakov's people alive as possible, so they can be conditioned to forget what happened and returned to their own times. Each one of them constitutes a potential disruption in the timestream."

"I don't see how you can avoid killing a lot of them," said Martingale. "Stunners don't have the same range as lasers do and they'll be shooting at your people. You're going to have to take a good number of them out, any way you look at it."

"I know," said Lucas. "We can only hope the show of force will intimidate most of them into surrendering. All we can do is hope that temporal inertia compensates."

"If their having been taken from their own time periods hasn't caused any disruptions, then killing them all might—"

"We don't *know* that," Lucas said. "A surgical strike would be nice and clean, even if it did take all of us with it, but it would be taking too much of a chance. Forrester will know he doesn't have that option. For all we know, their having been taken from their own time periods *has* caused disruptions. Maybe not, if we're very lucky. There have already been disruptions, thanks to Drakov's actions. Temporal inertia will only compensate for so much. It might be irreversible already. All we can do is hope.''

"You'll lose a lot of people," Martingale said.

"It can't be helped," said Finn.

"You'll have to clock out to signal the attack at the proper time," said Lucas.

Martingale frowned. "Why me?"

"Because Drakov will be expecting us to try something like that," said Lucas. "You'll have the best chance of getting out without being missed."

"I wouldn't count on that," said Martingale.

"We'll try to work that out," said Lucas. "I can show you how to program a fugue sequence on your disc. That way you'll be able to clock out and clock back in almost at the same time."

"But if Drakov is going to send you back to Forrester with his demands anyway, why not let him? He won't know you have the location of the base and you'll be able to clock back in—"

"No, I told you, the attack has to occur while we're still there," said Lucas. "For one thing, I don't trust him. For another, even if we could do that, it would leave only you behind at the base. We have to make absolutely certain Drakov doesn't have a chance to fire the missiles or escape on the sub. And someone has to protect Verne and Land, as well."

"Okay, I see your point."

"We're going to have to—"

"Lucas—" Andre said, squeezing his arm suddenly.

He glanced at her, then quickly looked in the direction she was staring. Martingale turned and looked as well, then relaxed and expelled his breath audibly. "It's about damn time," he said.

A man was standing by the fireplace. He was tall and slender, with dark, unruly hair and a neatly trimmed moustache. He was gaunt-looking, with deeply set, piercing eyes and a sharp, prominent nose. He was dressed, incongruously, in tweeds—a Norfolk jacket and stovepipe trousers with a matching vest, a button-down white shirt and a necktie with a regimental stripe. He wore a watch chain and a tweed driving cap pulled low over his eyes. In his right hand, he held a heavy, knobbed walking stick carved out of dark wood. For a moment, he appeared to be transparent, then he abruptly solidified, though not completely. Various portions of his body seemed to become substantial, then ghostly once again. When he spoke, his voice was rich and vaguely Continental.

"I am Robert Darkness," he said. "I perceive we are alone. Do we have time to talk or are we likely to be interrupted at any moment?"

"We should have some time," said Martingale. "If any of the servants should come in—"

"Yes, yes, I know," said Darkness, impatiently. "We mustn't frighten the help. Let's get on with it. Have you managed to learn anything of significance?"

"I've figured out the location of the base," said Martingale. "It's—"

"I already know where the base is," Darkness said.

Martingale looked both surprised and disappointed. "How did you find out?"

"Really, Martingale, if I had to count on you for everything, this affair would have dragged on endlessly. When you told me it was inside an extinct volcano, that narrowed it down considerably. The underground canal meant it had to be an island, the blacks being used as ersatz cannibals to scare off possible landing parties also gave me a clue and it meant it couldn't have been a very modern period or a pre-exploratory one. It was a simple matter of elimination. It merely took some time."

"Have you notified the Temporal Corps?" said Finn.

"No, I've kept it to myself," said Darkness. "Of course I've notified them. I'll be happy to get this out of the way finally. I have a great deal of work to do and these constant distractions are annoying."

"You call Drakov and his group a *distraction*?" Finn said.

"Everything that happens on this silly planet is a distraction," Darkness said. "That's why I moved. I find people to be generally bothersome. The more I deal with people, the better I like dogs. Unfortunately, it becomes necessary to deal with people from time to time."

"I wonder how you stand it," Finn said.

"I do my best to allow for their stupidity," said Darkness. "Playing deus ex machina for you is mildly amusing, but it does tend to rob one of time."

"Well, I'm glad you could spare a minute from your busy schedule," said Finn.

"Delaney, I wouldn't push it," Martingale said softly.

"Doesn't the potential of a timestream split disturb you?" Andre said.

Darkness gave her an annoyed look. "Very little disturbs me," he said. "I think a timestream split would be quite interesting. It would make a good opportunity for study. However, I'm in no great hurry to conduct that sort of research at the moment. I'm still working on perfecting my teleportation process. Oh, and speaking of perfecting things, I think I've finally ironed out the bugs in the disruptors."

"You *think*?" said Finn.

Darkness fixed him with a baleful glare. "You are starting to irritate me, young man. If you were better at doing your job, I wouldn't have to waste my valuable time with this nonsense. Come here."

"Don't get too close," Martingale whispered.

"Are you serious?" said Finn. "This guy looks about as dangerous as my Aunt Martha."

He approached Darkness, who stood motionless by the fireplace. The moment he was within reach, Darkness swung his walking stick and it connected with the side of Finn's head with a sharp crack.

"That's for your impertinence," he said.

"You son of a—" Finn swung a hard right at his jaw and almost lost his balance when his fist passed right through him. "What the . . . ?"

"I warned you," Martingale said.

"Here, take this," said Darkness, disregarding the attempted punch. He handed Finn a weapon. Gingerly, Delaney reached out and took it. It was solid. He looked totally confused.

The weapon looked like a small flamethrower without a fuel pack attached. It had a knurled metal pistol grip and a peculiar-looking barrel.

"Its method of operation should be simple enough even for a mind like yours to grasp," said Darkness. "The rest of you come here and watch; I'm not going to repeat this."

They gathered around and Darkness pointed out the features of the disruptor.

"It's activated by this control," he said, pointing. "Activating the disruptor allows a small portion of a very powerful magnetic field tapped through an ERG to enter the weapon. The magnetic field forms a sort of invisible cone around the muzzle of the disruptor, shaping the energy flow. It allows you to fire either a stream of neutrons on a tight beam or a spray of neutrons on a wide sweep. It's really quite uncomplicated. You turn the field adjuster, here, to select the firing mode. Turn it to the left and you get a tight beam about one inch in diameter. Turn it to the right and you have a spray. There isn't any recoil, naturally. It's just like holding a water hose, only there isn't any sensation of pressure. Try it out."

"On what?" said Finn, still dazed.

"God in heaven, man, you needed a weapon, I designed you a weapon. Now you want me to tell you what to shoot with it? What in hell do *I* care? Try it on yourself, that ought to be amusing."

Finn walked over to an open window and sighted at a palm tree. He turned the magnetic field adjuster to spray and carefully squeezed the trigger. There was a brief flash of barely discernible blue mist, Cerenkov Radiation, and the palm tree disappeared as if it had never been there in the first place.

"Shit," said Finn.

"Such eloquence," said Darkness. "Now give it back, please."

Finn carefully handed the warp gun back to him.

"You think you can remember how it works?" said Darkness, dryly.

"I'll manage," Finn said.

"Good. They will be delivered to you at the proper time."

"When?"

Darkness sighed. "When the signal for attack is given. All the soldiers of the First Division have been recalled and they are on standby alert, awaiting your signal. Try not to screw it up. Now, are there any more foolish questions? No? Fine. Good-bye.''

Suddenly, he simply wasn't there anymore.

"How does he do that?" Andre said. "He was solid one second and then when Finn tried to hit him . . ."

"Tachyons," said Lucas. "Amazing. He's faster than the speed of light. Or can be when he wants to."

"Is he always like that?" Andre said.

"No," said Martingale. "Sometimes he can be pretty abrasive."

"If he ever perfects that process," Finn said, "the warp disc will be as obsolete as an electric train."

"That's if he ever gives it to anyone," said Martingale.

"Why wouldn't he?" said Lucas.

Martingale shrugged. "Why should he? He's got an ego bigger than the whole damn planet and he really doesn't care all that much about what happens here. He lives somewhere on the other side of the galaxy and only drops in when he feels like it or when he needs something. He's a very hard man to figure out. If I were you, I wouldn't even bother trying."

11 _____

It was all they could do to get to sleep that night, knowing that in the morning they would be leaving Barataria for Drakov's island base. There were still unanswered questions and the frustration they had been feeling at being unable to do anything, combined with the anticipation of it all coming to a head at last, made it impossible to relax.

Verne didn't make things any easier when he returned from his night out on the town. They had been given rooms upstairs in Lafitte's house. Verne and Land shared one, Finn and Lucas shared another and Andre had been given a room of her own. Land had still not put in an appearance, so Verne, lacking for company, ensconced himself in Finn and Lucas's room and talked endlessly about his trip to New Orleans with Drakov and Lafitte. Paris nightlife, he had thought, would have prepared him for anything, but he was not ready for New Orleans. He had resolved early on to drink very sparingly, so he could remain sober and observe with his writer's eye, but that went the way of so many resolutions and he came back roaring drunk. Unfortunately, while he was quite a pleasant drunk, he was one of those who cannot shut up and even feigning sleep was not enough to put him off. Finn, miraculously, finally managed to fall asleep, but Lucas remained wide awake, his eyes closed, breathing heavily, hoping Verne would notice that his audience had departed for the realm of

Morpheus and take the trip himself.

Frustrated, Lucas finally was reduced to timing Verne's sentences, which kept getting longer and longer, though they remained perfectly grammatical. To his astonishment, Verne, his accent growing thicker, launched into an extensive monological sentence which went on for forty-five minutes without a break, ending *finally*, incongruously, in a question. Verne actually paused at that point, awaiting an answer. None was forthcoming. *Please*, thought Lucas, for God's sake don't start up again! The silence became lengthy and finally broken by a window-rattling snore from Finn, and Verne belatedly became aware of the soporific effect of his conversation.

"Oh, well, never mind," he said, and fell asleep the very next instant, slumping forward in his chair, chin on his chest.

"That's one for the books," Lucas mumbled to himself. He was just starting to drift off when there came a faint knock at the door and it creaked open slightly.

"Lucas? Finn?"

It was Land.

"Oh, no," said Lucas.

"Are you awake?" said Land.

"Ned, whatever it is, can't it wait till morning?"

"No, no, I must tell you *now*," said Land. "I will not be here in the morning."

Lucas came fully awake. "What are you talking about?"

The others slept on, both snoring loudly.

"I am leaving," Land said. "Tonight. Within the hour."

"What do you mean, you're leaving? Where?"

"I'm going with Marie," said Land. "We are running away together."

Lucas sat up in bed. "I thought she didn't want to leave Lafitte," he said.

"That was before," said Land. "All that is changed now. I love her. And she loves me."

"Ned, she's young enough to be your daughter."

"She doesn't think me old," said Land. "And she's no child, believe me. She knows her mind."

"Perhaps, but it does seem changeable," said Lucas. "You realize this is very foolish, don't you?"

"I know what you're going to say," said Land. "There's no

point in running off. Lafitte was willing to make me a present of her before, why not just ask if he still stands by his offer? No. I will not have any man make a present of a woman as if she were a horse."

"So you'll steal her as if you were a horse thief," Lucas said. "Ned, don't be an ass. Where would you go?"

"She knows her way through the bayous," Land said. "She's getting some things together. She'll meet me on the back side of the island in a pirogue and we'll paddle to New Orleans. Then we'll make our way to Boston. I can get work as a harpooner. I'll buy a house and we will marry. She's very light, no one would think she was a Negro. We can have a family."

"Ned, has it occurred to you that you don't belong in this time? It's 1812. You haven't even been born yet."

"What does that matter? I don't care. I'm leaving, I tell you and nothing you can say will change my mind. I only came to say good-bye. You will say good-bye to Finn and Andre for me, won't you? And to Jules."

"Well, if you've made up your mind. . . ."

"You can't talk me out of it. There's no use trying."

Lucas got out of bed. "All right, Ned, I won't. I wish you the best of luck. I hope you won't regret this."

He offered Land his hand and the harpooner took it.

"I will have nothing to regret, I promise you."

"I wouldn't be so sure," said Lucas and, still holding onto Land's hand, he gave him a savage kick in the balls.

Land wheezed and doubled over and Lucas nailed him with an uppercut to the jaw. The harpooner dropped to the floor, unconscious. Verne and Delaney kept up their steady cadence of snoring.

"Marie's going to have a long wait by the boat," said Lucas. "And by the time morning comes around, I don't think she'll love you quite so much."

He pulled down the curtain cord and proceeded to tie up the unconscious Ned.

Lucas woke up with someone shaking his shoulder gently. He opened his eyes to see Finn bending over him.

"Is it morning already?"

"Rise and shine, Major," Finn said. "Time to get ready to hit the boats and weigh anchor."

"It feels like I just closed my eyes," said Lucas.

"What happened here last night?" said Finn.

"Huh?" Lucas sat up in bed, rubbing the sleep out of his eyes.

Finn ponted.

Verne had fallen off the chair onto the floor, where he was curled up in a fetal position, dead to the world. Beside him, struggling against his bonds, glaring ferociously and growling into his gag, was Land. The door opened and Andre walked in.

"I must have missed a hell of a party," she said.

"Verne passed out and Ned was going to run off with Marie and set up light housekeeping in Boston," Lucas said, getting out of bed. "I tried to talk him out of it, but he wasn't very reasonable."

"He's liable to be a lot less reasonable when you untie him," Finn said.

"You're probably right," said Lucas. "Let's not untie him."

Land thrashed on the floor.

Andre stood over him, hands on her hips. "You cad," she said. "The minute my back is turned, you're playing around with another woman. You're a heartless brute."

Land rolled his eyes.

"Never trust a sailor," Finn said.

"He was just going to go off and leave us in the lurch," said Lucas. "Here we are, needing all the help we can get, and he's sneaking off to hide under some woman's skirts."

"Ned Land, the great harpooner, running away from a fight," said Andre. "I should have known he was all bluster."

"The hell with him," said Finn. "Let him go. Who needs a friend like him? We'll just have to handle Drakov by ourselves."

Land stopped struggling.

They looked at each other.

"You think maybe he's ready to be untied now?" said Andre.

"I think so," said Finn.

Moments later, Land was on his feet, looking sullen and rubbing his chafed wrists.

"Friends?" said Lucas, offering his hand.

Land grunted, then took his hand. And swung a haymaker at Lucas's head. Lucas easily ducked underneath it and jabbed Land twice in the solar plexus, hard enough to sit him down on the floor, winded.

"You didn't really think I was going to fall for that, did you?" Lucas said.

Land glared at him from the floor, then a smile spread over his face and he started to laugh. They all joined him.

"I should probably be thanking you," he said. "I would've married the girl."

"That's okay," said Lucas. "We all come down with temporary insanity every once in a while."

Land sighed. "You're right, for certain, it would have been a very foolish thing to do. Still, some things are worth being foolish over." He shook his head. "She must have been waiting all night at the boat. What am I to tell her?"

"Tell her you were tied up," said Lucas.

Land laughed and put his arm around Lucas, then quickly shifted his grip, caught him in a headlock and brought his fist down in a punishing hammerblow on top of his head. Lucas felt as if a gong had gone off inside his skull. He sat on the floor, palms pressed to his temples, rocking slightly.

"You fell for that one," Land said. "Now I'm in the mood for breakfast."

"*Sacre bleu!*" moaned Verne, from the floor. "I beg you, do not mention food!"

They took their leave of Jean Lafitte and rowed out to the *Valkyrie*, which sailed on the morning tide. In the early morning sun, with the wind blowing through their hair and the salty sea spray misting in over the decks, they all felt relaxed and invigorated. It was hard to imagine that in a short time, they would be involved in the most dangerous conflict of their careers.

Drakov was strangely silent as he stood by the helmsman, his gaze on the horizon. There was an air of tense anticipation among his crew.

"It's almost as if they know there's going to be a fight," Lucas said softly to Finn as they stood on deck.

"You think they're onto it?" said Finn.

"I don't know," said Lucas. "I sure as hell hope not. We need the advantage of surprise."

"Maybe it's just the thought of returning to the base," said Andre. "If they know Drakov is ready to put whatever plan he's made into action, that could account for it."

"I'd feel a whole lot better if we had our warp discs," Finn said.

"We'll have to try to get some," Lucas said. "Maybe Martingale can help. If not, we'll have to take them from Drakov's men."

"We may not get that chance," said Andre.

"I just wish we didn't have to depend on Martingale to get the signal out," said Finn. "Are you sure he's straight on the fugue sequence program?"

"I showed him as best I could," said Lucas. "He'll be all right. He's a pro."

"If something goes wrong and he winds up in the dead zone, what happens then?" said Andre.

"Then nothing's changed," said Lucas. "It will still be up to us, just as it was in the beginning. One of us will have to try and get out to signal Forrester. The others will have to stay and destroy the sub. It will still leave a mess, but the sub has to be destroyed, no matter what. All Martingale and Dr. Darkness can do is improve our odds. We've still got to get the job done."

"What about Verne and Land?" said Andre.

Lucas sighed. "We protect them, if we can. If not, well, they'll just have to fend for themselves."

When they were well out of sight of land, Drakov signaled the *Nautilus*. Within a short time, they saw its dark bulk rise up out of the waves, dwarfing the small ship they were on. Verne, who had shrugged off most of the effects of his hangover with the help of the tangy sea air, had joined them at the railing and he gasped as he saw the *Nautilus* rise.

"I have never seen her surface before!" he said. "What an incredible sight! She breaks the surface of the water like an island rising from beneath the waves. Small wonder sailors took her for a sea monster. She looks both terrifying and majestic.''

As the lines were tossed, bringing the schooner and the submarine closer together, men came up behind them, two for each of them, one on each side. They were grasped firmly while others, standing before them, covered them with pistols. This time, they were not black powder weapons or revolvers. These were lasers.

"Henceforth," said Drakov, coming up to them, "you will be kept under constant guard. I shall not make the mistake Falcon made in underestimating the three of you. You shall be separated, from Verne and Land as well as from each other. Two men will remain with you at all times. Two more will serve to reinforce the first two. I know you had planned to search my cabin for the warp discs. Land told me. Perhaps he is sincere in wishing to join me. Perhaps it is a plot you hatched. In either case, I will not trust him quite yet. He will be watched, as well. If all goes according to plan, and I see no reason why it should not, you will all come away from this unharmed."

"Just what is—" Lucas began, but Drakov interrupted him.

"No questions, Mr. Priest. T-Day is approaching. I have no more time for pleasantries nor for being a gracious, tolerant host. Take them below."

They were escorted down into the submarine and immediately separated. The orders given to their guards were clear. They were not to be let out of sight even for a moment, not even while going to the head. The guards would say nothing to them and they kept well apart, both holding lasers at the ready, so that if one was jumped, the other could fire, killing his shipmate if need be. Drakov had not exaggerated. He was taking no chances whatsoever.

Each of them, in their separate areas of the ship, kept thinking the same thing. Whether Martingale could bring help or not, the missiles must not be fired. There was only one way to guarantee that. Kill Drakov and destroy the sub. There were three against more than a hundred and that number would grow sharply when they reached the secret base in the volcano off New Guinea. And they could not act, even if they were able to, before they reached that base. For the present, there was nothing to do but wait.

They did not have to wait for long. Soon after they had submerged, the transition signal sounded throughout the submarine. They each felt the effects of temporal teleportation as the mammoth sub translocated to another time. Lucas bit his lower lip and stared at his two guards, who returned his gaze unblinking, both their lasers pointed directly at his midsection.

Whatever happens, Lucas thought, it won't be long now.

Moses Forrester sat in a straight-backed chair behind a small table on the raised stage of the briefing room on the sixty-third floor of the Temporal Army Corps Headquarters building at Pendleton Base. On the table before him was a steaming mug of coffee, which was periodically freshened by his orderly. Beside the coffee mug was an ashtray into which he tossed his wooden matches, an archaic affectation, and tapped out his pipe. He smoked continually and, to pass the time, watched the terminal before him, which he had switched to outdoor scan.

The cameras showed him different views of the Departure Station sixty-three stories below. There was no sound, for he wanted none, but he could imagine the sounds out there. It was part of the world he lived in every day. Down there in the Departure Station, men and women of the Temporal Army Corps congregated in groups in the center of the giant plaza as ground shuttles zipped through the crowds, carrying the supplies and personnel to their clockout points. Many soldiers sat in the bars which ringed the plaza, enjoying a last drink or two before being clocked out to their missions. Overhead, skimmers wound their way through the maze of pedestrian spans which connected the various buildings of the base. A computer-generated voice announced departure codes and grid designations for the soldiers to report to.

Code Yellow 38, Grid 600. To the Spanish-American War.

Code Green 67, Grid 515. To an arbitration action in Korea.

Code Indigo 14, Grid 227. Destination—the Asteroid Belt in the 24th century, scene of the last modern, non-temporal war.

Soon it would change. The departure grids would be replaced by warp discs, but meanwhile, the new technology had not reached the regular corps yet. Only the First Division had them. Only the temporal adjustment teams and a group of renegade time pirates led by Forrester's own son.

The soldiers sitting before him in the briefing room were very different from the regular troops assigned to arbitration conflicts, though they had all come from those ranks. Unlike those outside in the plaza, who were dressed either in disposable green transit fatigues or in period costumes—Cossacks, Mongols, Waffen SS, Rainbow Division, Vikings, Celtic knights—the commandos in the briefing room were dressed for action in blue battle suits woven from nysteel, lightweight, flexible one-piece garments that would deflect most ammunition but not, they all knew only too well, laser beams or plasma from an auto-pulser. All the commandos had their equipment at their sides, weapons and floater-paks, ready to be donned in an instant. Each had programmed his or her warp discs with the partial coordinates for the attack. They lacked only the final coding for the sequence—the precise time.

As they sat there, some napping, some talking quietly, some smoking, some eating sandwiches, others just simply staring straight ahead, the time had already passed long since. But the event of that long past time they were awaiting had not happened yet. They waited for history to change. Each hoped the change would not be significant enough to overcome temporal inertia and affect the timestream. History did not report a battle taking place in the interior of an extinct volcano on an island off the coast of Papua, New Guinea, in the 19th century. With luck, history never would report it.

Sergeant Wendy Chan, a small raven-haired, delicate-looking woman whose outward appearance gave the lie to her thin, yet exceedingly fit body which had been wounded scores of times in temporal conflicts, sat talking quietly with Staff Sergeant Martin, who nibbled on a pastrami sandwich. Captain Sullivan kept running his hands through his close-cropped black hair and rubbing his temples, trying to calm his nerves. It had been a long time since he had seen any action and he fervently hoped his battle instincts were still sharp. Lieutenant

Bryant, his face calm-looking and world-weary, sat staring off into infinity, creating an aura of dispassionate isolation about himself. They were all in the same unit, yet they had never gone into battle together en masse. Outside the briefing room, the hectic activity of the base proceeded as usual. Only a few were aware of what was about to take place.

Forrester would be leading his people into battle. No one could guess his thoughts as he sat there, waiting with the rest of them, smoking his pipe and sipping coffee. He appeared perfectly composed. No one knew he was being eaten up by guilt. None of the people in the briefing room knew Drakov was his son. The last time they had met, father and son had confronted each other in deadly combat. Forrester should have killed him then, but he had been unable to. Now the time had come to pay the price, and he stared at the screen before him to avoid seeing the faces of those under his command, many of whom would soon be dead because he had failed to kill his son when he had the chance. A part of him had not been able to do it, even while another part told him that he must. He had hesitated, and he had lost. As the minutes lengthened into hours, he steeled himself for what was to come. He did not wonder if he would survive the battle. He no longer cared.

They were brought out on deck, still under guard, for their first glimpse of Drakov's base. Verne and Land, neither of them knowing what to expect, were both awed by the sight which greeted them.

The submarine was on the surface of a giant lake inside the volcanic crater. High above them, the walls of the hollow mountain tapered to the opening, across which birds flitted as they darted from one side of the volcano to the other, their cries echoing down to them. To their left, they saw the tiers of buildings that were the quarters of the base personnel, modular units built into the rock, with catwalks connecting them. Above them, spanning the lake, were the pedestrian cable bridges across which people walked several abreast, carrying equipment or pushing dollies. To their right, the larger area of the complex was the heart of Drakov's base. In the water near the dock was a submarine tender, toward which they slowly moved. The crewmen of the tender stood ready to receive them. Beyond the tender, in a large slip, was berthed the *Valkyrie*, her sails neatly furled. Overlooking the entire complex, like an eagle's aerie, was Drakov's house, partly carved out of the stone wall and partly built of white brick. It looked like a cross between a cliffside Pueblo Indian dwelling and a lamasery.

"Unbelievable," said Verne, his voice almost a whisper.

"You will experience much that defies belief here, Mr. Verne," said Drakov. "Pay close attention. You shall record all this for posterity. Here, in this burnt-out caldron, an age will end and a new one will begin. You shall see history in the making and I shall be the one to make it. Literally to make it, to shape it out of nothing."

Finn glanced at Drakov sharply. "What are you talking about?"

"You will soon see," said Drakov. "The time has almost come."

The submarine was made fast to the tender and they disembarked. With Drakov leading the way, they walked down the dock and across a short stretch of beach to the main building.

They entered a large hall, with several corridors branching off from it. Lucas fought the temptation to look over his shoulder at Martingale. Their guards conducted them through the building, past the mess hall and recreation rooms, past a library, a computer center and a generating plant, toward the rear of the building and an elevator which took them up to Drakov's house. They came out directly underneath it and circled round to a wide stair cut into the rock face, ascending to the entrance of the house.

They climbed the stairs to a small portico and a large, carved wooden door, which one of the men opened for them. They entered into a foyer with a mosaic floor and large planters placed around it. A winding stairway led to the upper story of the house. Thick carpeting covered the stairs. Oil paintings hung on the wall, mostly Pre-Raphaelite art. There were several busts, one of Julius Caesar, another of Napoleon. A crystal chandelier hung from the ceiling. Drakov's boots echoed on the tile floor as he turned to the left and walked out onto the veranda, a wide, tiled plaza with a brick wall running round it at about waist height. The view was spectacular. They were halfway up the side of the volcano, looking down onto the lake, the submarine and the schooner, the cable span-bridges not far below them. Drakov leaned on the wall and looked out over his domain.

"Today is T-Day," Drakov said, still looking out over the base. "T for Transition. Transition from one age to another." He turned around to face them. "This has been my base of operations, my sanctuary from temporal agents and soldiers like yourselves who have dogged my heels ceaselessly since the Zenda affair. I spent my entire fortune to construct this place. Here I gathered and trained my people, preparing them for the tasks which they will embark upon today. Until now, not even my officers knew the full extent of my plans. What one does not know, one cannot reveal, no matter what the temptation may be. Now, it is safe to reveal all, for no one can stop it. Within the hour, it shall be done." He took a deep breath of relief. "It has all gone well. Everything is ready. Shiro, bring champagne."

"What are we celebrating?" Finn said.

"The ultimate disaster," Drakov said. "The end of time as you know it, Mr. Delaney. From today, the entire character of time will change. And you will have a ringside seat. All three of you. After we have our toast, Santos will prepare a disc for you, one which will send the three of you back to the 27th century, back to my father and the war machine he serves to tell him he has been defeated. You had assumed, no doubt, that I would emulate my old compatriots in the Timekeepers and attempt to blackmail the war machine into dismantling itself. Perhaps that might have worked, but it would not have provided an ultimate solution. Perhaps nothing ever will. But I think I can increase the odds in its favor."

He looked down at the submarine below.

"I have twenty chances," he said, "twenty opportunities to make a better world, a better universe. I have had some of my people clocking out to various periods of time, preparing other bases for us, not as ambitious as this one, but they will serve. It has taken time, it has taken money, and it has taken backbreaking labor, but all is done now."

He looked at Martingale, von Kampf and Benedetto.

"I am sorry to have kept you in the dark," he said. "I felt it was necessary. There was too much at stake to share my plans in full with anyone. Everyone has had a task. Some worked on our new bases, others disposed of riches that we found in order to provide the funds for all the work, still others worked to establish connections for us in the places we shall be visiting. There was much groundwork to be laid. Many nights, while you thought I was resting in my cabin, I would return here to keep track of our progress. Shortly before we left Barataria, I learned that all was in readiness at last."

Shiro brought out the wine.

"In order to create something new and clean, there must be a purging," Drakov said. "I shall purge the human race, not once, but twenty times. Each ballistic missile in the *Nautilus* has been equipped with a warp disc in its guidance system. Each will be launched from here into a different time period. Each will change the course of history. One will strike the Soviet Union during the time of the Cuban Missile Crisis. Another will strike the state of Israel during the Six Day War. Still another will be targeted on New York City during the time of a crippling embargo against the USSR. All will strike different locations in different time periods. Each will result in events radically different from those of history as we know it. Each will result in a timestream split. We shall have twenty different timelines to choose from, my friends. We shall have twenty alternate universes to explore. By clocking back through time, starting with the most recent split we shall initiate, we can travel to our base moments before the split occurs and then clock forward, thereby finding ourselves in an alternate timeline. We will see the future we will have helped create and, if it is not to our taste, we shall clock back to the next most recent point before the split and try again, when that next timestream split occurs. We shall all be able to pick and choose our futures and work to influence them. And with twenty different timelines in existence, the effect on temporal inertia will be such that none of these timelines will ever rejoin. Yes, we will destroy, and that will be the purging. But just think of what we shall create!"

They were all speechless at the enormity of what Drakov

proposed. Even Benedetto, who had accepted the worst excesses of the Timekeepers with indifference, was so stunned he dropped his glass.

"The three of you," said Drakov, to Lucas, Finn and Andre, "will stand right here on this spot and watch each missile being launched. As the final missile leaves its silo, Santos will activate the disc and send you back where you belong. The Time Wars will end, because no one will have any way of knowing from then on which universe they will be clocking back to. And when you tell Moses Forrester of what I have done, tell him that I could never have accomplished it without him."

12 _____

Out of the corner of his eye, Lucas saw Martingale edge around slightly so that he stood just behind the guards who had their weapons trained on them. While all eyes were on Drakov, save those of the guards who were watching the commandos carefully, Martingale's right hand went to the warp disc strapped to his left wrist.

Drakov reached into his pocket and removed a small communicator. He turned it on and as he spoke, his booming voice came through a speaker system, filling the interior of the volcano.

"Attention," he said, looking out over the base. "Attention. We are now at T-Day minus one hour. All personnel have fifteen minutes to report to the assembly hall to begin transition. Clocking will commence by unit in twenty minutes. Control and missile crews of the *Nautilus* stand by your stations, all other submarine and tender personnel report to the assembly hall."

Martingale was gone.

The scene barely had time to register on Martingale's consciousness as he fugue-clocked into the briefing room. He prayed he had programmed the disc correctly. There had been so little time. He had only a momentary impression of seeing a man seated before him and a roomful of commandos in battle dress before he shouted out the date and time coordinates and winked out again.

Forrester was on his feet in an instant, shouldering the floater-pak and buckling the harness. "*Now*, people! *Move it!*"

Not a second's time was wasted. Those who were eating or smoking simply threw the cigarettes or food onto the floor and grabbed for their floater-paks. Warp discs were quickly programmed with the coordinates Martingale had shouted. Forrester repeated them loudly, several times, to make certain everyone had them right. As the floater-paks were secured and the discs were programmed, they took position where they stood, left arms cocked in front of their chests, discs facing up, right arms raised to indicate the discs were staged. Forrester didn't wait to check that everyone was ready. The moment a significant number of hands were raised, he gave the order.

"*Go!*"

No one noticed the barely discernible confluence of atomic particles making only the vaguest hint of a shadow in a corner at the back of the room. The tachyonic essence that was Dr. Robert Darkness did not wait for Forrester to give the attack order. The moment Martingale disappeared, Darkness hurtled across parsecs of time-space with a speed faster than thought. The First Division could stop the time pirates, but it was up to him to save Martingale and the three commandos.

Drakov stared. A flicker of movement had caught his eye and he blinked, puzzled. What had he seen?

"Captain," Verne said, finally finding his voice, "*this is madness!* If those explosives are as powerful as you say, hundreds of thousands will die!"

"More like millions, Mr. Verne," said Drakov, staring at Martingale. "But it is necessary in order to—Martingale, what did you do just now?"

Martingale frowned. "What do you mean, Chief?"

Drakov quickly glanced at the commandos, then at Martingale. "You . . . moved. I could have sworn—"

"Drakov, listen to me," Lucas said quickly, realizing what Drakov hadn't realized yet, but was about to. The fugue had been a second or two off. "You haven't—"

"Be quiet, Priest. Something just happened—"

"Nikolai, look!" shouted Benedetto, pointing.

Drakov spun around. Benedetto was pointing up at the mouth of the volcano. He squinted and saw what appeared to be birds high overhead, but they were too large and as he looked, more of them appeared, out of nowhere, descending swiftly.

"Sound the alarm!" he said, then, remembering his communicator, he turned it on. *"Red Alert! Red Alert! We are under attack!"*

Martingale karate-chopped one of the guards and wrenched his laser away from him, but Shiro was on him before he could fire. His right foot arced around in a lightning, spinning-wheel kick and the laser flew out of Martingale's hand and over the side of the wall. Only the mercenary's swift reactions saved him from the second kick, which followed the first with astonishing speed. Shiro had continued the spinning movement that initiated the first kick and came around with the other foot flying up at Martingale's throat. The mercenary deflected it, backing away as Shiro continued moving forward rapidly, spinning around and around, cutting loose with kicks as if he were a moving buzz saw.

"Kill them!" Drakov shouted to the guards, activating his warp disc in the same instant and vanishing from sight.

Before the guards could fire, they became briefly enveloped in a blue mist of Cerenkov Radiation and their atoms disintegrated. Darkness turned his disruptor on Shiro, but his target reacted with amazing and decisive swiftness, vaulting over the side of the wall and dropping forty feet to the ledge below. Darkness could not move to shoot him.

"Quick little bastard, isn't he?" said Darkness. He tossed the disruptor to Lucas. "Catch."

For a moment, von Kampf had been mesmerized by the sight of the guards disintegrating, but as Darkness tossed the gun to Lucas, he suddenly roared and charged him. He passed right through the Doctor's body and his momentum carried him over the wall and past the ledge. With a scream, he fell down to the rocks below.

"Quickly, take these," said Darkness, taking several more

disruptors off his belt and tossing them to Andre, Finn, Martingale and Land.

The moment he had sighted the attack force, Benedetto had shouted out his warning, then fled. Things had happened so quickly that they only now remembered him.

"The elevator!" Finn said, turning and sprinting for the door. Martingale was after him in an instant.

"How the hell do you fire this thing?" said Land, gazing at the warp gun in puzzlement.

As Andre quickly showed him, Lucas approached Darkness. "Thanks. You saved our lives. Can you get down to the submarine?"

"I don't have the coordinates," said Darkness. "I can't home in on it as I can on you and Martingale. You'll have to manage for yourself; I've done all I could. Good luck."

He disappeared.

They quickly followed in the wake of Finn and Martingale, but by the time they had descended the stone steps, they saw that Benedetto had already taken the elevator down.

"It's no good," said Finn. "He's jammed it. We'll have to get down another way."

"There *is* no other way!" said Martingale.

Without a word, Land stuffed the disruptor inside his jumpsuit and leaped out onto the cable. For him, it was like the rigging on a sailing schooner and he made his way down it hand over hand with surprising swiftness.

"That guy's nuts," said Martingale.

"Maybe," said Finn, "but that's the way to go."

"Gentlemen," said Verne, who had finally found his voice after the shocking appearances and disappearances he had just witnessed, "I fear it is impossible for me to make such a descent. I have not the strength. I should surely fall."

"Go back to the house," said Lucas. "Stay inside. We'll come back for you after it's over."

"God protect you," Verne said.

Finn leaped out into the shaft and grabbed the cable, wrapping his legs around it as Land had done. He started lowering himself, though not as quickly. Andre waited for him to get a slight start, then took a deep breath and jumped.

"You're next," said Lucas to Martingale.

"No, you go ahead."

Something in the mercenary's voice made Lucas glance at him sharply. The man was deathly pale.

"What's wrong?"

"Nothing!" Martingale snapped. "Go on!"

"You're afraid of heights," said Lucas.

"Yeah, so what? Don't worry about it, it's my problem."

"Okay, forget it. Stay here with Verne. You've done more than enough."

Martingale stared at him. "Like hell," he said. He swallowed hard and leaped into the shaft. For a second, he hung there precariously and didn't move, his eyes tightly shut. "Oh, *Christ*, I wish I hadn't done that! Jesus. Jesus."

"Open your eyes, Martingale!" shouted Lucas. "It'll be all right, just don't look down. Watch the cable. You hear me? Watch the cable!"

Martingale opened his eyes and began to lower himself hand over hand.

"You're doing fine," said Lucas. "Just keep it up. Watch the cable. Don't look down."

"Not for all the tea in China, Jack!"

"I'm right behind you," Lucas said. He jumped and grabbed the cable. Heights didn't bother him since he had taken the plunge off the wall of Zenda Castle into the moat during his last mission. He looked down and saw that Martingale was making steady progress. Land had almost reached the bottom of the shaft. But Drakov had a very large head start.

As the jets on the floater-pak carried him down toward the mouth of the volcano, Forrester heard the *whoop-whoop* of an alarm reverberating through the air. So much for a surprise attack, he thought. There was nothing for it now but to come in fast and hit them hard.

He unclipped the auto-pulser from its fastening on his flight harness and held it ready in front of him. Just then someone shot past him with his floater-pak jets on full, leveled out in a fully stretched-out position to offer minimum wind resistance.

"Bryant!" shouted Forrester over the com-circuit, but with the wind from the speed of his descent, Bryant might not have heard him. And if he had, he would not have listened in any case. Forrester knew exactly what the fool was doing. He was going in first, ahead of Forrester, in an effort to draw fire away from his commander.

Several more commandos hurtled by Forrester in the same position and he cursed them, then stretched out himself and kicked the jets in, plunging into the mouth of the volcano.

Laser beams and pulser blasts came up at them like flak as the commandos fanned out upon entering the volcano, so as not to give a concentrated group as a target. Sullivan was in a flat dive, heading directly toward the submarine, firing his auto-pulser. Plasma blasts screamed past him and Forrester saw his floater-pak on fire. As the jets cut out, Sullivan fell, still firing his weapon as he hurtled to his death.

Bryant flew down in a fast arc toward the catwalks high on the left side of the base, where groups of men stood firing their weapons. He came in high through a barrage of pulser blasts, then abruptly angled down, still going flat out, making it difficult for the gunners to lead him. As he swooped past the catwalks, he fanned them with his auto-pulser and they burst into white-hot flame as they were enveloped in plasma. Men screamed as they were cooked to a crisp and the steel sagged, as if it were taffy, finally melting through. The entire structure collapsed to the roofs of the buildings below. Bryant kicked in his pilot jets at the last possible moment before he would smash head-first into a rock wall jutting out into the crater. He missed it by scant inches.

"Damn cowboy," Forrester swore. He changed his own course and flew down low, feeling the heat of plasma blasts erupting around him. He angled up beneath the cable span bridges. Several other commandos followed him, providing covering fire. On the bridges, gunners tried to track them as they came in. One blast narrowly missed Forrester and hit Wendy Chan. There was nothing left of her.

As he came up beneath the bridges, Forrester cut loose at their cable supports while the others concentrated their fire on the gunners. Some of the commandos were using lasers, sweeping concentrated beams of coherent light across the spans. Several of Drakov's men were killed instantly, others had their legs amputated and they fell over the side, screaming as they plunged down into the lake below.

One of the bridges collapsed with a roar as the supports parted, sending men tumbling into the water. The entire commando attack force was now inside the crater and they separated in all directions, swooping around like angry mosquitoes, firing at anything that moved. The heaviest concentration of defenders was around the submarine, trying to protect it, but already its hull was blackened from pulser blasts and there had been at least one direct hit on the rear of the sub. The aft section had been ruptured by a grenade set on minimal intensity. But as each commando flew down to strafe it, a heavy barrage of laser and pulser fire filled the air above and there were many casualties.

Somewhere down there, Forrester knew, were Delaney, Cross and Priest. If they were still alive. A lot of his people were getting hit. He didn't want to lose any more.

"Set down!" he shouted over the com-circuit. "Set down! Red Squad, secure the buildings on the side opposite the docks! Blue Squad, take the high ground on the same side and trap them between you, hammer and anvil! Green Squad, take the rocks on the far side past the main buildings! Gold Squad, follow me down to the rock cover near the docks!"

Finn took his disruptor and sprayed a blast of neutrons at the roof of the elevator, opening up a hole for them to jump through. He went first, followed by Andre, then Land, then Martingale and Lucas. Finn went out first into the hall, firing his disruptor as he ran. There wasn't much resistance. Most of Drakov's people were outside, engaging the attack force. The few men they encountered opened up on them, but against the disruptors, even auto-pulsers made poor weapons. The plasma blasts disintegrated as they ran into the neutron spray and in moments, Drakov's people were retreating.

"You were right," Finn told Martingale. "It's a lovely little sidearm, this warp gun."

"Drakov's got too much of a lead on us," said Lucas. "Come on, let's make a run for the tender."

They sprinted through the building, firing as they ran, taking a chance that they wouldn't catch any fire from the corridors and chambers to their sides. They made it to the building entrance and kept right on going, running full tilt toward the docks. The *Valkyrie* was in flames. Several buildings on the opposite side of the lake were burning, sending up clouds of smoke. They heard men screaming as they burned, caught between the flames and the commandos. One cable span bridge had been utterly destroyed, the other dangled by a single support over the lake like a broken toy. Black smoke was coming from the *Nautilus*.

A plasma blast struck the ground before them as they ran, bursting into a cloud of flame. Martingale was caught in the wash. He caught fire as he ran through it, screaming, moving on like a flaming juggernaut.

Finn tackled him and started rolling him over and over in the sand, heaping sand upon him and trying to snuff out the flames. Lucas, Andre and Ned Land ran on. A laser beam lanced across their path. Andre was able to react quickly enough to leap over it and roll, coming up running, but Land was caught by it and cut in half. He fell to the ground in two parts, screaming horribly and writhing. There was nothing anyone could do. Lucas swore, pointed his disruptor at him and fired. The screams ceased.

They were dressed like Drakov's men and the commandos had no way of telling who they were at a distance. They were being fired upon by their own people. Andre was pinned down, having scrambled for cover behind a large outcropping of rocks near the lake. Only her constant firing of her disruptor kept the plasma blasts from cooking her. Lucas fell down beside her and saw where a group of Drakov's men had set up a firing base in one of the storage buildings near the tender, protecting the submarine. As they watched, several men came out on the deck of the *Nautilus*, casting her loose from the tender.

"He's getting away!" said Andre.

Two of the men on deck were killed. Lucas fired his disruptor at the others and they were briefly shrouded in blue mist, then they disintegrated. But the sub had already started to drift loose from the tender.

"*No*," said Lucas, gritting his teeth. "No, God *damn* it, *no!*"

One of the hatches on the deck of the *Nautilus* sprang open. Lucas jumped and ran across the beach, sprinting toward the tender. Andre laid down covering fire for him as he ran with all the speed he had, screaming to get the adrenaline rush going. As he ran across the dock, leaping from it to the tender, a shower of flame and splinters erupted behind him and he felt the heat wash from the pulser blast as it destroyed the dock. Without breaking stride, he tucked the disruptor into his jumpsuit and leaped for the sub. He just barely made the deck and he scrambled for a hold, then was almost trampled by the men who came running out of the hatch to dive into the water. They didn't pay any attention to him. All they wanted was to get off the sub, which was in flames and taking on water.

Several more pulser blasts struck the submarine as Lucas dove through the hatch, sliding down on the handrails. His feet hit water at the bottom. It was up to his knees and rising fast. Smoke was everywhere. Several of the oil lines had ruptured and were spraying scalding hot, pressurized oil across the companionway. The watertight hatch before him was closed. He didn't waste time trying to open it. He took out his disruptor, set it on spray, and fired.

"Captain, we must abandon ship!" cried Sasha, leaving his station at the helm.

"Sit back down!" said Drakov.

Unable to resist the conditioning, the Russian sailor returned to his post, looking around at the control room helplessly. Smoke was seeping in.

"Sir, we don't dare submerge," said one of the other crewmen. "We're taking on too much water. We've been badly damaged. I'm shutting the reactor down."

"Switch to diesel engines," Drakov said.

"No!" shouted one of the other men. "It's useless, don't you see? We'll die!"

He grabbed Drakov, but Shiro tossed him aside as if he weighed nothing. Water was now coming into the control room. Despite the immense strength of the submarine's titanium double hulls, a pinpoint warp grenade explosion had caused a rupture and a spray had burst into the room, soaking down three of the men at the controls. They jumped at once and ran for the stairs leading to the hatch. Shiro turned to stop them, but Drakov called out, "Let them go! They're useless now."

At the words "Let them go," the rest of the control room crew bolted.

"The key, Shiro!" Drakov said.

As they fought to get up the stairs, the Soviet sailors were caught in a blast of neutrons and ceased to exist.

Drakov inserted his key into the box containing the arming and firing mechanisms.

Lucas came sliding down the hatch, into the rapidly accumulating water on the control room floor.

With a snarl of rage and frustration, Drakov hit his warp disc and clocked out. Shiro had just inserted his key into the box.

"Don't do it, Shiro," Lucas said softly, aiming the disruptor at him.

Two coal-black eyes stared at him with loathing.

"It's over," Lucas said. "He's deserted you. There's no point in—"

Moving with dazzling swiftness, Shiro turned the key and flipped open the box. Lucas fired. Shiro's atoms were scattered just as he was reaching for the buttons.

Lucas sloshed forward through the knee-deep water and gently closed the box, then took the keys out. He let his breath out slowly.

A glance at the indicators told him the reactor had been shut down. None of the missiles had been armed and all the silo hatches were still closed. But the attack was still continuing. He felt the sub shudder and roll and he was thrown into the water on the floor. For fear of exploding the missiles, they were using only the lowest setting on the warp grenades, using them as depth charges thrown into the water close to the sub, to rupture its hull. It was working very well. Blasts of water were coming in everywhere now and he had to fight his way through it to the ladder leading up to the hatch.

He tucked his disruptor inside his suit and climbed up, his feet slipping off the rungs. As he opened the hatch, he heard footsteps on the deck and before he could cry out a warning, a warp grenade came dropping down through the opening. He caught it, lunged through the hatchway and threw it as hard as he could out into the lake. The pinpoint blast went off, sending a gout of water up into the air. He looked up at Lieutenant Bryant, standing on the deck of the submarine, holding an auto-pulser pointed at him. Bryant lowered the weapon and without a flicker of expression, shrugged.

Lucas simply glared at him.

It was over. The remainder of Drakov's force had surrendered and they were being gathered together to be clocked back to Plus Time for conditioning and return to their own time periods. The stolen warp discs were found in one of the supply rooms in the main building.

Forrester landed on the beach by Andre, after taking to the air briefly to survey the scene. Finn was kneeling in the sand beside Martingale, his hands badly burned from putting out the flames. Martingale was unrecognizable. His entire body had been severely burned and he lay on his back in the sand, a charred lump of flesh, barely breathing.

"He's had it," said Forrester.

Finn shook his head. "No. No, he's in a real bad way, but we've got to try to pull him through. We *have* to."

"Who is he?" said Forrester.

"The guy who saved our asses," Finn said.

Forrester nodded, grimly. "Then I guess we'd best try to save his." He beckoned one of the other men forward, then he unstrapped his warp disc, quickly reprogrammed it, then bent down and gently put it around Martingale's wrist. Martingale's own warp disc was burned into uselessness, melded into the crisped flesh of his hand. "Hardesty, give me your disc," said Forrester.

The soldier quickly unstrapped his disc and tossed it to the colonel. Forrester programmed it and gave it to Finn. Delaney tried to put it on, but couldn't manage it and Hardesty had to help him.

"They're set for TAMAC," said Forrester, referring to the Temporal Army Medical Complex in Colorado Springs. "Get yourself taken care of and you tell 'em if they don't pull this guy through, I'll be down there to kick some ass."

"You got it," Finn said. A moment later, they clocked out.

"Verne!" Andre shouted.

"What?" said Forrester.

She was looking up at Drakov's house, perched high up on the wall above the lake. It had caught several pulser blasts and was in flames.

"We have to get up there," Andre said. "Now! Get me up there! We've got to get him out!"

"Hardesty!" said Forrester. He turned on his jets and picked Andre up in his arms. Hardesty flew up alongside them as they rose to the burning house. Verne was out on the veranda, trying to shield his face from the smoke and flames. "Get him!" Forrester shouted to Hardesty.

Hardesty swooped up and grabbed Verne under the arms, lifting him off the veranda floor. Verne shut his eyes tightly and let loose with a rapid torrent of French. Hardesty understood French. He grinned as he heard The Lord's Prayer. They quickly descended to safety and watched from the beach as the house fell down the side of the sheer wall and crashed onto the rocks below. Lucas and Bryant came up to join them and together they watched the *Nautilus* sink below the surface of the lake, into the depths of the volcano.

EPILOGUE ─────────────

Verne sat at a table in the First Division lounge, looking incongruous in his black base fatigues as he signed autographs for the commandos who clustered around him. Lucas sat across from him, drinking Irish whiskey and Andre sat on his right, sipping a Scotch.

"You have no idea what this means to me," said Verne, who was completely overcome by the experience. "I must be the only writer in history to know for certain that his work shall live on after he has died! To think that after so much time has passed, people will still read and enjoy my books. I could not have received a finer, more wonderful gift! Thank you. Thank you."

"All right, people, give it a rest. Let the man breathe for a minute," said Forrester, coming up to their table. "He'll be able to stay for a little while yet, so give us a few minutes, okay?"

The crowd reluctantly dispersed as they all went back to the bar and to their tables. Forrester pulled out a chair and sat down.

"Col. Forrester, I must tell you how grateful I am for this incredible experience," said Verne. "To have seen the future! And what wonders it holds in store!"

"Well, that's what I wanted to talk to you about, Mr. Verne," said Forrester. He signaled for a drink. "You can appreciate, I think, why it would be dangerous for someone from another time to have knowledge of what will occur in the future. Temporal inertia is a strange thing. It takes a great deal to overcome it, which is very fortunate for us. Our occasional interferences in history don't always cause disruptions in the timestream and, when they do, unless they are tremendously disruptive, they can usually be fixed. That's our main job in the First Division."

"Yes, I think I understand," said Verne. "That was how this entire episode began."

"Well, the people Drakov took from their own time periods and recruited into his group have all gone through a conditioning process and been returned to their own times," said Forrester. "Those of them who had not been killed, of course. Fortunately, none of those people were significant, historically speaking, so chances are their deaths won't cause any major problems, though we'll be on the watch for that. The point is, they have now been returned to where they belong and none of them will remember anything of what has occurred."

Verne's face took on an expression of profound chagrin. "I see," he said. "I understand. Naturally, I cannot be permitted to recall any of this. Of course. I will have to submit to this conditioning process of yours and have all these priceless memories erased."

Andre reached out and took his hand. "I'm sorry, Jules," she said. "I wish there were another way."

"No, no, do not apologize," said Verne. "It is perfectly understandable. I would not wish to cause any problems. If I must forget, then I must forget. *C'est tout dire.*"

"I admire your attitude, Mr. Verne," said Forrester. "However, that isn't quite the case here. We have a particular problem with you."

"What do you mean, sir?" said Lucas, frowning.

"I mean I've just come from a conference with the Referees," said Forrester. "Your case, Mr. Verne, has given them some mighty vicious headaches. You see, historically speaking, you are an important person. You are an important writer. And, at the time this entire thing began, you had still to write some of your greatest books. The Referees, who are very highly educated people and understand these things much better than I do, tell me the creative process is extremely delicate. Evidently, the least little thing can disturb it."

"Ah, yes," said Verne. "*Cela va sans dire.* How well I know!"

"And there we have our problem," Forrester continued. "The Referees are afraid to risk doing anything that might affect your delicate creative faculties. Which means, Mr. Verne, that they have decided it would be too risky to have you conditioned."

"Son of a bitch!" said Lucas.

"There seems to be only one thing we can do about you, Mr. Verne," said Forrester. "A great deal will depend on your cooperation, of course. We don't really *need* your cooperation, but it would make things very much easier, both for you and for everyone else concerned. I think you're perfectly capable of understanding the situation and the necessity for it; that's what I told the Referee Corps. So, they propose to do the following: to return you to your own time and allow you to continue with your life as you would have otherwise. You must never reveal, in any way whatsoever, anything you have seen here or any of the technology or information you have had access to in any manner that might affect the course of history. You understand? It will be necessary to keep you under observation, which will be done as discreetly and unobtrusively as humanly possible, although it will be imperative for one of our Observers to . . . read through your manuscripts before you submit them, just to make sure there is not any potentially damaging information in them. Now, I understand how an author might feel about something like this, but it need not be censorship, Mr. Verne, if you will exercise caution and restraint in what you write, strictly in terms of technical matters. That's the way it's going to have to be."

"Then . . . then I am going to be allowed to remember all of this?" said Verne, brightening.

"That's right," said Forrester.

"But I cannot use any of my experiences in my writing," Verne said, the brightness fading into gloom abruptly.

"Well, that depends," said Forrester, choosing his words with great care. "For example, if you were to write a work of *fiction*, suitably identifiable as such, about . . . oh, a submarine, for example . . . so long as there was nothing in the book to actually enable anyone to build one and so long as certain scientific principles were not revealed—"

"You mean if I were to make it entirely imaginary," said Verne, "obfuscate technical details, merely draw on my experience to write a sort of fantasy—"

"Precisely," Forrester said. "It would depend entirely on how you handled it, of course, but I don't think something like that would present any problems."

"But this is wonderful!" said Verne. "I shall be completely circumspect, Colonel. The secrets of the future will be safe with me."

"That's all we ask," said Forrester.

"Colonel, if I might ask one favor, if it would be possible . . . ?"

"Certainly, Mr. Verne."

"It is about Ned Land," said Verne. "If I could be allowed to somehow pay tribute to a brave man by remembering him in my work—well, it would be a small thing, but it would mean a lot to me."

"I think that would be appropriate," said Forrester. "Now if you will excuse us, we'll leave you to your admirers, who have been *specifically* instructed not to discuss your future work with you. It's been an honor, sir."

As they moved away from the table, Lucas cleared his throat.

"Did I just hear you give him the idea to write *Twenty Thousand Leagues Under the Sea*?"

"Don't be ridiculous," said Forrester. "*I* didn't put him aboard that sub. Besides, a writer has to write what he knows, doesn't he?"

"I think I just heard a hair being split," said Andre.

"As you were, Sergeant," Forrester said.

"Sergeant?"

"You've been promoted. Congratulations. Priest, you've made lieutenant colonel. You keep this up, you'll wind up outranking me. Since we can't have that, you're going to have to settle for a decoration next time."

"How about just giving me a raise, instead?" said Lucas.

"I'll submit your request through channels," said Forrester.

Lucas grimaced and looked at Andre. "A decoration," he said.

Finn was sitting up in the bed next to Martingale's when they walked in. His hands were swathed in bandages. Martingale's entire body was encased in a sterile cocoon with openings for the eyes, the nostrils and the mouth. Forrester tossed a small box onto Delaney's bed.

"What's this?" said Finn. He couldn't open it.

"Lieutenant's bars," said Forrester.

"Oh, no!" said Finn.

"You might be interested to know there's a pool going to see how long you'll keep them," Forrester said dryly. "Meanwhile, I'm sure you'll be interested to hear the wrapup. Salvage operations have been completed and the missiles disassembled. What's left of the sub will be repaired and placed on exhibit in San Diego. The base has been dismantled and most of the warp discs have been recovered. The Referees are extremely concerned about possible temporal disruptions as a result of this affair. We'll just have to wait and hope for the best. The TIA has managed to trace several of the bases Drakov had established."

Forrester paused uncomfortably.

"I'm afraid he's given us the slip again, along with Benedetto. We haven't heard the last of them. There were computer records kept at the base, but they were incomplete. Temporal Intelligence is still working on them and, as I've said, they've managed to find some of the other bases that were established, but there's good reason to believe a significant number of those people have escaped, so we're not finished with them yet. However, we did manage to avoid a multiple timestream split. But it cost us. We lost some of our best people. Still, we owe a considerable debt of gratitude to our friend here."

He approached Martingale's bed.

"The doctors tell me you should have died. They tell me you've got to be the stubbornest son of a bitch in the world.

Personally, I think the stubbornest s.o.b. in the world is in the bed next to yours, but I won't argue the point. You'll be good as new before too long and I was very glad to hear that. You did a good job, soldier."

Martingale gave him a faint nod.

"You know," said Forrester, "just to raise a point of idle conversation, the law concerning deserters is very strict. No exceptions, regardless of the circumstances. I just thought I'd bring that up. I don't really know why it occurred to me. It doesn't apply to you, of course. Does it, Lt. Hunter?"

Lucas and Andre both stared at Forrester. "*What?*" said Lucas.

"When Finn checked this patient in as Lt. Reese Hunter," said Forrester, "they ran the standard records check. Imagine their surprise when they discovered that Lt. Hunter had been reported MIA on an Airborne recon mission in 12th-century England. We all thought he was dead, right? I'm not too clear on it, myself, seems to me I heard a different story. Something about a Lt. Hunter being killed by the Timekeepers in 17th-century Paris. Well, I guess I heard wrong. Anyway, since Delaney was the one who checked him in, they came to him to get the facts. According to Finn, here, Lt. Hunter was marooned in 12th-century England and, as chance had it, he was one of those people recruited into the time pirates. Since then, he's been working undercover, independently, trying to help neutralize a threat to temporal continuity. The powers that be were properly impressed. Needless to say, since Lt. Hunter was listed MIA and since his actions have been heroically above and beyond the call of duty, no one would think of charging him with anything. In fact, it's been decided to reward his initiative by promoting him to the rank of captain."

Andre started to laugh.

"And since he has displayed such outstanding ability in a temporal adjustment situation," Forrester continued, "it's also been decided to transfer him from the Airborne Pathfinders into the First Division. So, welcome aboard, soldier. The First has the finest record in the corps. I'm glad to have you. I only take the best. I don't take people who can't cut it.

We've got spirit in the First. We've *never* had a deserter.''

He turned and walked towards the door, then paused and looked back.

"A man like you should do well in the First . . . *Captain Hunter*. We fight the good fight.''

He winked, then closed the door.

Although the *Time Wars* novels are historical science fantasy, it is my hope that readers, particularly younger readers, might be interested enough to read the *actual* history some of these books are very loosely based on, as well as the classic novels which inspired them. In that light, I add this note about Jean Lafitte.

A number of excellent biographies have been written about him, but his history, particularly his past prior to his appearance in New Orleans, is considerably cloudy. Lafitte, himself, did much to help keep his past a mystery. He is said to have claimed having been born in France and having seen the events of the French Revolution. A number of biographies report this as fact, as well as several entries in encyclopedias. In *Time Wars #3, The Pimpernel Plot*, Jean Lafitte appears as a supporting character, a young street urchin in Paris at the time of the Revolution.

However, in his own journal, which is mentioned in this story and which may be found in your local library, Jean Lafitte writes that he was born and raised in Port-au-Prince. Therefore, according to Lafitte himself, he could not have spent his childhood in France or seen the events of the Revolution. The reader might find it interesting to read several of the biographies written about him and then compare them with Lafitte's account of his own life. The reader can then make up his or her own mind about one of the more fascinating characters in American history.

As a final point of interest, Lafitte died without ever revealing a number of locations in the bayou country of Louisiana where he claimed to have hidden treasure. In his journal, he wrote that he was too old to go and look for it and that he didn't care, in any case.

So far as I know, it's still there somewhere, waiting to be found.

Simon Hawke
Denver, Colorado